LOVING ANNA

Piper S. Winn

Copyright © Piper S. Winn 2018

Published by PPR Publishing,
19 Kingswell Road, Northampton NN2 6QB.

www.pprpublishing.co.uk

A CIP catalogue record for this book
is available from the British Library

ISBN 9781916434714

Printed and bound in Great Britain
by Ingram / Lightning Source UK Ltd.

Chapter One

Shepherds Bush   Autumn 2017

It was another unremarkable working day for Cassie Davies, or so she thought. How fortunate that we do not know what lies in store for us. As Cassie took another gulp of her coffee and squinted at her image in the mirror, little did she know that, before the day was out, her destiny would be changed forever.

She was trying to put on some eye shadow but, without her glasses, even the magnifying mirror did not help her see well enough to apply it skilfully. She slathered on some lip gloss and raked the comb through her brown hair – 'mousy' most people would call it. Her bob reached to chin level and, unfortunately, rather accentuated the length of her face. She was not vain but, she did like to try and make the most of her dubious assets. She always acknowledged, to anyone who was interested, that it was an uphill struggle.

"Enough," she muttered at her reflection and threw down the comb.

She grabbed her coat, bag and briefcase and left, slamming the front door behind her, and ran down the stairs of the once spacious, three storey Victorian house that had now been mutilated into poky bedsits.

It was Friday, thank God, and, after work, Cassie and some of her colleagues would adjourn to *The King's Head* to celebrate Jennifer's thirtieth birthday. Cassie had remembered to leave an extra pouch of food for Kit, her noisy and rather greedy Siamese. She walked briskly down the Goldhawk Road. It was a lovely autumn morning, crisp and windy, and the low sunshine glittered off the window panes and car windshields and turned the stonework to a mellow gold. She made a left to cross diagonally through Ravenscourt Park. It was a slight detour on her journey but she relished the changing of the trees as the seasons rolled around. Today they were a riot of gold, red, copper and orange. Exiting the park, she headed right toward the school. Although her bedsit – or studio flat, as it was grandly called – was small, it was within walking distance of St Anne's Primary school. When she had been appointed, five years before, she had chosen the flat because of that proximity. She knew what a saving it would be, not to have to commute on trains or buses.

St Anne's was her first teaching post after qualifying. She had done a placement there, whilst training at Roehampton. She had immediately felt at home in the school and the Head and the staff had liked her.When a post became vacant, they had been more than happy to appoint her, despite some stiff competition at interview.

The staff room was fairly full by the time Cassie entered and she fought her way to her locker.

"Still on for tonight?" Jennifer called from across the room.

"You bet!" Cassie laughed, "Mine's a pint – of wine, that is!"

Jennifer smiled and picked up the bell to go out on playground duty. Cassie managed a coffee and a quick perusal of her day's lesson plans before heading off to Year 2's classroom. Her pupils marched in from the playground and took their places around the tables.

"Good morning, children," called Cassie, once the banging and scraping of chairs had ceased.

"Good morning, Miss Davies," the children chanted in return, folding their arms on the table tops, as required. Cassie looked around at their faces. Martha Bond grinned at her, showing the gap where her front milk-teeth had come out.

"I got a whole fifty pence from the Tooth Fairy, Miss. Can you believe it?" she had told Cassie. She was a delightful child – sunny, bubbly and confident. Cassie knew she should not have favourites, but, out of this year's intake, Martha was certainly the child she warmed to the most.

Cassie loved her work as a teacher, despite her family being rather patronising about her choice of career. Her two older brothers looked down on her, just as they always had, so her choice of work did not surprise them. Her mother, who had transformed herself from Elizabeth Davies of Pontypridd, into the well-known actress, Portia Portman, had always made it plain that she thought Cassie a disappointment in every possible way. The choice to be a teacher was just another confirmation of her daughter's failure to live up to Portia Portman's expectations for the baby daughter she had christened Cassandra. Cassie had never been a Cassandra. She never would be a Cassandra. She didn't mind. She only wanted to be normal and happy – and to be loved. That state of affairs, however, seemed to be as much out of reach as becoming the Cassandra her mother desired. A few short-lived and unsuccessful relationships through college had left her with nothing but dented self-confidence and the loss of her virginity.

She started her lesson on *Mathematics and Numeracy* and lost herself in her enthusiasm for motivating the children to absorb the information. The class was lively and responsive and, before she knew it, the bell rang for break. She was scheduled for playground duty during the morning break. She was standing shivering in the autumn wind, having mistakenly decided she did not need her fleece, when she smelt coffee.

"Here, girl, you look like you could do with warming up," Jenny said, and thrust the mug toward her.

"You are an angel, Mrs Moore," Cassie grinned, as she took the proffered mug.

"Never mind the 'Mrs Moore', have you thought any more about that dating app I told you about, *Ms* Davies?"

Cassie wrinkled her nose at Jenny.

"I am not now, nor have I ever been, a member of the dating app contingent."

Jenny laughed.

"You are a stubborn woman, Cassie Davies. I'll just have to do some match-making myself for you – you poor spinster of this parish."

"I might remind you that I am only twenty seven, and we are living in the twenty-first century – not Jane Austen's times. I am not in want of a husband, no matter what you think. That's the trouble with you married lot, you want everyone else to be neatly matched and labelled, just like you. It's the same for people with kids who are always egging you on to reproduce, even though their eyelids are held up with matchsticks."

Cassie could have bitten her tongue out. Why did she

always put her foot in it? What was the matter with her?

"Oh God, I'm so sorry, Jen, I was just trying to be funny. I wasn't thinking."

Jenny and James had been trying for a baby, without success, for the last three years. Cassie knew their entire sorry tale in great and painful detail. Why was she so unthinking?

Her mother had always said, "Engage your brain before opening your mouth, Cassandra."

She had been right about that, at least.

"It's fine, Cass. I know you were just sounding off, with no malicious intent. Don't sweat it."

The light-hearted banter had taken a darker and more serious turn for Cassie, and the atmosphere had changed.

"Well, gotta go and work at the coal face," said Jenny, with a forced jocularity. "See you later, Alligator."

Cassie thought she heard a catch in Jenny's voice. She swallowed the remains of the coffee and felt wretched. She was such a *klutz*. When would she ever learn?

As the bell announced the end of break she tried to put these thoughts to one side and immerse herself in her teaching of *The World Around Us*. Lunchtime came soon enough and, with it, her recollection of the break-time conversation. She reluctantly retired to the staff room, but Jenny was not there.

"Ok if I sit by you, Angela?" Cassie asked.

Angela nodded, as she chewed a mouthful of food, and waved her hand encouragingly in the direction of the empty seat. Cassie sat beside her and took out her healthy, but boring salad. It did not make any difference how low-calorie her meals were, for she never seemed to lose more than a couple of pounds. She still kept trying. Her mother never said a word when she saw her daughter, after yet another long period of no contact. She merely looked Cassie up and down with a sweep of her eyes, before saying something totally unrelated to the physical imperfections she had, so obviously, swiftly and silently, catalogued. Cassie was left in no doubt that her mother had examined her and, yet again, had found her wanting. She was given to understand, however, that her mother was, tactfully and sensitively, trying hard not to show her disappointment. Cassie was never fooled, nor, she suspected, was she meant to be.

"That looks healthy," said Angela, waving her fork in the direction of Cassie's Tupperware box.

Angela was an excellent teacher, but she examined everyone's lunch or break-time snacks, with an obsessive interest that was both irritating and repellent. Cassie estimated that Angela weighed at least twenty stone. She was currently shovelling a tub of pot noodles into her mouth.

"Not very appetizing, though," Cassie replied, and hoped that had ended the discussion.

"Do you make it yourself, or buy it ready made?"

"I make it myself. It's cheaper."

"Oh, isn't that commendable? I never have time to make something myself, too busy seeing to my husband and kids."

Angela had a stick-thin husband and two obese children.

"Hi guys."

Thank God, Cassie thought, Jenny had arrived to cut off Angela's oft-repeated paean to her happy family.

"Hi," Angela and Cassie replied, in unison.

Jenny flopped into a chair and slapped a packaged

sandwich on to the coffee table. She winked at Cassie. Cassie felt anxiety lift off her shoulders. She was forgiven.

"Well, not quite as healthy as this paragon here," said Angela, tossing her head sideways at Cassie, "but healthier than mine, I suppose," and she eyed the sandwich.

Jenny looked nonplussed and shot a glance at Cassie, who kept her head down over her salad. She must not laugh.

"Are you joining me for my birthday celebration at the pub?" Jenny asked, ignoring Angela's mysterious declaration.

"I'd love to, Jennifer, but I have to take Ethan to his violin lesson and then I have to drive Anastasia to ballet. That's the lot of a working mum, I suppose. We're always being cook, cleaner, nursemaid and chauffeur – at the beck and call of our children. Not that I mind, of course. I love being a mother."

Neither Jennifer nor Cassie said anything. This endorsement of motherhood hit a raw spot for both women, and besides, neither could bring herself to envision the rotund Anastasia in tutu and leotard, so they avoided each other's eyes. Anastasia was eleven years old and heavily overweight. Angela never missed an opportunity to underline her role as a martyr to parenthood, as if her entire identity and self-worth was predicated upon pushing out two slippery neonates, who grew quickly into mammals with enough blubber to protect them from swimming in the Arctic sea. Unfortunately the only cold they had to endure was the temperate winter of a city in the grip of global warming, and, even then, they were swaddled in large padded coats from Uniqlo, and cashmere gloves, hats and scarves.

Deidre and Morag, the school secretary and Deputy

Head, came and joined them, so the conversation was able to move on from Angela's self-absorption. Nevertheless, Cassie was relieved when the bell rang for the start of the afternoon session. She imagined that Jennifer was too, judging by the smiling glance she shot at her.

All the staff welcomed the bell that marked the end of the school day for the children. It was not the end of their day, however, for they now had their own clearing-up and tasks to do. Following that, there would be paperwork and administration, before they even thought about marking and lesson planning. Some of them also had to run school clubs and activities. It was not a job for the faint-hearted and it was gone six when Jenny tapped on Cassie's classroom door.

"Ready for the pub, Miss Dedication?"

"More than ready," Cassie sighed, putting down her pen and reaching for her bag and briefcase. "Lead the way, Birthday Girl," and she pulled out the wrapped present and the card and handed them to Jenny.

"You shouldn't have, Cass. You know you don't have to get me anything!" Jenny exclaimed.

"I wanted to, silly. Go on, open it."

Jenny read the card first and gave Cassie a hug, after reading the kind words Cassie had written in it. She tore the paper off the parcel to reveal a beautiful wool shawl in shades of blue.

"Oh, Cassie, that's just beautiful, and in my favourite colours, too."

She draped it around the shoulders of her navy coat.

"Look it goes really well with what I'm wearing."

"You look lovely," said Cassie, linking arms with her

friend, as they turned to go.

By the time they shouldered their way into the lounge of *The King's Head*, half of St Anne's staff was there, together with workers from what seemed like every office and shop in the vicinity. It was Friday, after all, and the huddled masses of Shepherd's Bush and Hammersmith were heaving a collective sigh of relief.

There were no tables available so, after fighting their way to the bar, Cassie and Jenny joined the St Anne's contingent on the pavement. They huddled together in an attempt both to keep warm and to be close enough to hear each other over the din. Relaxing customers raised their voices, in order to be heard over the tumult, in an escalating babble of noise.

It was when they broke into *Happy Birthday* for a grinning Jenny, that Cassie caught sight of her. People had turned to see who the birthday girl was, and she was watching their group from the vantage point of an outside table. She continued to stare, as Cassie ploughed her way to the end of the song, looking back at the woman as she did so. She was small and neatly fashioned. Her face was a pale oval, framed by a mass of auburn curls. She exuded a self-confidence, that was glamorous and riveting, like a young Helen Mirren or Kate Moss. She was an 'it' girl, someone with that *je ne sais quoi* that Cassie could only admire. She wished that she had even a pinch of the sexual witchcraft that seemed to emanate from this woman.

Everyone was congratulating Jenny and wishing her everything she desired for the coming year. Cassie, however, could not keep her eyes from straying over to *her* table and *she*, in turn, kept looking at Cassie.

9

Cassie had never had a crush on a woman; she had no experience of gay relationships and she had never had any thoughts of one. It seemed ridiculous, considering that she had been at a single-sex boarding school, from thirteen to eighteen, but it was true. There had been girls there whose crushes had led to physical experimentation, but she had been too busy with hockey and homework to have any such interests. She could not deny, however, that she was attracted to this woman, nor that the attraction was sexual. The woman's stares were making Cassie feel self-conscious, but also excited. She had never felt any emotion, apart from a squeamish repulsion, when watching gay sex scenes in films, or when reading about them in books. Yet here she was feeling moved and awakened by a strange woman staring at her across a pub frontage, on a busy road in West London, on a cold September evening. *Get a grip!* she thought, and turned toward her neighbour, in order to block out the sight of the woman.

"It's getting chilly, isn't it?" she said inconsequentially to Deidre O'Connell.

"It is. The nights start to draw in now. Won't be long before it's Christmas again. Will you be with your family for Christmas, Cassie?"

"No, our family don't really do Christmas. My mother lives in California, one of my brothers is always travelling and the other one has his own life, with two sons and a wife and the whole catastrophe! I usually have a quiet Christmas, sometimes with a friend, or sometimes just me and my cat."

Deidre looked at her, shock and pity showing on her face.

"But that's terrible. I can't imagine being on my own for Christmas. I know we don't have kids of our own, but there are always nieces and nephews living in London temporarily, or other relatives descending from Dublin. Why don't you come and join us? The more the merrier, we always say, Brendan and I."

"That's really kind of you Deidre, but it's ok, really. I'm fine with it. I enjoy my time on my own, just pleasing myself. Honestly."

Deidre looked at her as if there were something wrong with her. Perhaps there was.

"Hi there!"

Cassie spun around, to come face to face with *her*, holding her hand out to be shaken. Cassie shook hands with her, and felt a jolt of connection, as she pressed the woman's flesh.

"I'm Anna Hardwick, and you are?"

Anna held on to Cassie's hand a little longer than necessary.

Cassie felt a blush creep up her neck and suffuse her face. "I'm Cassie, Cassie Davies."

Deidre, thinking a friend had hailed Cassie, had turned away to talk to Jenny. It felt to Cassie as if there were only the two of them in the whole pub – she and Anna.

Now Anna said, "What's a nice girl like you doing in a place like this?"

Cassie laughed, her blush deepening.

"We come here quite often. Tonight we're celebrating my colleague's birthday; we're all teachers at St Anne's Primary."

11

"Oh, a teacher! And are you a strict teacher, Cassie Davies?"

Anna arched one eyebrow, and her comment hung heavy with innuendo and sexual tension. Cassie felt her stomach flip and tighten. How could this woman have such an effect? What was happening to her? She could not think of any response. She merely stared at Anna, her mouth open, but her vocal chords paralysed.

"I would like to see more of you, Cassie Davies – much more," and her eyes lingered on Cassie's body.

"Can we make a date for tomorrow? Say here – at seven?"

"That sounds very tempting, but I should probably tell you that, um, I'm not gay."

Anna threw back her head, to expose a white, slender neck, and let out a rich belly laugh, so infectious that it made you want to laugh with her.

"Oh Miss Davies, you are priceless! I like you already. I'll see you at seven, darling. You'll be here?"

Cassie nodded, her cheeks aflame.

"Till seven, then. *Au revoir*, Cassie," and she turned on her heel and returned to her table, where she collected her coat and a carrier bag. With a last look over her shoulder at Cassie, she turned her back and set off up the road in the direction of Chiswick.

Cassie turned back to her group, hoping her face was not too red.

"Who was that?" asked Jenny, digging her friend in the ribs.

"Oh, that was Anna. Just someone I know," Cassie said

with a forced lightness.

Jenny gave her a knowing look.

"You're a bloody liar, girl, I just heard you both introduce yourselves."

Cassie blushed again. Would she never stop?

"You're right, sorry. I feel embarrassed 'cos she's just a random woman I've never seen before. She came up to me. I suppose she was hitting on me. She wants to meet me here tomorrow."

"Well don't be embarrassed, Cass. I just didn't know you were bi, it's not an issue."

"But I'm not bi!" Cassie protested and then stopped and stared at her friend. "Or perhaps I really am, and I didn't know it?"

Jenny chuckled and put her hand on Cassie's arm.

"Well all I can say is – have fun finding out, girl! She's certainly a looker," and Jenny continued to watch the receding back of Anna, as she marched purposefully up the road.

Chapter 2

Later that night, Cassie stared back at herself in the bathroom mirror as she brushed her teeth. Was she gay or bi-sexual? She certainly could not get Anna Hardwick out of her mind, and yet the thought of meeting her the following day filled her with a mixture of excitement and apprehension. Gay, bi-sexual, heterosexual, what did it matter? The real mystery was how someone like Anna Hardwick could be interested in her. She carried a few pounds too much, her chin was too long, and her nose was too small. Her blue eyes were her best feature – large and clear and bright – but they were hardly enough to attract such a woman. She tried to remember Anna's features. She recalled that her face had been small, with fine, delicate features. She had very white teeth and an amazing smile. The whites of her eyes were clear and sparkling, yet Cassie could not remember what colour the irises were. Anna's hair was magnificent – the russet colour of the trees that she had admired that morning, or the copper of a polished conker. It fell into Pre-Raphaelite tendrils. Cassie's impression was of someone petite, beautiful and animated – someone totally captivating, in fact. Yet she knew nothing about this woman. What sort of person was she? Would she like her? More importantly, would Anna like Cassie, once she had a chance to talk to her? She would find out tomorrow, no doubt.

Cassie slid under the duvet, and Kit jumped up on the bed and started purring. He stretched himself out, with his head resting on Cassie's feet. Soon both were fast asleep, dreaming their separate dreams.

Kit stood on her chest and butted his head softly against her face. Cassie pushed him off.

"Bugger off, Kit, it's too early!"

She squinted at the bedside clock's fluorescent hands. It was 7 am and the alarm was set for 7.30. She turned over, and Kit jumped off the bed and stalked off.

The thought came to her that, after work today, she was meeting Anna Hardwick. Her stomach lurched. She was wide awake now. She depressed the alarm switch, and sat up. Kit heard her and started, with strangled little mews, to demand his breakfast. Cassie padded across to the little kitchen area and opened a pouch of wet food and squeezed half into his bowl. Kit impatiently wound himself around her ankles with urgent and increasingly loud mewing. When she straightened up, he tucked himself onto his haunches and bent his face into the bowl.

She was free to fill the kettle and reach for the Lavazza. Two strong cups were enough to set her up for the day. After showering, Cassie deliberated what to wear with more than her usual care. She would be going straight from work to meet Anna at the pub, so she needed to look as good as possible. After several rejected choices, she finally settled on her knee-length black boots with a red, woollen, cable-knit mini dress over her black, skinny jeans. She added some red glass earrings and a long black, silk scarf. She approved the final look, and turned to her make-up. It had to be more fully and carefully applied today: eyeliner and blusher, foundation and eye shadow were all required, topped off with a matt scarlet lipstick that matched her dress.

"What do you think, Kit? Will I pass muster?"

Kit half closed his eyes and gave a small meow in assent. She put the lipstick and perfume in her black tote in preparation for a reapplication at the end of the day. She felt too keyed-up to eat breakfast, so she switched on the television, whilst she drank her second cup of coffee. She steeled herself to tackle the litter tray with her poo bag and scoop.

The news was, as usual, upsetting: more harrowing pictures of refugees, injured and starving; another raid on a girls' secondary school by Boko Haram, with more young girls snatched and disappeared; the blowing-up of a Christian church in Pakistan, killing sixty two people, who were worshipping there.

"The human race is going to hell in a handcart," Cassie told a disinterested Kit. "How come our natures have not evolved by now?"

The brutality and madness that featured every day in the media never ceased to sadden and depress her. She thought of those eager, innocent faces, in her classroom. How did a child grow into someone who could murder, or enslave others? What nature or nurture could account for it? She could understand how children, who had been kidnapped and forced to be soldiers, could become brutalized, to the point where any capacity to feel for another was extinguished. But what of the young people who were brought up in civilised and affluent countries, but came to believe they were justified in killing ordinary, blameless people in the name of religion? How did that happen? She switched off the television, even though it was now showing a vanilla interview with some soap actress, of whom she had never heard. As she tackled the litter tray, she tried to remind herself of the positives in her world: her favourite pupils, her friends, her cat, a walk in Richmond Park, a holiday in the sun. She must remind herself that life was not all doom and gloom.

She donned her coat, hat, and gloves and gathered up her bags and briefcase, before remembering to fill Kit's bowl with dry food, to last him through to the evening, as she would be home late. Finally she set off for school.

Later that morning she prepared to take her class to the hall for a PE session. They were supposed to wear T shirts and shorts. Cassie clapped her hands together, and called out, "Now, children, time to go and change for PE. Does everyone remember what we do?"

"Yes, Miss Davies," they chanted in unison.

"So let's go over it together. We line up, boys on this side of the classroom, girls over there, on that side. When you have made your straight lines and you are all quiet, you can march into your separate cloakrooms to change. Quietly please, remember. When you have changed, line up again and I will come and collect you all. We will march together to the hall. Does everyone understand what to do?"

"Yes, Miss Davies," they chorused again, as they clattered off their chairs and lined up against the walls.

When all was quiet, Cassie clapped her hands again and called out, "March off, children."

The children proceeded out of the classroom, but Nazia Qureshi hung back and then sidled up to Cassie.

"Please, Miss I don't feel well. I don't want to get

changed."

"What's the matter, Nazia?"

"My tummy hurts, Miss."

Nazia was a subdued and quiet child; she seemed generally fearful, and became anxious when she attracted any attention. Cassie thought that she must feel very unwell to have the courage to approach her teacher in this way.

"Oh you poor thing, Nazia. Has it just begun to hurt or did it hurt before you left home this morning?"

Nazia nodded, but to which question Cassie could not tell.

"Before you left for school?"

Another nod.

"Did you tell your Mummy?"

Nazia shook her head and looked at the floor. She looked very uncomfortable.

"Should we try and ring Mummy to come and take you home, if you feel so ill?"

The child looked up quickly and shook her head. Tears rolled down her face. She looked terrified, and Cassie felt something was not right, but she did not know what to do.

"Can you show me where it hurts?"

Nazia gingerly patted her stomach, and shot Cassie another frightened look.

"Well, I think we need to take you to the quiet room, so that you can rest, while I take the session with the other children. Is that ok, do you think?"

Nazia nodded. Cassie put her hands on the child's shoulder, to guide her out of the room, but Nazia winced, took a sharp intake of breath and let out a little cry.

"What is it? Did I hurt your back?"

Cassie knew that her touch had been a gentle one. Nazia shook her head, and began to cry more vigorously, but now Cassie felt she knew why Nazia did not want to get changed, nor have her mother come to the school. She gently plucked the neck of Nazia's top away from her back and glanced down the child's back. She could see red weals, some beaded with blood. Even such a quick look made it clear that the child had been beaten with a rod or belt.

"Nazia," she said gently, "I think you are hurt. I think we need to have someone check out your hurt. Let's go and speak with Miss Underwood."

Mavis Underwood was both Headmistress and the school's safeguarding lead. Cassie took Nazia's hand and led her to the Head's office. As they reached the door, Cassie could see that Mavis and Deidre were bent over some papers on the desk. Mavis looked up and beckoned them in, as Deidre straightened up.

"Miss Underwood, you remember Nazia Qureshi, don't you?"

"Yes, of course. Hello Nazia."

"Nazia seems to have some hurts on her back, Miss Underwood, and does not feel well enough to change for PE."

Cassie put a slight emphasis on these words, and widened her eyes at Mavis.

"I think we might need to have a quick peek and talk to Nazia, but I have my class waiting for their PE lesson."

Mavis instantly understood.

"Oh my! Poor you, Nazia. Come and sit with me while

Miss Davies goes to PE. Mrs O'Connell, can you get Andy on the phone for me? He's just the right person to know about hurts, Nazia. Tell him I'll ring back when I've spoken to Nazia."

Andy was their contact, to male a referral to Social Care. Cassie knew Nazia would be in safe hands now.

"Of course, Miss Underwood, I'll go and telephone right now," said Deidre, as she left to return to her office.

Mavis settled Nazia in the armchair across from her desk. Cassie turned to leave.

"Bye for now Nazia," she said.

"Might I have a quick word, Miss Davies, before you go back to your class," Mavis said and, closing the door quietly after her, she followed Cassie out into the corridor. "What happened, Cassie?"

"She didn't want to get changed, said she was ill with a bad tummy, but something wasn't right. She looked terrified, and didn't want me to call her mother. I was going to take her to the quiet room, but when I placed my hand on her shoulder to take her, she winced and cried out. I peeked down her top and could see all these welts and some blood, so I brought her straight here. It makes sense now of her behaviour in class, if she's being physically hurt at home."

"Well done, Cassie, for spotting this. We'll set the wheels in motion, but you know I have to inform her parents of the referral to Social Care. They won't see them, otherwise."

Cassie screwed her face into an expression of distaste.

"I know that will be difficult for Nazia, and for you, if she feels you have betrayed her trust. My hands are tied, though. I'll have a quick look at her back as tactfully as I can, ask her how it happened, and then speak with Andy. Hopefully, this way she'll get the help she needs. Are you ok?"

Cassie dropped her eyes and nodded, though she felt sick and upset and angry. How could anyone do this to a child?

"Yes, I'm ok. Thanks, Mavis. Let me know what happens."

Cassie squared her shoulders and hurried off to her waiting class.

The whole drama with Nazia had eclipsed thoughts of Anna Hardwick from Cassie's mind for the rest of the day, so it was only when the bell sounded for home time that she remembered. She hurried through the clearing up and the daily paperwork before going to the staff toilet to freshen up: she washed her face and hands, combed her hair, and applied more lipstick and perfume.

Finally, with some trepidation, she set off for *The King's Head*. When she entered, she could see Anna already at the bar. She, in turn, had spotted Cassie in the mirror behind the bar. She turned and waved her over. Anna was wearing a tight, black, leather jacket and a yellow, mini-skirt with thigh-high, black suede boots. Someone else might have looked rather slutty in such an outfit, Cassie thought, but instead Anna looked stunning. She exuded both class and sensuality.

As Cassie came up to the bar, Anna leant over and kissed her lightly on the mouth. She put her hand on Cassie's upper arm, and pushed her away a little.

"Let me look at you. You look lovely, darling."

Anna's eyes travelled up and down Cassie's body, coming to rest on her eyes, with an intensity that made Cassie's body respond, like Pavlov's dog. Up close, Anna's eyes were a pale green, like a cat's.

"Chardonnay ok for you, hon?" Anna asked, breaking the gaze, and turning back to the bar.

"Yes, that's fine," Cassie agreed. Anna paid the barman and, picking up a tray with two glasses, and a bottle in an ice-bucket, she led the way across the bar to a small table in a dark corner. Cassie followed her, and they sat down.

"Well now," said Anna, totally in charge, as she poured the wine and handed a glass to Cassie. "Let's get to know each other, and tell each other absolutely everything about ourselves. I can't wait, can you? *Salut!*" and she clinked glasses and looked into Cassie's eyes.

"Go!" she urged, as Cassie sat speechless.

Anna took a sip of her wine and licked her lips. Cassie stared at them. They were fuller and more prominent than would be expected for such a fine-featured face. There were a smattering of freckles on her face and one prominent freckle at the side of her mouth. Cassie could not take her eyes off it. Anna watched Cassie's gaze and then licked her lips, slowly, and with deliberation, showing her sharp, pink tongue. She was smiling, teasingly.

"Well?" Anna said finally, raising an eyebrow at her.

Cassie finally looked her in the eye.

"Where to begin?"

"Start at the beginning and go right on to the end," laughed Anna, taking another sip of wine. Cassie nervously drank some of her own, and then set the glass down.

"Well, as I told you yesterday, I'm a primary school teacher, qualified for five years now, and working locally at St Anne's. I love my work," and, as if to prove it, her face softened and shone.

Anna watched her closely, as if fascinated. "I can see that you do. You're positively glowing."

Cassie felt herself blush again. This is ridiculous, she scolded herself, you're behaving like a school girl.

"So you're – what – twenty seven?"

Cassie nodded.

"And your beginnings?"

There was a pause as Cassie took another sip of wine and wondered how much to say.

Eventually she said, "I was brought up in Wimbledon and sent away to boarding school when I was seven. I have two older brothers, Sebastian and Rafe, who also went to boarding school at seven – a different boarding school – so we weren't terribly close, either then, or now."

"What about your parents?"

"They were both actors, but my father's dead now. He died when I was thirteen. He drank himself to death, my mother said, but when he was around, which wasn't that often, I just found him good fun. My mother lives in California now, she has done for about ten years. She has a part in a long-running soap. She's quite famous over there."

She nervously took another sip of wine. "What about you and your family?"

Anna waved an elegant hand past her ear and over her shoulder, as if relegating her family to oblivion.

"Nothing to declare, really: 2.4 children originally, as it were, though just me left now, since my brother died."

"Oh God! I'm so sorry. When did that happen?"

"Oh, years ago, so no need to be sorry. At the time, of course, it was shocking and I was very sad."

"What happened?"

"He died in a car accident."

"How old was he – and how old were you?"

"He was sixteen. I was fourteen."

"How did your parents take it? It must have been awful for them."

"Oh, my father had buggered off back to Australia years ago, when I was just a baby. That's where he was from originally. I never really knew him so, of course, he didn't know about Paul. It was awful for me and my mother, but time passes and life goes on, doesn't it?"

"I suppose so."

Cassie thought that Anna must be making light of what had to have been a traumatic time for her.

"Where is your mother?"

"She lives in Provence, where I was brought up, before I was sent away to school. We're not close."

"So what do you do, work wise, Anna?"

"I'm a writer, Cassandra. Can you believe it?"

Cassie stiffened. No-one but her mother called her Cassandra, and it sent a shiver through her.

"How do you know my name is Cassandra?" she asked.

She must have sounded very stiff, because Anna laughed.

24

"Cass, darling, the name Cassandra is usually shortened to Cassie or Cass. It's not rocket science! I take it you don't like your full name?"

"It's just that the only person who calls me Cassandra is my mother, and she always sounds disappointed or cross when she says it!"

"Ah!" Anna breathed it out with relish, "*Zo*, you don't like *ze* mother or she does not like *ze* child, is *zat* not *zo, mein liebling*?" she continued, in a poor imitation of Sigmund Freud.

Cassie both laughed and coloured. It was too close to the bone, but also quite funny.

"No, it's not that, I just prefer Cassie. It sounds friendlier."

Anna patted the back of Cassie's hand as it lay on the table, next to her wine glass.

"It's ok, my pet. Don't fret. From henceforth you shall only be Cass or Cassie for me."

Cassie smiled a thin, uncomfortable smile.

"Well, enough of history talking," said Anna, leaving her hand resting on top of Cassie's, "let's get down and dirty – do you fancy me and how much?"

Cassie choked on her swallow of wine and, spluttering and laughing, she nodded, holding her hands elbow width apart to indicate lots of attraction.

"I'm not practised at this, I'm afraid, so you'll have to bear with me," she added.

"Oh, I'll bare with you, any time," breathed Anna, leaning in toward her, "because I fancy the pants off you."

There was a silence, while Anna watched Cassie and Cassie tried to still the tumult in her mind and body.

"I won't rush you, darling."

Anna tightened her hand on Cassie's.

"It will be ok, I promise," she murmured.

She released Cassie's hand and leaning back, she asked in a teasing voice, "Will you come home with me tonight?"

Cassie's stomach flipped, and yet her thoughts were not about the rights and wrongs of such an outcome, but about the fact that she was terrified.

She must have looked it too, because Anna laughed again and said, "I'm just joking, my pet. Don't be scared. I don't want to do anything that you don't want to do. Let's just get to know one another as friends and see how it goes."

She paused. "I do want to take your pants off, though!"

They both laughed.

By the time they had finished the bottle of wine, they had learnt a little more about each other. They agreed that they wanted to see each other again. They had flirted and laughed and enjoyed being with one another. Cassie was sure that, with time, she would want more with this woman than just a friendship. For now, however, this was all so new and shocking that she could scarcely come to terms with it, or cope with the strange new feelings that were engulfing her.

She walked home that night in a daze, totally unaware of her surroundings, and completely preoccupied with the thoughts and physical sensations that were overwhelming her.

Chapter 3

The following morning, Jenny had hurried up to Cassie as soon as she arrived in the staffroom.

"Well, how did it go? Are you a lesbian or not?" she whispered, not to be overheard by any of the other teachers, who were milling around in the usual early morning rush.

Cassie burst out laughing, much as Anna had done when Cassie had said she was not gay.

"Jen, you are incorrigible. *I* don't know, do I? We had a good time. I enjoyed her company. We agreed we should continue seeing each other, but just as friends for now. There's definitely an attraction – on both sides – but we're just going to take it slowly, and see what happens."

"Fair enough. Sounds sensible, if you ask me. What's she like then? She's certainly beautiful enough to turn anyone's head."

"Is that what's happened to me, I've had my head turned?" laughed Cassie.

"Oh you know what I mean, Cassie Davies," Jenny said, flipping Cassie's arm.

Cassie chuckled again. "She's as you would expect, from the way she looks. She's sexy, glamorous, sharp and funny. She seems very confident, and in control of things. I don't know what she sees in me."

"Oh, you are hopeless, Cass. You have no idea how intelligent, and attractive you are, and what a lovely figure you have. You're funny, and kind, and dedicated and thoughtful and…"

"Stop!" cried Cassie, her face flushing. "Look, you're making me blush!"

"Well, if you don't want me to make you blush, stop with this self-flagellation all the time. It's not big, it's not funny, and it's not clever!"

They both laughed.

"Ok, let's get a coffee before the madness starts."

"I'm with you there," said Cassie, as they both headed for the kettle.

After a long day, Cassie and Jenny had to attend a PTA committee meeting. Neither of them was looking forward to it. It was the first they would attend, after both being voted in at the last AGM. The new chair was Deidre, and the treasurer was a parent, Ray Dickinson, who was, suitably enough, an accountant. Other new members were Martha Bond's mother, Stella, and one of the dinner ladies, Nicola Gray.

Introductions were made, and the agenda was circulated. Deidre made a good chair, and the meeting bowled along reasonably painlessly. Jenny took the minutes. The liveliest discussion took place on the subject of the PTA pantomime, to be held in February, and the summer fete, in June. Dates and requests for participants would be published in the newsletter.

There was already a willing core of PTA members, who

could be relied upon for help with organizing and executing the events, but they were always looking for new parents to join in, and offer fresh blood. Jenny and Cassie usually involved themselves actively in both events, which was probably why they had been voted on to the committee this year.

As the meeting drew to a close, Jenny looked around the table and said, "Cassie and I are planning to go for a drink after this. Anyone or everyone is welcome to join us."

"Thanks ladies, but I'm beat, and I'm straight home to put on my slippers," Deidre laughed.

"I'm afraid bath time routine, and bedtime stories, await me," added Ray.

Nicola and Stella, however, both enthusiastically accepted the offer.

The women headed in a gaggle to *The King's Head*. As they all wanted a glass of Chardonnay, it was agreed a bottle should be bought, and they repaired to an empty table by the fire.

Both Cassie and Jenny knew Nicola well, as she was one of their longest serving dinner-ladies. She was a warm, motherly woman with a great sense of humour. She was probably in her mid-fifties, and had grown-up children. Both teachers had seen Stella in the playground, and Cassie, of course, as Martha's class-teacher, had spoken with Stella, but neither she nor Jenny, knew her well.

After they had settled themselves down and clinked glasses, Cassie said, "Stella, your daughter is just gorgeous!"

She looked across at Nicola.

"Martha Bond, in my class, Nicky, do you know her?"

"Oh goodness, yes, she's a little poppet."

"Well, thank you very much. Of course, I'm partial, but we think so too – my husband and I."

She laughed.

"Have you any more like her at home?" Jenny asked.

"Yes, actually, we do, we have another little girl, who is three, called Sophie. We think she's gorgeous too."

"Oh, yes, Martha's talked about Sophie," said Cassie.

"What do you and your husband do, Stella?" asked Nicola.

"I'm a child psychotherapist, and my husband's a psychiatrist," and Stella laughed at the looks on their faces.

"Goodness, no wonder Martha's so lovely, you both must know how to parent, brilliantly," said Jenny.

"Oh, I don't know about that," said Stella, with a chuckle.

"You don't look old enough to be a psychotherapist," Cassie put in.

Stella shook her head. "That's very flattering, but I'm afraid I was an elderly *prima gravida*, as the medical profession so flatteringly puts it. I was thirty-four having Martha."

The other three women reacted with surprise and incredulity, whistling and blowing in unison.

"What's your secret, pet?" asked Nicky, "I could do with a bit of whatever you've got!"

They all roared. They had all warmed to one another, and realised they were having a really good time, making each other laugh, and swapping funny anecdotes.

Another bottle of Chardonnay was ordered and drunk, before they reluctantly readied themselves to leave.

"Listen girls, Jenny and I meet here some Fridays, for a wind-down before going home, but we always make the last Friday of the month. If, and when, either of you could join us, then we'd be delighted, wouldn't we Jen?" Cassie said.

"You bet, I've had a whale of a time tonight, with the four of us," answered Jenny. "Stella, it's been great to meet you properly, and as for you, Nicky, it was lovely to get to know you better, outside of school."

They hugged, and made their farewells. Both Nicky and Stella promised to join Cass and Jenny, whenever they could, for their monthly Friday catch up.

Since that first night, Cassie and Anna fell into a rhythm: they would take turns to telephone each other, in the week, when neither of them had any other commitments, usually on a Monday and Wednesday. They would talk for up to an hour. On Saturdays they would meet up and go out. These were very much date nights, though the term was not used by either of them.

They went out exclusively as a couple. They would go to a restaurant or to a pub. Sometimes one or other of them would undertake to arrange a surprise, and they would book a concert or the theatre, buy cinema tickets, or go to a comedy club.

On these outings, Anna would dress to kill. She seemed to enjoy Cassie's reaction, when she turned up looking stunning. Cassie soon learnt, however, from Anna's responses to her own choice of outfits, that she preferred

Cassie to dress a little more conservatively. On the odd occasion that Cassie had dressed more sexily, Anna would either say nothing about Cassie's appearance, or she would joke about Cassie wanting to provoke lascivious attention. It left Cassie in no doubt that to please Anna, she should not draw too much attention to herself.

Cassie was a conservative dresser, anyway, unlike her mother, so it was no great hardship to be even more conservative. It was familiar: Cassie had never chosen particularly glamorous or sexy clothes, as she had never wanted anyone, least of all Portia, to think she was competing with her mother. Despite Portia nagging her daughter to be more like her, Cassie had never been convinced that her mother would really have liked it.

Anna had been as good as her word, in not rushing Cassie to make their relationship more sexual and, despite flirting outrageously with her, she had made no move to be more physically intimate. This had the paradoxical effect of making Cassie yearn for Anna to touch or kiss her. On several occasions, unable to stand it any longer, she had initiated things. She had kissed Anna and on one occasion had fondled her breasts. She had held her and moved against her.

When this happened, Anna would sometimes respond affectionately or gently remove herself, saying, "This isn't fair on me, darling. You know I want you so much. We don't want things to get out of hand, do we? You have to be certain you want me, certain that you're ready for us to move the relationship on. I don't want you to feel I'm rushing you, or seducing you, until you're really sure it's what you want, and that you feel ready."

Cassie would feel guilty then, as if she was leading Anna on, but not really giving herself to her.

After one of these incidents, one Saturday night, Cassie rang Flick the following morning. She and Felicity had been best friends during their training. After qualifying, Flick had returned to her native Swansea, where she was now a Deputy Head at a local primary school. She was still unattached. She and Cassie spoke nearly every week and met up whenever they could.

"Bloody hell, Cass, what's the time? It's the middle of the night, isn't it?"

"Oh sorry, Flick. It's half past nine. I forgot you like a lie-in on Sunday. I've been awake ages, so I assumed it was later."

She could almost hear Flick sitting-up in bed and willing herself awake.

Her voice sounded so different when she next spoke. "Ok, what's up? Even you aren't 'awake for ages' on a Sunday."

Unaccountably, Cass found herself starting to cry, and for a moment she could not speak.

"Is it this Anna? Is that why you're lying awake and crying? It had better bloody not be, or I'll be jumping in my mini, and coming up to deck her for you."

Cassie laughed, despite herself.

"It's not Anna herself; she's lovely, and I do think I love her. No, it's just the situation, really. We're neither fish nor fowl – more than friends, but not yet lovers. It's getting us both down, I think. Neither of us knows how to behave, and I seem to be making things worse when I do try to get more physical."

"Jesus, Cass, it should be pretty simple: do you or don't you want to shag this woman?"

"But I don't know what shagging a woman means," wailed Cassie.

At that, Flick burst out laughing, and Cassie had to laugh, too. She sounded so ridiculous, even to herself.

"Do you want to find out?" Flick said, growing more serious.

"Yes, I think I do, even though it scares me. I really am sexually attracted to her, and I've never felt like this about a woman."

"What, you've never fancied me?" Flick asked, in a mock hurt tone.

"Oh Flick, don't tease me!"

"Yeah, sorry kid, bad joke. Look, just tell her you want to move things on. If you shag, and you decide it's really not for you, what have you lost? Just chalk it up to experience and move on. The world's not going to come to an end, is it? You're not going to be traumatised for life, or have your sexual identity screwed-up forever. I mean, you're not a teenager, you're an adult, mature woman – well an adult woman, anyway!"

"Bog off, you cheeky cow, I'm very mature – most of the time, anyway. But you're right, I should just say I want it, shouldn't I? I'll still have a choice how I want to proceed after that, won't I? That's really helped, Flick. Thanks my love. Now that you've picked *me* up off the floor, how are *you* doing?"

"Same old, same old. No simmering passion for good old Flick. There's no glamorous, sexy person in my life, I'm afraid. Work, work and more work, apart from my boozy weekends, that is."

"Where do you booze and with who?"

"With *whom*, my dear! Do watch your grammar!"

"Sod off, you piss taker," Cassie laughed.

"Well I share a bottle of wine with a mate, or mates, after school on a Friday."

"Me too."

"I know, where do you think I got the idea? I usually have choir rehearsals or performances on a Saturday night and then we usually end up in the pub, or at someone's house till late. Sundays are usually at Mum and Dad's, with the bro', if he's free."

"How are they all?"

"Great, yes. They ask after you all the time."

"Give them my love, won't you?"

"I will, darling, I will. And theirs to you, as always."

They talked on, about this and that, and by the time Cassie put down the phone she felt a different woman: happier and clearer about the whole situation. She thought about ringing Anna, but decided against breaking their routine. She would wait until they talked on Monday. It was Anna's turn to ring. That would give Cassie time to reflect and decide how to talk about it with her.

Kit mewed at her, clearly fed up with her being preoccupied and upset, and not giving him enough attention. Feeling a surge of happiness, Cassie bent and scooped him off the bed and leant him back into her arms so she could rub his tummy. He half closed his eyes and commenced to purring.

Chapter 4

When they spoke on the Monday, Cassie told Anna that she wanted them to progress the relationship, and sleep together. After making sure that Cassie was certain, Anna made plans for Cassie to come for dinner at her house on Saturday, and stay the night. Cassie was nervous for the rest of the week and by Saturday she was in pieces.

As she walked up Chiswick High Road she began to feel sick and by the time she knocked on the door of the little terraced cottage that was Anna's home she had begun to tremble.

Anna was warm and calm and teased Cassie gently and affectionately about her anxious state.

"Anybody would think you are a nineteenth century virgin, darling, not an experienced twenty-first century independent woman."

But Cassie did not feel like an experienced woman. She had never as much as kissed a woman before Anna. Though not a virgin, she was hardly much more experienced with men. There had been a rather unsatisfactory coupling with Jed, at university. It had carried on for a while but then fizzled out. It had been a pleasant, but not exactly earth-shaking, introduction to sex. Later, there had been a couple of one-night stands, followed by a year-long relationship with Steve. The sex had been better, but she felt she had always held something back. Steve had eventually dumped her, saying she was too needy and always put the worst spin on anything he said or did. Flick had said she was driving him away, making him reject her, because she was too scared of loving and being loved. Cassie was not sure she had ever really loved anyone, or knew what love was. Somehow, however, she was sure that she loved this woman, instantly and overwhelmingly. She had not believed that was possible.

After Anna had fed her, and plied her with an excellent Malbec, she took Cassie's hand and led her upstairs. They lay on Anna's bed and stroked each other. Soon their kissing became wet and deep and passionate. Taking off their clothes and exploring the skin and bones of each other took Cassie to another place. The things Anna did to her played her body like a symphony orchestra. She lost count of the number of times she climaxed.

Finally, however, she had turned the tables: she used what her body had learned from Anna, to give the same back to her. It gave her a sense of sexual power, of pride and satisfaction, to bring her lover to orgasm for the first time. She did not recognise the person she had become. She had never felt this passionate or shameless ever before. She suspected she was the Cassie that had been resting dormant within her all her life, just waiting for Princess Charming to give her the kiss that would awaken the sleeping, sexually voracious monster within.

For most of the night they made love until, exhausted, they fell asleep in one another's arms. When Cassie awoke late on Sunday, Anna was still asleep, her arm across Cassie's breasts, and her mouth parted. Cassie stared at her lover as she slept. She marvelled at the blue tinge to the closed eyelids and the paleness of the skin beneath its dusting of golden freckles. She looked at the damp tendrils of Titian hair at Anna's temples and the faint pulse of a vein at the side of the slender neck. Thick dark eyelashes shadowed the small high cheekbones. She was so very beautiful that Cassie could not believe that she was hers. As if the intensity of Cassie's gaze had penetrated her slumber, Anna's eyes opened and she looked directly into Cassie's, as a smile lit up her face. In the morning light, her irises were the green of the sea. It seemed to Cassie that Time seemed to hold its breath, as they both lay there, locked into one another, marvelling at their brave new world.

They spent the whole day in bed dozing, or making love. One or other of them paused long enough to make a foray to the kitchen for titbits, or more champagne, but, otherwise, the day rolled slowly into night as they lay together. It was as if the world had gathered itself together and tiptoed away. Cassie was glad she had taken the precaution of leaving lots of dry food for Kit. She had not consciously planned to stay the whole weekend, yet, unconsciously, she had managed to cover that eventuality.

By dawn on Monday, they were both sore and spent, and stank of sex. Cassie reluctantly drew her arm from beneath the dozing Anna. Anna stirred and, grasping Cassie's wrist, she mumbled sleepily, "No, don't leave me, Cass. Don't go. I love you. I need you every minute of my life from now on."

"Darling, I have to go. I have to get home to feed Kit, shower and change and collect some files I need. I have to go and be dynamic in front of some irritating Governors at a breakfast meeting, and all that before teaching a class of thirty adorable, but exhausting, seven year olds. And all I want to do is to fuck you, and then fuck you again, until we physically are incapable of moving!"

"I am already physically incapable of moving," Anna giggled. "Be back here straight after work or I'll probably die."

"Don't die, and don't worry, I'll be with you straight after work – and I'll bring a take-away and a bottle of wine."

Anna moaned, and turned away from the lamp light. Cassie scrambled into her clothes, and tip-toed down the stairs. In the hall, she shrugged on her coat and let herself out of the front door. She power-walked all the way down Chiswick High Road, up Turnham Green, and finally reached her bedsit in Shepherds Bush. She was sweating and panting, and charged with electricity throughout her tingling body. She had never felt so alive and buzzing with energy. Kit instantly read her mood and could see from his lashing tail that he felt angry and betrayed by her long absence: he yowled, communicating his fury and distress, and, for good measure, ran around the bedsit like a demented thing before tearing his way up the curtains. She had to sit and calm him, before he would look at the food she put out.

How was she going to go to Anna's again tonight, without sending Kit into a psychotic meltdown? Perhaps she would have to ring Anna, and have her come here tonight. She looked around at the shabby bedsit and her miserable single bed and wondered how she could ask anyone – least of all Anna – to this dump. She compared the decor of Anna's bedroom and the span of her comfortable king-size bed to this. *Why did Anna have a king-size bed anyway?* she suddenly wondered. *Who else had been in that bed with Anna?*

"Stop it!" she told herself. She had never felt jealousy before, and it was a disconcerting and unpleasant experience.

So this is what love does? she thought.

She made herself coffee, and took a long and scalding shower. She dressed carefully, but hurriedly, gathered her files, and spent some time clearing-up, and sorting out food and water for Kit. He gazed at her balefully, as if he knew more was to come to disrupt his comfortable world. Accordingly, he refused to purr, and kept stalking off whenever she tried to pet him. Eventually, the clock won out and she had to leave for work.

During break time, Jenny came out to the playground, where Cassie was on duty, to say, "How goes it? I must say I haven't seen you glowing like this before. If I didn't know better, I would say you're in love, or, at the very least, you have had a very good shag."

"You are a terrible person, Mrs Moore. What a filthy mind you have. As it happens, however, both things are true: I *am* in love, and I *have* had a very good shag, very good indeed."

"Not Anna?" asked Jenny, her eyes widening.

"The very same."

"Wow! Way to go, Cassie! So you *are* gay?" and she laughed.

"Must be, and I never knew it – until now. Hey ho!"

"Well, if you look like this on it, I'm all for it!"

"And so you should be."

"But be careful, I've heard lesbians can be promiscuous and temperamental!"

"That is the most non-PC and prejudiced statement I have ever heard. Shame on you, Jennifer Moore!"

"I know, I know, but that's what a gay cousin of mine told me - anecdotally."

"Rubbish! Gay people are just like everyone else – some are temperamental and promiscuous, and some are, like you, me and Anna, calm and faithful and perfect!"

Jenny laughed, "So now you are an expert on gays? Anyway, good on you, kid. Enjoy it – you deserve it," and she chinked coffee cups with Cassie.

Cassie felt surprisingly moved, and had to fight back tears. She had never felt happier, and more in love with the whole universe. She thought of Martha Bond, who had been such a funny, little angel this morning.

"Miss, you look lovely today."

"Why, thank you, Martha!"

"I want to look like you, when I grow up, Miss."

"What a very nice thing to say, Martha."

At lunchtime, Cassie rang Anna. The phone rang and rang before Anna answered.

"Hello, darling. It's Cassie."

"I know, sweets, you're on my screen. How are you doing this morning?"

"I'm fine – missing you already. Listen, I haven't got a lot of time, but Kit was so distraught this morning, having been left alone so long, that I'm not sure I can leave him all night, again. I can't be without you, though. Is it possible for you to come to me tonight, so he's got company?"

"Oh darling, how sweet you are to worry so much about a little moggie. Cats are independent creatures, though, aren't they? I'm sure he doesn't really need people in order to survive one night – you just think he does 'cos you want to be needed."

"It's not like that, sweetheart. Kit's a Siamese, not a moggie, and he's an indoor cat; he has to be, as we're on the third floor and on a really busy road. That makes him dependent on me for company and stimulation. So, please, please, come to me tonight. Would you?"

Anna hesitated, and then went on, "I wasn't going to tell you, Cass, but the truth is, I'm horribly allergic to cats. I haven't told you before because I know how much your cat means to you. Your face lights up when you talk about him, just as it does when you talk about your work."

"Oh, I see. I'm so sorry to hear about about your allergy."

It was Cassie's turn to hesitate.

"Look, why don't we postpone meeting until tomorrow night? That way Kit won't be as distressed as if he was left alone for two nights running."

There was a silence on the other end.

"Anna?"

"Yes, I'm still here. It's just that I'm so disappointed and hurt, Cassandra. I thought we felt the same way about each other. I can't imagine, after what's grown between us this weekend, giving up a chance of being with you for anything – leave alone a bloody cat. Clearly you don't feel the same about me, as I do about you. So, ok, come round tomorrow, if Kit needs you more."

The line clicked off. Cassie stared at the screen. There was no time to ring her back before she had to take her class.

43

In any case, she needed time to think about what had just happened. She wanted to cry, but there was no time for tears; she couldn't go into class with red eyes. Anna calling her 'Cassandra' had also stung. It had taken her right back to when her mother was disappointed in her, and would say her name with that same tone of voice. 'More in sorrow than in anger', was how her mother would have expressed it.

It was not until she was walking home that evening that she had the space and time to think about the conversation with Anna. She felt sad that a canker had appeared on their burgeoning happiness, so soon after such fantastic love-making. Perhaps Anna was right, shouldn't Cassie put her new lover before a cat, even her beloved Kit? They had both declared their love for one another, so she needed to demonstrate it. She could see why Anna had felt hurt. If Anna could not come to her, she should go to Anna. As she had said, Kit was not going to die if she left him again tonight. She made up her mind: she would surprise Anna. She would give Kit a tin of tuna, as a special treat, and spend time petting him, before heading over to Anna's with the promised take away and bottle of wine.

Kit was delighted to see her and rubbed himself tirelessly against her ankles as she opened the can, changed his water and topped up his dish of dry food. While he was still eating, she scooped out the litter tray, before showering and quickly donning fresh clothes. She played with Kit, throwing his favourite catnip mouse for him to chase and worry. Eventually he jumped on her lap, with a little mew of greeting. He had forgiven her.

She petted him while he purred like a diesel engine.

Eventually she was able to scoop him up, and put him beside her on the sofa. He curled up into a contented sleep, making faint snoring sounds. She put on some make-up, collected a few toiletries and some clean underwear, and stuffed them into her tote. She was good to go.

Nearer to Anna's house, she called into an off licence and chose a good bottle of red wine. A few doors up, she went into an Indian restaurant and ordered a take-away. She took a seat by the window, while she waited for her order to arrive and idly watched the people passing by on the street outside. Suddenly, she saw someone who looked just like Anna. The woman was walking briskly in the direction from which Cassie had just come. Cassie jumped up and raced out of the door. She ran after the figure, calling, "Anna, Anna!"

The figure turned. It was indeed Anna. Cassie ran to her, and flung her arms around her.

"Oh Anna, how lucky I saw you. I was going to surprise you, but it would have been awful if you weren't there. I've got some wine, and I was just waiting for the takeaway in that restaurant, when I saw you pass. You were right, I shouldn't sacrifice a night together, just because of Kit."

Anna put her hands on Cassie's shoulder and held her at arm's length.

"Cassie, darling, why didn't you ring me back? Why didn't you tell me you were coming over after all? I took you at your word, and now I've made other plans for tonight. I'm going to the theatre with a couple of old friends I haven't seen for ages."

Cassie's face crumpled and she started to cry.

"I've messed it all up, haven't I? Do you have to go?

45

Can't you make your excuses? The food's just coming."

Anna regarded her with a sympathetic face, but she made no move to take Cassie in her arms.

"Oh sweetie, I'm so sorry, honestly I am, but there's nothing I can do now. I'm already late, my friends will be arriving from out of town, and I can't just tell them I'm blowing them off. I don't let people down."

Cassie felt rebuked – she did let people down, apparently. She had let Anna down.

"It's ok, I understand. It's my own fault. It's my turn to be disappointed. I suppose it serves me right."

Anna leant forward and kissed her hard on the lips. Sliding her hands into Cassie's coat, she squeezed her breast, until Cassie gasped.

Anna whispered hoarsely into Cassie's ear, "I'll see you at my place, tomorrow, as you originally said. We'll have a wonderful time, darling. And I forgive you," and she turned on her heel and walked away.

Cassie stood on the pavement, aroused and bereft, tears coursing down her cheeks as she watched Anna's figure disappear into the throng of returning commuters. She was beginning to attract looks from people passing. She dashed the tears away, and turned toward the restaurant to collect the redundant food, and make her dejected way back home to her empty bedsit. At least Kit would be pleased.

Chapter 5

Cassie spent most of the night crying, so that by the morning her eyes were puffy and red and she had to work hard with the make-up bag to prepare her face to meet the day. She was just doing her lips when her mobile tinged. She reached for it, and there was a text from Anna:

Darling, so sorry about last night but longing to see you. We'll make up for it tonight. xx

Cassie did a poor impersonation of a Native American dance, together with some whooping. Kit was so alarmed he hid under the bed. She felt relieved and elated. All was not lost, Anna had forgiven her.

The weather had suddenly become unseasonably cold. Cassie donned hat, gloves, scarf, and a warm coat, to walk to work. When she arrived, and joined Jenny for playground duty, they huddled together, and nursed their mugs of coffee.

Jenny quizzed her, "So how was the next round of passion?"

Cassie explained what had happened.

"Oh God, poor you. I'm so sorry, Cass. I don't understand, though, what's the difference between you choosing Kit over her – if you want to read it like that, and I'm not sure I do – and her choosing her theatre date over you?"

Cassie's eyes remained fixed on the huge lime tree, that stood outside the playground boundary.

"It's not like that Jen; she thought I wasn't coming, so she'd made other arrangements. She could hardly cancel them,

47

and let other people down, could she?"

"So she let you down instead?"

"That's not fair."

"You're probably right. Don't mind me, it's just that I care about you, and so I worry. I don't want to see you get hurt, that's all. You have a lovely time tonight. I really hope that it works out for you both, if it's what you want."

"I do want it, Jen. I do want her."

Jenny squeezed Cassie's arm, and gave her a smile.

"Miss Davies, Miss Davies!"

Martha Bond had dropped her mother's hand and was running across the playground toward Cassie and Jenny.

"Morning Martha," Cassie called, waving a gloved hand at the approaching figure.

Martha skidded to a stop in front of Cassie, her breath steaming before her in the frosty air, her cheeks burnt red by the wind.

"Look, look Miss. Look what I have," and Martha held out a mittened palm, in which rested a shiny brown conker.

"Wow, Martha, what a beautiful conker. Are you going to bring it to our *Show and Tell*?"

Martha grinned her gappy smile and nodded vigorously. Joy dripped from her every pore, and Cassie wanted to hug her, and put her in her pocket, and take her home.

"I love your conker, Martha," added Jenny, smiling broadly at the child. They both waved at Stella, and Martha danced off, back to her mother. Jenny and Cassie smiled at each other.

"She's gorgeous, isn't she?" asked Cassie.

"She certainly is," agreed Jenny.

Cassie enjoyed her working day. Her mood was good and she was full of excited anticipation for the evening ahead. Her upbeat attitude even helped her cope with the news that Nazia Qureshi had been taken into care, on an emergency order. She had been placed with foster parents the other side of the borough, necessitating a change of school.

Cassie tried to imagine what it would be like to be ripped from your family, even an abusive one, taken to strangers, and have to start a new school, with no friends. She felt sad and angry for the Nazias of this world. She, however, was going to go home and take better care of Kit than people had of Nazia. She would collect the wine, and the takeaway, from last night, which they could microwave later, and head over as fast as she could to Anna's. Life was not fair when some people were happy, while others suffered.

When Cassie arrived at the Chiswick house, Anna greeted her effusively, throwing her arms around her neck. She kissed her deeply, her tongue sliding into Cassie's mouth. Cassie was breathless and already aroused, when Anna let her go, and ushered her into the kitchen.

"Oh my sweet, I've been waiting all night and day for this. I'm starving – but let's eat first," and she burst into laughter at her own *double entendre*.

Cassie joined in, feeling as happy as she could ever remember herself being. If this was love, no wonder so much fuss was made about it.

They devoured the chicken jalfrezi, talking little, but looking at each other the whole time, with a growing sense of desire and urgency. By the time they had finished the wine and the meal, they could barely make it up the stairs, before starting to tear off their own and each other's clothes, in their haste to feel their skin against the other's. If anything, the passion this time was more intense than ever, and they devoured each other with the same hunger and enjoyment with which they had devoured their food. Finally sated, they lay against each other's damp and cooling flesh.

"It's at times like these I wish that I still smoked," Anna laughed.

"You smoked?" asked Cassie, incredulously.

"In another lifetime, poppet — another lifetime. I haven't smoked for years."

"How old *are* you, again?"

"I didn't say, my darling. You know the saying 'you should never ask a woman her age'? But we mustn't have any secrets, must we, sweet thing? So I will confess that I am thirty-seven. You can see why I wasn't keen to volunteer that little fact to you. It makes me a decade older than you. I could be accused of cradle-snatching, couldn't I?"

"Oh don't be daft, Annie, Ten years is nothing. I wouldn't have said you were that old anyway. You certainly don't look thirty-seven."

"Very flattering, my angel, but also quite ridiculous. I look every one of my thirty-seven years."

"Shut up, you beautiful thing!" Cassie laughed, but Anna suddenly became serious. She grasped Cassie's hands.

"Cassie, my love, I want us to be together for the rest of our lives. I want you to live with me. I want you to marry me. Do you feel the same?"

Cassie smiled and nodded, a tear trickling down her temple, and dropping into the pillow.

"Yes, my love. Oh yes!"

Anna drew her close, and gently kissed the top of Cassie's head, her temples and, finally, her mouth.

They lay together in silence. Cassie was overwhelmed by the momentous direction her life was taking. She was committing to a same sex relationship, and, not only that, but they had known each other for such a brief time. Were they both mad? How could she really be this sure? What would they do about children? Cassie had wanted children for as long as she could remember. She had wanted children from the time she had been a child herself. She and Anna would have to talk about this. All she knew was that she was head over heels in love with this woman, and now she could not imagine her life without her. It was incredible. She felt as if she had come home. She felt blessed.

They fell asleep, in a jigsaw of limbs and breasts and hips. The alarm woke Cassie at six. Anna groaned and turned over. Her breathing said she was still asleep. Cassie slid gingerly from the bed and, by the light of the electric clock, gathered her things from the wicker chair, and tip-toed out of the bedroom. She carefully closed the door, and padded down the stairs. She had brought a toothbrush and some toiletries last night, and had placed them in the bathroom. She decided, however, to leave quickly and quietly, and make her way home to Kit.

As she strode through the clear and frosty dawn, she wondered what she could do about Kit, when they moved in together. Why did Anna have to be allergic to cats? She thought of those slim, pale, freckled limbs and the tousled russet curls and knew that nothing could come between her and Anna, not even her beloved cat.

She was feeding Kit, when her phone buzzed. It was Anna.

"Hello darling?" Cassie said, smiling into the phone. "How are you this lovely morning?"

"Cass, why did you go without a word to me? I woke up, and the bed was empty."

"I'm sorry, babe, but I didn't want to disturb you. I left quietly to come back and feed Kit, and get ready for school."

"But you brought your stuff over. I thought we would have breakfast together before you left."

"That would have been lovely, but you know I have to feed Kit and clean his litter tray before I go to work."

"Oh, sod that bloody cat! Aren't I more important?"

"Of course you are, Anna, but I still have to take care of him, and I had things for work I had to sort out."

"Well, we're going to have to talk about this. We can't go on like this. I have to be away tonight and tomorrow, but we can talk on Friday? What time will you come over?"

"It's the last Friday in the month, Annie, I'm so sorry but Jenny and I always go to the pub on the last Friday in the month, and now Nicky and Stella are joining us. It's a long standing arrangement. I can't stand them up with no notice."

There was a silence.

"Anna? I'm so sorry. Say you're not angry with me."

Silence.

"Anna, look, why don't you join us? I'd like you to meet Jenny and the others and I know they'd love to meet you."

"I wouldn't dream of imposing on your arrangements, Cassandra. Let's agree we won't meet for a few nights. I'll ring you Saturday. We can see then if we want to get together."

"Anna, don't be like this. I can't help that I have a commitment. It's the same as you not feeling you could let your friends down at the theatre, the other night, I don't feel I can let mine down, either."

"Of course you can't. I'm just disappointed, that's all. Last night was so marvellous and I am madly in love with you. I just want to be with you all the time. Is that so wrong?"

"No, my darling, of course not – and I feel the same. I want to be with you all the time too. I could come over after the pub, if you'd like. Why don't I do that?"

"No. I don't want to be fitted in like an afterthought, Cassie. Let's leave it, and I'll ring you Saturday morning."

"Please don't be angry with me. I love you, Anna. I can't bear it, if I've upset you."

"It's fine. You go and enjoy your evening on Friday. We'll talk at the weekend. Have a good week," and she had gone, leaving Cassie holding the phone and staring at the 'call ended' message.

She felt agitated and close to tears. Should she have cancelled Jenny and the others, just this once? She and Anna were, after all, only starting their relationship. It was a crucial time. Maybe she would speak to Jenny at lunchtime, and get her take on it. She could always ring Anna later. She showered and dressed hastily, gave Kit a cuddle, and issued forth to face the day.

At lunchtime, she did take Jenny to one side and shared what had happened.

"What do you think I should do, Jen?"

Jenny was quiet and thoughtful for some time, and her eventual reply seemed considered and careful.

"As far as I'm concerned, I wouldn't take offence or be upset, if you wanted to cancel our pub date on Friday. I doubt Stella and Nicky would mind either. You're my friend, Cass, and I enjoy your company, but I wouldn't want you to stick to an arrangement with me, if it's going to be difficult for you, or if it means upsetting someone else you care about. Clearly, you're both head over heels in love, at the moment, and everything's very charged, but I think it might be a dangerous precedent, to give in to her reactions, and give up something of your own, merely because she's pissed at you for not being there when she wants you to be. That's not love, is it? That's more akin to possession."

"Oh God, Jen, you're over-dramatizing it! It's not like that! It's just that we're both completely bowled over by what's happening between us. We want to be with each other the whole time."

"Then Cass, for Christ's sakes, just cancel our pub date, and don't give it another thought. I want whatever makes you happy. It's simple. If you feel that at this stage you need to be with her, then go be with her, with my blessing, honestly. I think it's a bit odd though that she's not available for the next two nights but *you* haven't got upset with her because she has other things to do. That doesn't feel very equal to me."

Cassie was shocked. It had not even occurred to her, until Jenny had pointed it out, that there was a discrepancy here. She felt totally unable to think straight, or decide what was the right thing for her to do, or feel. She felt confused and conflicted between the two messages she was being given, by her lover and by her friend.

She hesitated and then said, "I'll see you on Friday, Jen, just as we'd planned. Sorry to lay all this on you. It's my problem. I'm completely at sea with all of this. I apologise for dragging you into my tumult."

"Don't give it another thought, Cass. We all go a bit mad, when we fall in love for the first time. I pissed my friends off, big time, when James and I first got together. I'll spare you all the embarrassing details but, take it from me, I was a dickhead. I totally get it and, don't forget, I love you. I'm on your side."

Cassie felt like crying, but she gave Jen a hug, and told herself how lucky she was to have such a good friend.

Before the end of lunch she took herself to the loo and texted Anna:

Darling, so sorry that I have this arrangement on Friday and hope you're still not too upset. Hope your things go ok on Wednesday and Thursday, whatever they are. I love you and hope we can talk things through. Missing you. All my love, Cassie

Chapter 6

Cassie enjoyed the Friday evening. Stella and Nicky did come, and the four of them had a great night. At the back of her mind, however, were thoughts of Anna and how she might be feeling, and what she was doing. When they left the pub, she was desperate to go straight to Anna's, but she knew she could not: Anna might have gone out, or perhaps she would be cold and rejecting because Cassie had gone against their agreement not to meet. Instead she returned home to a delighted Kit, who greeted her with much leg rubbing, mewing and, eventually, when she flopped into bed, a steadfast purring that soothed and comforted Cassie until she too fell asleep.

Despite it being a Saturday, she awoke early the following morning. When she drew the curtains, on her way to make coffee, and feed Kit, she was greeted by a leaden December sky. It was emptying a deluge over rooftops and tarmac. She shivered involuntarily, and wrapped her dressing gown more tightly around herself. It was a miserable day that matched her mood. She felt in limbo: she could not make any plans for the day until she heard from Anna. She took her coffee back to bed, and tried not to obsess about the situation.

When she could lie there no longer, she rose and dressed listlessly. She pottered around the bedsit, changing her bedding, putting on a wash load, vacuuming and polishing, and washing Kit's litter tray, before filling it with fresh litter. Next, she cleared her overflowing ironing basket.

All the while, she kept one eye on the clock, as morning turned to afternoon. Still there was no call from Anna. She made herself a late lunch of cheese on toast, and turned on the radio. She was restless and tense. Why was Anna not calling?

When her phone did eventually ring, she dashed to pick it up, only to find the screen displaying Felicity Williams' face. She clicked on 'accept.'

"Flick! How are you girl?"

"I'm ok. No news from the Principality, unless you count my joining a Zumba class."

"Really? Well that's enterprising. Any male talent in your class?"

"You have got to be joking, it's mainly women, and the only men that are there are all dorks or ancient."

Cassie laughed. "Good exercise though. Very noble of you. I bet you're on a diet too."

Flick was always on a diet, but she never seemed to grow any slimmer – or fatter – just like Cassie.

"Of course. This time I'm trying the Atkins. I'm trying to lose a few pounds before Christmas so I've got some room for sinning! So what's new with you? Have you shagged her yet, this Anna?"

"Yes, as you so delicately put it, we have shagged and it's great! Who knew I was gay?" Cassie was laughing now.

"Cassie Davies is a lesbian? I can't believe it. You have always been so – well – heterosexual!"

They both burst out laughing.

"Heterosexual, Flick? What the hell is that, when it's at home?"

"You know, never showing any interest in women, in that way, having boyfriends, and fancying men – all of that. Anyway, you don't look like a lesbian."

Now, they were both laughing so hard, they could hardly speak.

"What does a lesbian look like?" Cassie eventually managed to splutter, and that set them both off cackling again.

When they finally sobered up, Flick said, "Well tell me everything."

"She's called Anna, as you know – Anna Hardwick. She's small, petite, beautiful, with pale skin, green eyes and auburn curls. She's a writer and she's lovely. I'm in love and the sex is brilliant."

"Oh Cass, I'm so pleased for you. When and how did you meet her?"

"Middle of September. She picked me up in a pub."

"What? Just three months? You don't hang around, do you!"

"I know, but I'm in love and she loves me."

"Wow," Flick breathed, "change of sexual orientation, and falling in love, all at once? You are something else."

"*She* is something else, Flick, believe me. You have to meet her."

"So where is she? Why aren't you in bed right now, or entwined in each other's arms?"

"Aye, well there's the rub: she's pissed off with me, I think, 'cos I went out with Jenny and the girls last night, instead of going round to hers. She's supposed to be ringing me, to see what we're doing this weekend, but I've waited in all day. She still hasn't rung. I think she's punishing me."

"That's a bit much, isn't it? If you are both crazy with love, it's a bit shit to be punished so soon."

"Oh, it's probably not like that at all, it's just as likely that I'm being paranoid. She's probably just busy and she'll ring soon."

"Well, I certainly hope so. It wouldn't bode well if she was 'punishing' you. That would make her a control freak, and you don't need that, my darling."

Cassie knew that Flick was thinking of Cassie's mother. Flick and Portia had met on three or four occasions, when they had been doing their training, and neither had liked the other. She knew that Flick's mother was a typical Welsh 'mam', strong, loving and warm. Cassie knew that Flick considered Portia to be cold, controlling and manipulative. She had never said as much, of course. She would not be that unkind to her friend. Cassie, however, could tell from her attitude, and one or two throw-away remarks she had made, what Felicity Williams thought of the real Elizabeth Davies.

"Who would know, when you see the charming Portia Portman being interviewed on chat shows, or see her twinkling on stage as Mary Poppins, that that creature is your mother, Elizabeth Davies?" she had once remarked to a mortified Cassie.

It had been after a particularly spiky visit by her irritated and waspish mother, when Flick and she had been sharing a flat in Roehampton. She did not want Flick to have a similarly negative view of Anna.

"I'm just being hypersensitive, because it's a new relationship, and it matters so much. Once we've settled down together a bit, you must meet her. I'm sure you'll like each other. I really think you will."

She wondered if she really believed that. She had an uneasy feeling that she did not.

"If she's going to be this important to you, I certainly hope so too. Now, I'd better get off, so your line is free for this very important call. We'll catch up in the week. I'll want to hear all the gory details. In return I'll tell you all about my brother's engagement party. 'A bit of a do' had nothing on his event."

Cassie did want to know about it, especially as Flick was a very funny raconteur, but she too wanted the line free for Anna, so she did not demur.

"Ok, Flick but I can't wait to hear all about it. I'll ring you in the week. Take care, mate."

After the call, Cassie tried to distract herself. When the light began to fade, however, she had to close the curtains, and put on the lamps. She knew, at that point, that she would have to be the one to call, if there was to be any hope of the evening ahead being salvaged.

She clicked on Anna's number, but the phone rang and rang, and, eventually, it went to voicemail. She did not know if Anna picked up her voicemails, or was one of those people who would not pay the tariff, so, instead of leaving a message, she texted:

I'm hoping we can be together this evening. Please ring me. I'm missing you. All my love, Cassie. xx

It was almost nine p.m. when Anna eventually telephoned.

"Cassie, darling, I'm so sorry. You must have wondered what on earth was going on. I've been on a writer's retreat all day, which I had totally forgotten about, when we last spoke. We had to switch off our phones. We only finished at 8 pm so I didn't see your text until I got out. I wanted to get home before I rang you. I'm home now and I'm dying to see you. Could you come over now, sweetheart? Please, please, pretty please? I hope you haven't been worrying. You must have thought I was just ignoring you.'"

Cassie's anxiety, and growing anger, instantly evaporated, and her heart burst open.

"Oh Anna, I have been so worried. I thought you were cross with me, about last night. I thought you were deliberately not ringing me, or not answering my texts. I've had a horrible day, just waiting and worrying."

"Oh, my baby girl, I am devastated that I've upset you. I should have texted you before I went into the retreat, but we started at eight o clock this morning, and I thought it was too early. I thought we would have a break, when we could switch our phones back on, but we all ate together, and it was not possible. The contract was to have no contact with the outside world for the twelve hours of the retreat. Come over now and let me make it up to you, and I *will* make it up to you, you wait and see. I'll make it up to you, big time, I promise."

Cassie was already in Anna's house, in her head. She was so relieved, she could not wait to take Anna in her arms. She immediately wanted to ring Flick, and tell her that her lover was not the punishing sort, that she had misjudged her. She dialled Flick's land-line number. She somehow expected it to go to answer phone. It was nine o clock on a Saturday evening, after all, but Flick picked up. She said she had been too tired to go out, and was having a quiet night in front of the box, with a bottle of wine.

Cassie explained to her what had happened. "How could I have doubted her?"

"*Cariad,* you know that you expect every relationship to be painful and betraying, because of your bloody family. It becomes a self-fulfilling prophecy, though. You expect to be hurt, so you interpret everything as hurtful, even when it's innocent, and that can drive people away. I saw you do it with Steve, remember ?"

Flick's comments hit home. She had to remember this insight, and act on it, so that she would not screw-up this relationship.

"I'll try harder this time. It's too important."

"I wish you the very best, my darling. Keep me posted. Now go and put on your best knickers and let me get back to watching *Strictly,*" laughed Flick.

Cassie was too eager to waste time dolling herself up. She grabbed her bag, double-checked Kit's bowls, and slammed the front door behind her.

Chapter 7

Cassie greeted Anna with a passionate kiss, when she opened the door. The two of them shared a magical evening. After they had made love, they had remained in each other's arms, making plans for their future. They agreed that they wanted to live together, and as soon as possible, as they could not bear to be apart.

"It makes sense for you to give up your bedsit, as it's rented and, from what you say, too small. You should move into my house," Anna said.

"Yes, I only have to give one month's notice, and I don't have much stuff. But what can we do about Kit?"

"I know, my darling, but I just don't know what to suggest. There is no way I could live with a cat, without getting really sick. What's to be done? Could you find him a good home with someone you know?"

"It'll break my heart – and his."

"He's a cat, Cassie, just a cat. They're independent creatures, and they'll go to anyone who feeds them, and gives them some fuss. He'll be absolutely fine."

Cassie could not decide whether Anna was right, or whether she just did not understand the bond with an animal.

"Did you ever have a pet?"

Anna hooted with laughter.

"Darling, can you see me drooling over some furry thing, even without my allergies? No, we never had pets as children. It was not allowed. Grandfather could not have coped with the competition for love. I didn't want any pets, anyway."

Cassie looked thoughtfully at her lover. How much did she really know this woman? What experiences had Anna had, that Cassie could only guess at? Despite her pleasure at being with Anna that weekend, the thought of what to do about Kit weighed heavily on her.

When Cassie told Jenny the problem of Kit on Monday, Jenny had immediately offered to take him.

"I know how much you love that cat – and he you. I've seen enough of him to be very fond of him, too. I'll have to run it past James, but I'm sure he'll agree that we should take him; that way you'll be able to see him whenever you want, without it affecting Anna."

Cassie had shocked them both by bursting into tears. Thank goodness they were alone in the staffroom at the time.

When she was able to compose herself, Cassie said, "Oh Jenny, sorry for that. I had no idea I was so stressed about all of this until, you resolved the problem for me. The thought of losing Kit completely was unbearable."

She reached unsteadily for her coffee cup.

"I can't tell you how relieved I am to know he'll be in good hands, and that I'll be able to see him sometimes. You are such a good friend, Jen," and Cassie flung her arms around Jenny and gave her a bear hug. "I owe you big time, you and James."

"Don't be silly, Cassie. You don't owe us anything, you'd do the same for us, if the situation was reversed. Anyway, you've been a good friend to both of us. Look at all the times you've come over to our place, to sit with me or stay the night, when James was on late shifts or night duty. You calmed me down, and mopped my tears, when I was so terrified whilst he was on that undercover job."

Remembering that difficult time made tears spring into Jenny's eyes so that she had to reach for a tissue.

"No, we'll just love having Kit, and he'll be company for me when James is working. I don't know why I didn't think of having a cat before: I'm quite excited. And when do we get to meet the lovely Anna?"

"I'll arrange something as soon as possible. I'll speak with Anna."

When Cassie did speak with Anna, however, she said she wanted them to get through the move, and settle in together, before meeting Jenny and James.

"It would be better at our place, Cassie, so I'm on home territory, when I'm scrutinized by your friends."

Cassie rolled over in the bed, to face Anna.

"Anna, it won't be like that at all. Jenny and James just want to meet you, and get to know the person who's made me so happy. I want you to know them, and like them as much as I do. I'm sure you will: they're lovely people, both of them."

Anna kissed Cassie's forehead. "I'm sure they are, sweetheart, so all the more reason that we're all settled in, and able to give them a lovely evening, when we do invite them round."

"Flick's dying to meet you, too."

"Flick?"

"Yes, you know, my best friend in Wales, Felicity Williams? I told you about us sharing a flat, when we were training?"

"Of course, I just didn't know you called her Flick."

"I thought I said."

"I don't think so, I don't remember that."

"Maybe, we can invite her up for a weekend, not before we're settled, of course. And what about your friends? Who would you like me to meet? I want to know all about you, and get to know all the important people in your life."

Anna reached across to her bedside cabinet, picked up her wine glass and took a sip.

"Right at the moment, my lovely, I don't want us to meet anyone. I want you all to myself for a while, like an extended honeymoon. We'll meet each other's friends and family, soon enough. Don't get me wrong, I want that too, but all in good time. I think we'll need some time and space to really get to know one another, and get used to living together. Don't you agree?" and Anna grasped Cassie's hands, above the duvet.

Cassie smiled and nodded.

A month later, the Saturday before Christmas, Cassie made the move from Shepherds Bush to Chiswick. Earlier that day, Jenny and James had driven over to collect Kit, and all his accessories.

Cassie had shed more tears as she placed him on the blanket in his pet carrier, and bagged up his litter tray, feeding bowls, toys, scratching post and bed.

James loaded it all into his car to take back to Esher. Though Cassie had a full driving licence, she had never bothered with a car in London, and Anna did not have a licence that could be used in the UK. Cassie, therefore, had booked a man with a small van to transport her clothes and possessions. There were also some small items of furniture that she had bought, when she first moved in, to augment the bedsit's sparse furnishings.

By early evening, she and the van driver were unloading all her stuff into Anna's narrow hall. As she waved the guy off, Anna came up behind her. She slid her arms around Cassie's waist and pressed her small breasts into Cassie's back.

"At last, you're here. At last, you're mine. Leave all this until tomorrow, and let's go upstairs. I have some champagne on ice. We are going to celebrate your arrival in style. Later, I've booked a meal at *L'Escargot.*"

Cassie felt exhausted but did not want to spoil Anna's plans. She had obviously put a lot of effort and thought into welcoming Cassie.

"But isn't *L'Escargot* horribly expensive?"

"Nothing is too good for us, my sweet, and, besides, it's really not that expensive. You have to learn to live a little, my darling Cassie."

They drank the champagne, and made love. Cassie would dearly like to have fallen asleep after that, but she went and showered with Anna, as requested. Anna was buzzing, and could hardly keep her hands off Cassie. Finally they dried each other, and started dressing.

"Dress up for me darling, let's knock them dead," said Anna, as she wriggled into an emerald-green, silk, sheath dress.

She moved to the dressing table to pin up her hair, and put on her make-up. She took Cassie's breath away. She looked stunning. Cassie thought how lucky she was, an ordinary and rather plain woman, to have the love of such a beautiful creature.

"You are so exquisite, Anna, you truly are," and she went and placed the back of her hand against Anna's cheek.

Anna pressed her own hand over Cassie's.

"Thank you, babe," she said.

Cassie tried her best to dress to please Anna. She went to one of her cases in the hall, and pulled out a purple, short, sheath dress, that she had bought on a whim, but had never worn. She felt oddly shy, and dressed hurriedly in the sitting room. Anna came down the stairs to find her.

"My beautiful Cassie, you look wonderful, but I don't want anyone else seeing you looking this hot. They may want to make a move on you, and I can't have that, can I? You're all mine, and only mine."

Cassie, despite her disappointment at not pleasing Anna with her choice, smiled and said, "Come and choose for me then," and she grasped Anna's hand, and led her into the hall, to her open suitcase.

Anna rummaged through, tutting and exclaiming in turns, as she held up first one dress then another.

"Darling, are you serious? We are going to have to get you some new clothes. These are all so, so... uninspiring! You are incredibly beautiful."

Cassie thrilled to hear this.

"But your clothes are not. Mmm, this just might do," and she held up a black wool dress with a cross over bodice and flared skirt.

"But I'll look like I'm going to work, if I wear that!" Cassie protested.

"Nonsense!" Anna said, passing the dress to her, and

returning to her rummaging. "You'll look beautiful and classy. Here, wear these with it," and she handed Cassie her knee-length leather boots.

Cassie did as she was told, and took the dress and boots up to the bathroom to change. When she came back down the stairs, Anna smiled approvingly and handed her the black coat that Cassie wore all winter.

"I'm starving. Let's go," Anna said.

The restaurant in Soho was a revelation: it was buzzing, full of life and noise, vibrant colours and wonderful artworks. Cassie had never seen anything like it, and she gazed around with fascinated pleasure. Anna was delighted with Cassie's awe-struck reaction and insisted that they both start with a cocktail called *L'Amour*.

"So appropriate, don't you think, my love?"

Cassie noted the admiring glances the confident, glowing Anna was receiving, and could only feel blessed to be the lover of a woman like this. Anna insisted they start with the snails and then she ordered the duck confit. Cassie chose the chargrilled, lamb cutlets. The food was wonderful.

Cassie chewed a morsel of lamb with relish, and said, "One thing a boarding school education does for you is to make you appreciate good food. The food was so disgusting at my school. Where did *you* go to school, my love?"

Anna placed a forkful of pak choi into her mouth and chewed slowly. Eventually, swallowing her mouthful, she replied, "I went to St Paul's actually, on a scholarship, of course."

"My God, St Paul's, and on a scholarship! Wow! You

must be even cleverer than I thought. Did you go on to University?"

"Yes."

"Where?"

"I went to Bristol and did English and Drama, but I took a gap year first. I went to Africa, and did voluntary work, in a primary school, in the middle of the bush, in Zambia."

"How exciting. I was so dull in comparison: I went straight from school to teacher training at Roehampton. I wish, now, I had taken a gap year and gone somewhere interesting. Rafe, my youngest, older brother, if you see what I mean, went to St Paul's. He'd be two years older than you, but maybe the girls' and boys' schools came together sometimes? You might have crossed paths?"

"No, we didn't mix much and I certainly don't remember any Rafe Davies. What does he do now?"

"Actually, he's a diplomat of sorts, can you believe? He's always jetting about the world. I don't think he'll ever settle down."

"And the older one?"

"Sebastian? Oh, he's a banker. He's married to Henrietta. She's a musician. They are a very unlikely couple, but it seems to work. They've been married now for about fifteen years. They live in Suffolk."

Anna refilled their glasses and gazed intently into Cassie's eyes.

"Have they got any kids?"

"Yeah, I've two nephews, Giles and Marcus. I don't see them much as they've been away at boarding school, since forever."

"How old are they?"

"Let's see, Marcus must be coming up to fourteen and Giles is ten. Apart from your mother, and your long-lost Australian father, have you any other family living, Anna?"

"I have a very old, and very senile, maternal grandmother in a care home in Sussex and that's it. That's why I'm so interested in your family. My grandfather died four years ago, and that was very hard for me. He was everything to me. I was closer to him than I ever was to my mother, and, as you know, I don't remember my father at all. Granny got early onset Alzheimer's, so she didn't really figure in my life much. She went into a home when I was quite young. My grandfather was my rock. I miss him terribly, but he was quite a difficult man, and we had a complicated relationship."

"That's so sad, baby. Never mind, I'll be your family from now on," Cassie said, and Anna kissed her own finger-tips, and gently touched them to Cassie's lips.

"You are all the family I could ever want, Cass. I love you so much."

Chapter 8

That first Christmas together, after Cassie had moved in, was magical. They saw no-one and hunkered down, with delicious food and drink and log fires. They listened to music or watched television, to amuse themselves in the intervals that they were not making love, feeding each other titbits, or taking long, hot baths by candlelight. They turned off their mobile phones, and set the landline to answerphone.

Cassie turned down the invitation from Jenny and James to join them for a Christmas morning drinks party. She would have loved to have seen her friends and, most especially, Kit, but she knew Anna would hate it, and would probably have a reaction to Kit's presence. Anna told Cassie to go alone, but Cassie refused.

They also turned down the New Year's Eve party to which Stella and Charles had invited her, and a 'plus one', to attend. Presumably Jenny had not told them yet of Cassie's move to Anna's Chiswick house, as the invite had been sent to her old Shepherds Bush address, and forwarded on by her landlord. That reminded her that she should circulate her change of circumstances and change of address to people.

After Christmas, when they turned their mobiles back on, Cassie found several, increasingly frustrated, messages from Flick:

Merry Christmas, cariad. Ring me.

Where the fuck are you? Why haven't you rung me back? Ring me!!!

Cass, now I'm seriously worried. Why haven't you been in touch?

What's going on? Have you emigrated with your lezzie lover, or has she kidnapped you to some tropical isle? Has she killed you in a fit of jealous rage? Bloody ring me or else!

Have you lost your phone? Are you marooned in a place without signal? I've e-mailed you too but still no response. I've even rung your mother, in case you decided, against all the odds, to go and stay with her in the States. She said she hasn't heard a thing from you. She just about managed to wish me a Merry Christmas, but I could tell it killed her.

A message from her mother said, *I have had a worried Felicity ring me, trying to track you down, but, as I told her, I don't get so much as a telephone call from you at Christmas, leave alone any other contact or information. I hope you are well, and had a good Christmas. Perhaps you would do me the courtesy of contacting me, to let me know if you are alive. Clearly you can see that I am, if it is of any interest to you. Rafe spent Christmas Eve with me, before going to Dubai to spend Christmas with his new boyfriend. Sebastian, Henrietta and the boys skyped me on Christmas morning, so all is well there. Hope you received my present. Thank you for the card and the book. Love, your mother.*

It took Cassie two long telephone calls to mollify Flick and her mother. Neither seemed impressed with Cassie's explanation of a quiet, incommunicado Christmas with her lover.

If Anna had any similar problems with her messages she said nothing, merely listening to Cassie's difficulties and replying, "Why don't they get a life? Jesus, you're a grown woman and you don't have to answer to anyone – except me, of course!" and then she giggled, and snogged Cassie so long, and so passionately, that they ended up back in bed.

After their hermitage over Christmas, life with Anna at the house in Chiswick soon settled into a familiar routine:

Cassie usually rose first, and made coffee for them both. She took the cups up to the bedroom, and the two of them sat in bed watching the news on TV, and chatting a little. Cassie missed Kit and her morning routine of feeding and petting him. She even missed scooping out his litter tray, but she never mentioned any of this to Anna.

They breakfasted together, and afterwards Cassie walked to work. She knew that, after she left, Anna would be showering, and dressing, and taking herself into the box room to write. Sometimes, she had meetings up in town with her literary agent, her publisher, or some of her literary friends. At the end of the day, Cassie would walk back, picking up any provisions they needed, and she or Anna would cook their evening meal. They might watch a little television or listen to some music together, but they went to bed early, to make love, or hold each other.

They rarely went out.

Cassie had offered to pay half the mortgage and utilities, once she moved in, but Anna had said there was no mortgage, as she owned the house outright, so she did not need rent. She agreed, however, to split the utilities, and said she would be happy for Cassie to buy the food, in lieu of any rent. Even doing it this way, Cassie was spending more than she had when she was living in the bedsit, but she felt it was only fair that she contributed in this way. She had no capital with which she could offer to buy a half share of the house so this seemed the only equitable solution.

Anna seemed to need a quiet routine, and appeared to only want Cassie in her world. In the six months they had been together, they had seen no-one as a couple, neither any of Cassie's friends, nor any of Anna's. It was as if they were in a sealed bubble. They went out occasionally, of course, to the cinema or to a pub or restaurant, but even then, it was just the two of them. Anna said she preferred to see her friends, or do any errands, when Cassie was at work, so she did not encroach on their time together. The unspoken rebuke was that Cassie should want to do the same. Cassie still tried to make her last Friday of the month rendezvous with Jenny, going straight from school and returning to Anna before ten o'clock.

They tended now to meet at Jenny's house so Cassie could see Kit, but it did make for a long drive to Esher. Stella and Nicky would join them when they could, and then they took turns to be the designated driver. Kit would invariably ignore Cassie at first, only gradually forgiving her, and allowing himself to be petted.

Anna said she did not mind Cassie meeting up with Jenny and the others, but she was always quiet and distant when Cassie returned, or else she was already asleep. Cassie tried returning even earlier, but it did not seem to make a difference to Anna: she still seemed hurt that Cassie should need others in a way she seemed not to, though she excused her behaviour as needing to avoid any contamination from Cassie by Kit's hairs.

When Cassie had her weekly, long conversations with Flick, Anna would take herself off upstairs, saying that Cassie needed her privacy. Yet, afterwards, she would question her lover about the call, and would seem upset and angry, if Cassie was reluctant to give her a detailed account. As a result, Cassie had taken to ringing Flick, or having Flick ring her, in the day, just after the children went home.

"Why are you doing this? Why are you ringing me just after school and making me do the same?" Flick asked.

"It's just that the evenings and weekends are so busy, now that I'm living with someone. It's easier to give you my whole attention at this time of the day." Cassie fiddled with the papers on her desk.

"Well that's just weird. What do the two of you do, that you can't spare the time for a phone call, on an evening, or over the weekend?"

"Nothing in particular, we just hang out together, you know?"

"No, I don't know. I've never lived with someone, have I? It all sounds a bit claustrophobic to me, but what do I know? It's probably just as well that I'm a sad and lonely spinster!"

Flick laughed, and Cassie tried to laugh too, but she felt too upset to carry it off. Flick picked up on it.

"Christ, Cass, what's wrong?"

Cassie could not speak. Her throat ached with the effort of holding back the tears. Her hand tightened on her mobile. The silence went on.

"Speak to me, Cassie! What's the matter? You're not happy, are you? What the fuck's going on? You haven't sounded like yourself for a while now."

Cassie found her voice. "I'm fine, Flick, really. It's just that it's all new, and a bit intense. Anna and I are head over heels in love with each other. It's all too overwhelming at times. It's a huge change for both of us, to share our space and our lives like this."

"I thought being in love was supposed to make you

happy, Cass, not bloody miserable, but what do I know?"

"I'm not miserable really, I just get a bit overwhelmed sometimes – my life has changed so completely."

"I want to meet this bird of yours. I want to see you together. Why don't you both come down for the weekend? We'll show her the attractions of Swansea, and the Gower coast. What do you say?"

"That would be lovely, Flick. It would be great to see you. I'll talk to Anna, but she might prefer for you to come up to us, for a first meeting. So that's she's on home ground, so to speak. She might feel a bit more comfortable. I think she's a bit scared of meeting my friends."

"Christ, we're not going to eat her. Have you met any of her friends?"

"Not really."

"What do you mean, 'not really'? Have you met any of them, or not?"

"No." Even to Cassie, this sounded peculiar. She went on, "She likes to do all her chores, and see any friends, while I'm at school, so we can have uninterrupted time when I am at home."

Cassie's eyes flicked nervously around the room. This was sounding peculiar, even to her, now she was saying it out loud.

"Well that's fucking odd, you must admit, Cass. You guys have been living together for over six months. She's not met me, nor Jenny – two of your best mates – and you haven't met one of *her* friends. Has she got any?"

"Oh Flick, stop it! You make her sound like a weirdo. It's not like that. We've just been so wrapped up with each other, we haven't felt the need to socialise much, yet."

"Well it's time you started, it's not healthy to be so isolated. Get your finger out, and sort it, girl, or I'll just turn up on your doorstep one weekend!"

Cassie wanted to say, "No, don't do that!" but she knew it would sound even stranger. She would have to persuade Anna to meet with Flick, or it would confirm Flick's view that something was not quite right in their relationship. She felt defensive of Anna, and of their relationship.

That evening she decided to raise the issue. As they sat at the dining room table, to eat the spaghetti Bolognese that Cassie had cooked, she looked at Anna and said as casually as she could, "Guess who rang me today, just as I was leaving school?"

Anna paused, her forkful of spaghetti halfway to her mouth, and raised an eyebrow, in lieu of the expected question, 'who?'

"Flick, you know, my friend from Swansea? She's dying to meet you. She's has invited us down for the weekend. What do you think? I think it's time we socialised a bit more, and started to meet each other's friends, don't you?"

Cassie was aware that she was gabbling. Anna took the forkful into her mouth, and chewed slowly, whilst regarding Cassie impassively. Eventually she laid her fork down and dabbed at her mouth with her napkin.

"This is clearly important to you, Cass, and, for that reason, it's important to me too. By all means, let's go down and stay with your friend. I don't have any burning desire to introduce my friends to you, any time soon, but if you would like that, then I'll arrange it too."

Cassie let out her breath, and it was only then that she realised she had been holding it in. She felt foolish and self-dramatizing, to have made such a big deal of this, and to have expected Anna's displeasure. Clearly she was attributing all kinds of stuff to Anna that were just not there. She felt giddy with relief and happiness.

"That's great. Flick will be delighted. I'm so looking forward to you two meeting. You'll love her, and I'm sure she'll love you. What weekend suits you best?"

Anna's expression was one of amused exasperation, and she shook her head at Cassie.

"Darling, are you serious? You know what a busy schedule I have at weekends – not! Any weekend will be fine, of course. You just organise it with your little friend, and I'll fall in with whatever you decide."

"Oh Anna, I'm so happy. Thank you. I can't wait."

Anna smiled at her fondly, but then, looking more serious, she said, "I do just feel, sweetheart, that you are constantly picking at our relationship, as if it's not quite good enough for you. That's a bit destructive, I think. Me? I'm just happy to be with you. That's good enough for me. Give what I've said some thought, why don't you?" and she continued to eat.

Cassie stared down at her plate. She had suddenly lost her her appetite, and all her excitement had drained away.

After dinner, despite Anna's last comments at the dinner table, Cassie telephoned Flick in Anna's hearing. They confirmed a date for the following month. That night, Anna's love-making was especially tender and intense. Cassie fell asleep in Anna's arms, feeling happy.

The weekend of their visit rolled around, and Cassie admitted to herself that she was feeling nervous about how things would go, and whether Anna and Flick would like each other. They had decided to hire a car, and that, obviously, Cassie should drive. Anna said she did not really enjoy driving in Britain, though she quite liked the long straight French roads or the endless motorways of America. She said it was for that reason she had never bothered to learn to drive, once she had settled permanently in London.

Anna, and she, had decided they would arrive on the Saturday, rather than the Friday night, so that this first meeting should not be too long. It had been Anna's suggestion, but Cassie had agreed it was a good idea. Flick had said that it was a ridiculous idea, but nevertheless she accepted their plan, if that was what Cassie wanted.

Anna managed to sleep through most of the journey down the M4, and woke, as they were crossing the Severn Bridge.

"If you've never been to Wales before, this will be quite interesting from here on in, so stay awake, sleepy head!" said Cassie.

Anna stretched and yawned extravagantly.

"I always fall asleep when I'm a passenger, but I'm wide awake now, I promise."

They chatted about the scenery, and what Flick had told Cassie about Wales, as Cassie motored past Newport and Cardiff, Bridgend and Port Talbot. Finally, she brought the car to a stop outside Flick's garden flat, at the bottom of a Victorian terraced house on the slopes of Sketty, just outside Swansea town.

Flick must have been watching as, before they could alight from the car, she bounded up the steps from her basement front door, waving like a maniac, and calling out, "Just in time for lunch, excellent timing Davies! You must be Anna. Welcome to Swansea, and my humble abode. I am, of course, Felicity Williams, or Flick as everyone calls me," and she came to embrace them both.

Anna was at her most charming. "Flick, how lovely to meet you. Cassie's told me so much about you."

"Ditto," laughed Flick. "Well, you are as beautiful as Cass said you were, Anna. Let me get your bags," and she tussled with Cassie for them, until they were both doubled over with the giggles.

"Let me settle it," laughed Anna, wrestling the two weekend cases from Cassie's and Flick's grips.

Flick showed them to the guest room, and then they all repaired to the garden. Flick had the BBQ burning, and a table laid for the three of them. Although only early spring, the weather was unseasonably warm.

"First things first," Flick announced, pulling a bottle of champagne from an ice bucket. "A toast to the happy couple," and, with a satisfying pop, she pulled the cork, and proceeded to pour three foaming flutes of the amber liquid. They solemnly chinked their glasses.

"To all of us," said Anna, looking from one to the other.

"To the two of you," insisted Flick.

"And a thank you to our host," Cassie smiled, saluting Flick with her raised glass.

The lunch was delicious and the wine flowed, so that all three were soon mellow and convivial. They chatted about inconsequential things, which was how it should have remained.

Chapter 9

They had eaten sausages and burgers, salad and French bread, Eton mess and some delicious cheeses, before Flick uncorked yet another bottle of oaked Chardonnay. The sun was hot for April, and the conversation wide ranging, but not controversial, until Flick started on the questions.

"So Anna, Cass tells me you're a writer. Anything I would have read or heard of?"

"That would be telling, Flick. I know it might seem a bit odd, but I write quite a few different things, and all under various pseudonyms. I've told Cassie that one of these days, I'll share some of it with her, but I like to keep my writing pretty private, so I wouldn't like to have you know which are my books."

"That *is* odd, Anna. I thought the point of writing was to communicate, not obfuscate."

"But I do communicate, Flick. You just don't know who it is that is communicating with you."

"Can't you even say what kind of things they are that you write? That's hardly baring your soul is it?"

Cassie began to feel anxious at the turn the conversation was taking.

She tried for a light, humorous touch, "Flick, let poor Anna alone. She's a very private person, don't you know?"

Anna smiled at her, but Flick was like a dog with a bone. Cassie knew, of old, how Flick would tenaciously pursue something, once her antennae were up. Her heart sank, and she wondered how she could head her off at the pass.

"Cass tells me you did Drama and English at Bristol."

"Yes, a while ago now, of course."

"When were you there?"

"2000 to 2003."

"Oh God, what a coincidence! My brother was in that year, also doing Drama and English. Gosh! I bet you two must know each other, Huw Williams? Do you remember him?"

Flick seemed to Cassie to be genuinely excited, but Cassie could tell by the set of Anna's mouth, beneath her large sunglasses, that she was neither happy, nor excited.

"The name doesn't ring a bell, I'm afraid, but it was quite a large department. I have to admit, also, that I was heavily involved with a guy from London for the whole of the time I was at Bristol, so I didn't exactly socialise much at Uni."

"But I must ask Huw if he remembers you. You wouldn't be an easy person to miss, looking like you look," Flick laughed.

Anna gave a thin smile. Cassie shifted uncomfortably in her garden chair, and tried desperately to think of a way to change the conversation to easier topics.

"So when are you going to meet Cass's mother, Anna? You have a treat in store, take it from me."

Anna shrugged, "Whenever Cassie wants me to, I guess."

"What about *your* mother?" Flick persisted.

"Ah, my mother! She's in Provence, so we don't get together very much, obviously. As Cassie knows, my relationship with my mother is not great. Cass and I have that in common, amongst other things," and she smiled flirtatiously at Cassie, cutting Flick out of the frame.

"It's so sad isn't it? Milly and I, and my brother Luke, all get on great with our parents. I've always felt sorry for Cass, that her mother's so difficult, and her brothers are so distant. I'm sorry it's like that for you too."

Anna didn't reply.

Cassie said, "Yeah, it helps us to understand each other, being in the same boat, doesn't it Annie? I don't have to feel envious of her, as I have always felt envious of you, Flick, for your amazingly close family. How I used to wish I could have had your family, instead of my own."

"You *have* got my family, babes. You know they all adore you. You are the honorary third daughter. They'd do anything for you."

"That makes *me* feel redundant," Anna tried to joke, but her mouth was tight.

Flick regarded her from behind her sunglasses, and Cassie knew that look. It was coolly appraising, and Cassie did not like it.

"You're very mysterious, Anna Hardwick, aren't you?" said Flick eventually.

"Am I?" Anna replied, with a coldness that made Cassie's heart sink. "I don't mean to be. I guess some of us are just more private than others. *Vive la différence,* I say."

"I'll drink to that," Cassie toasted, but with a hollow enthusiasm.

"So are you guys going to get married?" Flick asked, and Cassie choked on her swallow of wine.

Anna made much of patting her on the back.

"You ok, sweetheart?"

Cassie nodded, though her eyes were streaming.

"You're nothing if not direct are you, Flick?" Anna continued.

"That's me!" Flick replied, and Cassie knew the knives were out for both of them. This was worse than she had feared. She could see that now they disliked each other intensely. No amount of charm on anybody's part was going to paper over this. How were they going to salvage something from this weekend?

"Let me help you clear away, Flick," said Anna, standing and starting to stack the dirty dishes.

"Yes, we'll all pitch in," Cassie cried, a little hysterically, getting to her feet herself, and grabbing the salad bowl and bread basket.

"Clear away, kids, if you must, but I for one am going to sit here and finish this rather good Chardonnay, while the sun is still smiling on us."

Anna ignored Flick's statement and briskly continued to pick up the dirty plates, and head for the kitchen.

"I'll start the washing up, Cassie, if you bring the rest in," she called over her shoulder.

Cassie commenced, as she was bid, to collect the dirty cutlery, whilst at the same time trying to avoid Flick's gaze.

"Cass?" Flick murmured. Cassie held her hand up to silence her, because if she said anything more, Cassie was going to break down in tears. She could tell that Flick got it, and sipped her wine, saying no more.

Cassie made much of bustling into the kitchen with her dirty load and issuing forth again into the garden to collect more debris. Flick had also risen now, and started to clear the remaining shards of their difficult lunch. She followed Cassie into the kitchen, and addressed the back of Anna's head, which was bent over the sink.

"I do have a dishwasher, but I am not going to say no to you two doing the washing-up, if that's what you want to do. As a good hostess, however, I will make the coffee, and invite you back out to the garden to enjoy it in the sun – with a brandy, should you so wish.

"I suggest we have a rest for what remains of the afternoon. We can then sally forth to sample the delights of Swansea's night life. What say you? Cass? Anna?"

"Sounds lovely," said Cassie, trying for a renewed equilibrium.

"Thank you, Flick." Anna said evenly, "but I'll pass on the coffee and brandy. I've also had enough sun, so I'll finish washing-up and go and have that rest. Will you join me, Cass?"

"Oh, ok. I'll just have a quick coffee with Flick, and then I'll join you."

A silence fell, that was thick with pent-up feelings. Cassie wanted nothing more than to be on her own with Flick, or on her own with Anna, but not to be stuck here, caught between the two of them, fighting over her, for that was how it felt.

Anna finished the washing-up, and, without a word, took herself upstairs. The silence continued, as Cassie finished drying the dishes, and Flick made coffee. They returned to the garden to drink the coffee and brandies, but they were uncomfortable with the elephant in the room, that could not be named. They tried to converse about safe topics, their mutual acquaintances, work and family matters, but both were aware of the open windows to the guest bedroom that was just above them.

Eventually, and desperately, Cassie announced, with a forced jocularity, "I think I'll go and have that rest now, Flick. I feel really sleepy. That was such a delicious lunch, thank you so much."

"You're welcome," Flick offered, but her voice was strained.

"It's 3.35 now," said Cassie. "What time shall we reconvene?"

"Whatever time you want, my darling. I've booked a restaurant in the Mumbles for 8.30. We can go to that nice pub on the Front beforehand, or not – as you wish. I'm entirely easy."

"Are you going to have a rest?" asked Cassie anxiously.

"Probably not, mate, but don't worry about me, I've got lots of marking to catch up on. You go have a rest. That journey from London's quite a killer, isn't it ?"

Cassie nodded and gave her a sheepish smile. "Yes. Thanks Flick, see you later," and she headed upstairs, feeling churned up and nauseous.

When she entered their room, Anna was sitting up against the headboard, her legs outstretched, and a face that was stiff and pale with fury.

"Your friend is a cunt," she snarled, "and you have been a disloyal bitch. I wish I had never indulged you by saying I would come. I've a good mind to just get the next train back to London, then you and your friend can commiserate together about what a fucking horrible person you have got yourself involved with."

Cassie was paralysed with shock and dismay. Anna had

never behaved in this way to her, nor had she ever heard her swear like this.

"Anna, what is the matter with you? Don't call my friend that awful word, and how have I been disloyal to you? Neither of us thinks you are a horrible person. This is ridiculous. What's happening here? I'm so, so sorry that you are this upset, but I don't know why. What have I done? What has Flick done? Tell me why you're so angry and hurt."

"You don't know why I'm so angry and hurt? Christ, that's rich, that is. That fucking woman has interrogated me since we got here. She's made it clear that she doesn't like me at all, and that she doesn't trust me. She clearly thinks her precious friend shouldn't be with me, and you've placated her all afternoon, instead of sticking up for me."

Cassie felt assaulted and confused. She didn't even begin to know how to manage this.

"But – but Anna, sweetheart, I haven't done anything. I just wanted you two to get on. I don't think I've been placating Flick or being disloyal to you, at all. I've just wanted the two people that I love to like each other. Is that so wrong? What has she said, or what have I said, that's got you this distressed?"

"If you don't know then there's no point in me spelling it out. Jesus! I thought better of you, Cassandra, I really did. I can't tell you how disappointed I am. I am so hurt. Sorry, I don't want to go on with this. I don't know that we can get past this. Please, don't talk to me any more. I need to think. I need to be left alone."

"Do you want me to go out of the room?"

"What? Do I want you to go and be with your friend so

that you can bitch about me together? Do I want that? Are you fucking mad – or are you trying to drive *me* mad? You had better shut up and sit down or I'm really going to fucking lose it."

The hate on Anna's face was so shocking, and the violence of her words so disturbing, that Cassie was shaking. She could not order her thoughts in any way that would make sense of how Anna was behaving. It was like the ground beneath her feet had given way, to reveal an abyss so deep, she was certain she would die.

She could not think what she had done to make Anna into this person, that she had never seen before, and never wanted to see again. She sunk down onto the basket chair, positioned to the right of the bed. She could not go nearer to Anna, she felt too unsafe. She longed to run down to Flick, but knew she could not do that, if she wanted to work things out with Anna. They both stayed where they were, each wrapped in their own silence, Anna's the silence of fury and Cassie's that of desolation and fear.

The silence seemed interminable, and all the while neither of them moved. Cassie longed to know how long they had been sitting there, but she dared not look at her watch, for fear of another outburst from Anna. She wanted to check Anna's expression but could not risk turning her head. She tried to go over all that had been said to see if she could make sense of Anna's feelings, but nothing seemed to warrant her reaction.

Cassie knew that she herself had felt uncomfortable in the garden, as she sensed a mutual antipathy emerging between Flick and Anna. Yet she could think of nothing specific that had been said to explain it, apart from Flick's questions. Had Anna felt that Flick did not believe the answers she was giving? Was that why Anna had said Flick didn't trust her? What reason could Flick possibly have to disbelieve what Anna was saying? No, Anna was just being over-sensitive, surely? Perhaps, she had been more nervous about meeting Cassie's best friend than either of them had realised. How could they salvage the weekend now, and what on earth could she say to Flick?

Suddenly Anna was speaking. "Cass, I am really sorry I lost my temper and swore. I don't know what came over me. I so wanted Flick and I to get on, for your sake, and I just felt it was all going wrong, that she didn't really like me. I suppose I wanted you to rescue me, and make it all right, but you didn't. I know it wasn't fair, and I am so very sorry. Can you forgive me, babe?"

Anna held her arms out. Cassie found herself crying hot, urgent tears, that spilled soundlessly down her face. She allowed herself to be embraced, and her face folded into Anna's neck, wetting it with her tears, but she felt numb and switched off. Anna, however, was suddenly energised, and once again her normal self.

"Let's go downstairs and start again, and I promise, this time, I will charm the pants off your friend. Not literally, of course! That would never do," and she laughed.

Cassie tried to smile but failed.

Anna chucked her under the chin. "Come on, babes, forgive and forget and give me one of your fabulous smiles," she urged, leaning in to kiss Cassie's lips. "Are we good?"

Cassie nodded, though she felt far from good. Anna took

her hand and led her downstairs.

Flick was marking papers at the garden table as they emerged into the evening sun. Cassie glanced at her watch and confirmed that it was six o'clock. They had been immobile in their room for over two hours.

"Here we are at last! Sorry, Flick, to desert you for so long, but we both dozed off, didn't we, Hun?"

Anna grinned at Cassie and squeezed her hand.

"Thank you for a super lunch, Flick, and apologies if I seemed a little cranky after lunch. I was more tired than I thought, but I feel great after a sleep, and I'm raring to go for a night on Swansea town. And, by the way, dinner's on me."

Flick glanced from one to the other, as Anna and Cassie joined her at the table.

"That's really kind of you to offer, Anna, but I wouldn't dream of letting you pick up the whole tab, when you're guests in my town."

"You're hosting us, and beautifully, may I say, so I think the least I can do is stand you dinner, Flick."

Cassie knew Flick was observing her, and so she joined in with a jollity she was not feeling,

"Yes, mate, just you do as you are told. Anna and I are buying you dinner."

"No, babes, I am buying dinner for both you besties. My thank you for welcoming me to the fold, eh Flick?" said Anna, way off-key.

Cassie recognised the polite smile Flick flashed Anna. It did not reach her friend's eyes. Cassie felt it was going to be a long night.

Chapter 10

It was an odd trio, that sallied forth to the Mumbles that evening: Cassie thought she and Flick made a subdued duo, but Anna seemed to be on a high. It was Anna who did most of the talking in the taxi, asking Flick about Singleton Park, about Swansea University campus, and about the Mumbles. She waxed lyrical about the beauty of Wales, and the Gower peninsula in particular.

For Cassie, the evening had been a huge strain and not very enjoyable. She could tell that Flick felt the same. Anna had continued a single handed charm offensive, talking, questioning Flick with earnest interest, making jokes all evening, until both Cassie and Flick were exhausted.

When they finally arrived home, Cassie and Flick both agreed they were ready for bed.

"You're a pair of lightweights, and party poopers. I'm just getting into my stride. I fancy a nightcap – a nice brandy would go down well, if I may be so bold." Anna laughed.

"You are more than welcome to a nightcap, but you'll have to excuse me. I'm bushed."

Flick poured a generous measure of brandy for Anna, but Cassie waved away the proffered bottle.

"Sorry, my darlings, but I'm not up for any more to drink. I just have to go to bed too."

Flick and Cassie said goodnight and made their way up the stairs, leaving Anna sipping her brandy, and flicking through the channels on the TV.

When Anna finally climbed into bed, beside a sleeping

Cassie, she started to kiss her awake, and move her hands over Cassie's body. Cassie awoke. She felt rigid, cold and angry. She was not ready for this. She felt too bruised, hurt and confused.

"I'm sorry, Annie, but I'm just too tired. Do you think we could take a rain check?"

Anna removed her hand and, without a word, she turned over, with her back to Cassie, and her body close to the edge of the bed. Cassie now felt wide awake, and restless, but she lay uncomfortably still and silent, pretending to be asleep. She was sure Anna was doing the same.

Eventually, sleep did overtake her, and she slipped into a merciful oblivion. When she finally opened her eyes, the clock read 8.22am. The bed was empty and the house silent. Her heart sank. She shrugged on her dressing gown, pushed her feet into her mules, and padded quietly downstairs. It was empty, with no sign of Anna or Flick. Cassie even checked the garden.

She had just put the kettle on to make herself a coffee, when a bleary-eyed Flick came into the kitchen. She shuffled over and enfolded Cassie in a hug.

"How are you *cariad?* Where's Anna?"

"I don't know, she's not in our room. I don't know where she is. Oh God, wasn't it awful yesterday, Flick?"

Cassie began to cry, sudden hot tears falling on to her friend's satin housecoat.

"It was difficult, yeah, but don't be upset. These things happen. It'll all come out in the wash, you'll see. We were all a bit keyed-up, meeting together for the first time. It can't have been easy for her. Maybe she's more insecure than she seems.

Come on, dry your eyes, and let's have a coffee."

They were just finishing their second cup of coffee, having avoided talking honestly about Anna, when the front doorbell rang. Flick raised her eyebrows at Cassie, and went to answer it.

She returned, saying, "Look who's here, Cass. Coffee, Anna?"

"Yes please, Flick. I could murder a coffee. I hope I didn't worry you Cass? I was wide awake at the crack of dawn, so I slipped out to go for a long walk. I didn't want to disturb you guys, so I just quietly shut the front door behind me. I would have left a note, but I couldn't find any paper."

"No you didn't disturb me. I haven't been awake long," said Cassie, meeting Flick's eyes, and trying to smile.

"Oh, good, I'm glad you had a good sleep, you needed it. I slept very well too, even though I woke early. That bed's really comfy, Flick."

"Thanks," Flick replied, as she placed a mug of coffee before Anna.

"Well, girls, wha's occurring?" she continued, making them laugh with her impersonation of the Nessa character, in *Gavin and Stacey*. "Do you want to stay for lunch and dinner, and head off early evening? If that's too late, I could do an early lunch?"

"I think we should go before lunch, Flick," said Cassie, "lovely though your offer is. The drive will take us at least four and a half hours, even if the traffic's not too bad. It probably will be, though, with everyone heading back into London on a Sunday. What do you think Anna?"

"It's entirely up to you, my sweet. You're the driver, after all. I'm happy to go with whatever you think."

Cassie couldn't read Anna's true feelings, behind the smiling mask, and light tone. She looked at Flick, and closed her eyes briefly, in exasperation.

"Yeah, I think it best to get off after breakfast, Flick. That way, I'll have time, when I get back, to prepare for an early Monday morning start at the coal face."

"Tell me about it!" laughed Flick, "a teacher's lot is not an enviable one is it? To be honest, I've got a load of marking to plough through, too."

"You poor wage slaves. My heart bleeds. Anyone would think *I* didn't work for a living," said Anna, with a failed attempt at joking.

There was an awkward silence, then Flick said, "I'll rustle up a great, big, rib-sticking, Welsh, fried, breakfast. That will set you up for the M4. What do you both say to that – up for it?"

"Sounds great," said Anna, with just a tad too much enthusiasm, "your hosting has been superb, Flick, and I have so enjoyed meeting Cass's best friend. Thank you for a lovely time."

"You're more than welcome, Anna, and it was lovely to meet you, too. So, if you ladies can excuse me staying in my dressing gown, I'll crack on with breakfast, while you two sort yourselves out. Who's for laverbread with their fry-up?"

"What's laverbread?" asked a non-plussed Anna.

"It's our lovely seaweed," said Flick, "straight off the Penclawdd rocks. Delicious it is too, and so good for you. Over the years, I've converted Cassie to liking it."

"I'll take a rain check on that," laughed Anna. She turned

to Cassie. "I won't bother with a shower, now I'm already dressed, Cass, so shall I just pack up for us, while you use the bathroom?"

"Ok, thanks," said Cassie, and she set off up the stairs. Anna started to wash-up the coffee cups.

Cassie stood in the shower and let the hot water cascade over her. She tried to order her thoughts. Despite Anna's volte-face, after her outburst yesterday afternoon, Cassie still felt hurt, angry and bewildered. How had this important occasion turned so sour? Had she been responsible in any way for causing it? Her mother had often told her that she was difficult. She had accused her of always causing a row, or an atmosphere, whenever the family were together. Cassie could not bear to think that she, somehow, might have sabotaged this meeting. Poor Anna, and poor Flick, if that were the case. She needed to help bring them back together, not split them even further apart, as she had done by bursting into tears on Flick's shoulder, and making Anna seem the baddy. Before they left, she had to work hard at seeming happy and comfortable with them all being together.

When she arrived downstairs, dressed and made-up, Flick and Anna were dishing up the breakfast and talking about novels. Flick was a voracious reader and, although Cassie had not seen Anna read much, as a writer she was probably pretty knowledgeable about other writers.

"Oh look at my two favourite women preparing breakfast for me! What a heart warming sight!"

"Just don't get too used to it, princess," Anna laughed.

"Lazy cow, skiving off to the shower for hours, while we slave away over a hot stove!" Flick joked, whilst giving Cassie a searching look.

"So have you been putting the literary world to rights, you two?" Cassie asked brightly, as she slid along the bench to position herself before a groaning plate of bacon, sausages, eggs, baked beans and laverbread.

"No, we couldn't agree on anything," said Flick.

"And especially not laverbread!" put in Anna. "I have never seen anything that looks so disgusting in my life. Surely you aren't going to eat that slop too, Cass? How will I ever snog you again?"

She smiled lasciviously, and Cassie felt momentarily uncomfortable and could not look at Flick.

"I know what you mean," Cassie joked, "it does look disgusting, but Flick wore me down until I tried it and now I really like it."

Anna shuddered.

Flick chuckled and went on, "This woman of yours has no taste, Cass. She doesn't like Virginia Woolf and she doesn't like George Elliot. She doesn't even like Henry James! I ask you?!"

"I'm with her on George Elliot and Virginia Woolf, though I don't know how anyone could dislike Henry James."

"This girl can," said Anna.

"Shame on you," Cassie laughed.

"You're both peasants!" Flick said. "Let's have a chance to critique your work then, Anna Hardwick."

"All in good time, my girl. I don't show my brilliance off to every Tom, Dick and Harry that I've just met," Anna announced, and they all laughed, with more shared warmth than they had felt all weekend.

By the time they drove off, as Flick waved from her gate, the tension had dissipated, and Cassie's mood lightened considerably. Anna's energy, however, seemed to plummet as they went along. Soon her monosyllabic responses to Cassie's comments and questions were replaced by sleep. It was only as they limped along in the traffic, queuing for the slip road to Chiswick roundabout, that she seemed to rouse herself properly.

"What time is it?" she asked groggily.

"It's a quarter to five. You've slept all the way. It must have been getting up so early this morning, that's worn you out."

"No it's not that. Frankly I just found the whole weekend exhausting and a tremendous strain."

"Oh Annie, don't say that! Didn't you like Flick, really?"

"Cassie, I know you love her, and I'm sure she's really nice, but it was clear she did not like me at all. I think she found me a threat. She doesn't want to share you, don't you get it?"

"That's just not true, Anna. She wants me to be happy. She wants to be happy *for* me."

"Until she met me, you mean?"

"No, I didn't mean that. Please, let's not do this. Let's not argue."

"I'm not arguing. I'm just saying it as I see it, but you don't want to hear what I think."

"I just want you to like her and her to like you. I want you to meet my friends and family, and like them, and be accepted by them. I want the same for me too, to like and feel accepted by your friends and family. That's what it should be like, shouldn't it, when two people who love each other, come together?"

"I thought, from what you have said, that you don't feel particularly accepted and liked by your *own* family," said Anna.

Cassie was stung, and took her eyes off the road to see Anna's expression. It was inscrutable.

"Ouch!" said Cassie.

"What do you mean 'ouch'? I wasn't trying to hurt you, or be unpleasant Cass, I'm just reflecting back what you've told me."

Cassie once more felt in turmoil and confusion. She could not think clearly. She did not know what she thought or what she felt, what was true and what was false. Her sense of her own reality had begun to show sudden lurches and chasms, like an earthquake re-aligning the landscape.

"Let's not go there now, Anna. Let's just get home and relax. We can talk another time."

Anna lapsed into silence and, when they finally dropped the car off at the hire firm, and walked back to the house, she pleaded a migraine and repaired to the spare room.

Chapter 11

By the following morning, Anna was back on good form, and woke Cassie with a cup of coffee, and a tender kiss on the lips.

"Wake up, sleepy head. It's a beautiful morning, and I'm feeling on top of the world. My migraine's completely gone."

Cassie smiled and stretched languorously. It felt so good to have her Anna back. She was not about to spoil things, by bringing up anything difficult, or controversial, from the previous day's conversations.

Anna slipped under the duvet, and wrapped her legs over Cassie's, drawing her close, and kissing her eyelids, her lips, her neck, and her breasts. Soon the coffee was forgotten, and they were making love with a passion that neither had felt for a while.

By the time Cassie left for school, she was thrumming with happiness, and the spring sunshine reflected back the hope and warmth she was feeling.

In the staffroom, Jenny pounced on her.

"My God, Cass, you look radiant this morning. It must have been a great weekend with Flick and Anna?"

"Actually, Jen, it had its sticky moments, but, overall, it was ok."

"It must have been pretty good, for you to look like this."

"Stop it, you'll make me blush."

"I will have to meet this woman of yours. My curiosity is killing me. Now that you're ready to introduce her, why don't

James and I throw a small lunch party – you and Anna, us, maybe Nicky and Greg, Deidre and Brendan, and what about asking Stella and Charles too ?"

"That's quite a party! It sounds lovely, Jen. I'll talk to Anna. When are you thinking?"

"What about Easter Sunday? That'll give us all some notice and no-one will have to work on the Monday. I'll check with the others."

"Ok, great. I'll get back to you a.s.a.p."

That evening, as Cassie sat down to the chicken stir fry Anna had made, she told her what Jenny had suggested that morning.

"She says she's dying to meet the woman who can make me look so radiant," she added, laughing.

Anna smiled.

"That's nice to hear, sweetheart. You know I'm not much of a one for parties, but if you want me to meet these people, I'm happy to do it for you."

"They're all colleagues, and their partners, so you'll get to meet the people I work with, and the girls I meet with on my monthly Friday nights out."

"I thought you didn't go out to the pub any more, but to Jenny's, so you can see that cat of yours, that's so special to you?"

"We do, but you know what I mean – it's still a night out from here, isn't it?"

Anna gave her an indulgent smile, as if she were a child who was a little slow on the uptake.

"Anyway," Cassie went on, "they're all dying to meet you, so can I tell Jenny yes?"

"If you want to, why not? Let's get it over with – this meeting lark. You've gone on about it for long enough," and she took a sip of her wine and forked more beansprouts into her mouth.

Stung, Cassie protested, "That's not fair. I have not gone on about it. I asked you once, and I accepted your answer – that you felt it was too soon."

"Calm down, sweetie, I was only teasing. You really can be far too sensitive, sometimes, Cass. I worry that you can be hurt so easily by people. It's as if you're missing a layer of skin. You need to toughen up a bit."

Cassie forgot to close her mouth, as she stared at Anna in disbelief.

"You think I'm over-sensitive?" she finally asked. "Really? I would never have said I was easily hurt."

Anna smiled at her.

"Sometimes we don't see in ourselves what others see, do we? Yes, I think there's a fragility about you, baby, and I suppose from what you've told me about your family, and your childhood, that wouldn't be surprising, would it? Eat up. Look, your food is getting cold," and she took another sip of wine.

Cassie slowly picked up her fork and began to push her food about. She did not recognise herself, this Cassie that Anna was describing, but perhaps she was unaware of how others saw her. She must remember to ask Flick and Jen if they thought she was over-sensitive.

"I've just thought, if it's at Jenny's house won't your cat be there?" Anna cried.

"Kit? Yes, he will, but we'll only be there for a short

while. It won't be a problem, will it?"

"Cassie, you really don't understand allergies, do you? Of course it will be a problem. I can't go near a cat without sneezing and wheezing. I wouldn't be able to last five minutes in that house, if there's a cat living there. You know that's why we couldn't have your cat here."

"I didn't think it would be a problem, as long as you weren't living with a cat."

"But it will be," Anna said more firmly and shook her head in exasperation.

"I'll talk to Jenny, maybe Kit can go to her neighbour's for the duration of the party."

"There will still be cat hairs all over the house."

"Maybe Jenny can give it an especially good clean, or we can sit in the garden, if the weather's good."

"I won't risk my health just to meet some of your friends."

"You must know that's the last thing I would want, for you to risk your health, but I do want you and my friends to meet. I'll talk to Jenny tomorrow."

The meal ended in silence, and Anna announced that she had a writers meeting up in town, and had to leave. It was the first Cassie had heard of such a meeting.

She was asleep before Anna returned that night.

The following day, Jenny declared she would research cat allergies and find some solution. If all else failed, she would discuss with Deidre moving the venue to her house, if Jenny still did all the catering. Deidre had no pets.

Finally it was agreed that Kit should be shut up in the

spare bedroom, with a litter tray and food and water, and the house would be thoroughly cleaned. Jenny argued that if most of the party took place under an awning in the garden, Anna could be satisfied that she would be safe from possible anaphylactic shock.

Cassie felt bad for all the trouble to accommodate Anna's allergy, but she considered that Anna would have tried as hard to fit things around Cassie's needs. After all, wasn't that what love was about?

She told Anna, who was still dubious, but said that she would not go in the house at all, during the lunch party, and that Cassie was not to fuss Kit on the day.

The following weekend, Anna and Cassie were ambling back from a light lunch they had eaten in a local pub on the river. They were laughing about something, as they pushed open the gate, and walked up the short garden path. All at once, a grey-haired woman opened the front door of the house next door.

"Anna! I'm so glad I caught you. Could I have a word about Susan?"

Anna stopped laughing, and started to put the key in the door. With her other hand, she waved the woman away.

"Sorry Joan, Cassie's desperate for the loo. Cassie, this is Joan Carter, my neighbour. Joan this is my partner Cassie Davies. There you are, in you go, Cass, straight to the bathroom. I'll pop round in a minute Joan, if that's ok? I'll just take my coat off," and with that she closed the door swiftly behind them, leaning her back against it.

Cassie stared at her in astonishment. "What on earth was all that about? I'm not desperate for the loo, and who the hell is Susan?'

"Joan's a real pain. I didn't want us to get stuck on the doorstep. She never stops talking and you just can't get away. It's easier if I pop round there, then I can make a swift exit. Susan's the neighbour on the other side of Joan. Joan is always moaning to me about her: Susan's dog has shat on Joan's path, or Susan's bin was blocking her gate, or Susan's music is too loud. I don't know what she expects me to do about it. I guess she's just lonely."

"Oh poor thing, so what do you do?"

"Well, I *ooh* and *aah* sympathetically, say I'll have a word with Susan, then it all dies down for a while, until the next time."

"What's this Susan like?"

"She's all right, a bit younger than Joan, probably in her fifties, divorced with grown-up children, and out at work most of the time. Joan's never married, or had kids and she's a bit of an old maid in all sorts of ways.

"Look, you put the kettle on and I'll just pop across and soothe the old biddy. I won't be long," and Anna slung her coat over the newel post and went out the front door.

When she came back ten or so minutes later, she was smiling. Cassie had made a pot of coffee, and put two mugs on the kitchen table.

"Was she ok?"

"Oh yeah, after a bit of sympathy. Some nonsense about the fence between them in the back garden. Aunty Anna has worked her magic again."

"Well, come and work your magic on me, Aunty Anna."

The coffee was forgotten.

Chapter 12

By lunchtime on Easter Sunday, Anna and Cassie were driving to the party and the sun was shining on them. Cassie was nervous and excited about introducing Anna to everyone. Anna was cool and quiet. Cassie thought, she too might be nervous until she said, as they were entering Jenny's street,

"What perfectly ghastly 1930s semis. Don't tell me this is where they live?"

"Don't be such a snob, Annie, Jen's house is lovely and they have a beautiful big garden at the back."

Anna rolled her eyes, but said nothing more. Cassie parked the car, and prayed that the event would go smoothly, and that Anna would enjoy herself. She hoped that everyone would love her as much as she did.

As they went up the path, Anna took Cassie's hand, which was sweet. Cassie couldn't help wishing, however, that they would not, initially, display too much intimacy in front of her friends, until everyone was more comfortable with one another.

There was a sign on the front door saying 'This way to the back garden', with a large arrow pointing them to the path, at the side of the house. The path was narrow, so they had to walk around in single file, Cassie leading the way. As they came in sight of the back garden, there were cries of welcome from the others, who had caught sight of them. Anna came to Cassie's side, and linked hands again.

Jenny and James hurried toward them.

"Anna, at last," cried Jenny, shaking Anna's free hand.

"How wonderful to meet you finally. You are every bit as beautiful as Cass said you were. Isn't she, Jay? This is my husband James."

James shook Anna's hand, and laughed, "My wife is right, you are very beautiful, and we're glad to welcome you to our home."

"Thank you, thank you both. It's lovely to be here," Anna said, as Jenny relinquished Cassie from a hug.

James kissed Cassie on the cheek.

"Lovely to see you again, Cassie. Come on girls, let's get you a drink, and introduce Anna to the others."

Deidre and Nicky stood to shake hands, and be introduced to Anna, before ushering forward their spouses, Brendan and Greg, to do the honours. Jenny handed a glass of champagne each to Anna and Cassie, then turning to the others, she raised her glass and said, "A toast, everyone, to friends, and to this happy couple. Anna and Cassie. Jay, you too, raise your beer."

Everyone raised their glasses, and parroted "to friends, and to this happy couple," before bursting into laughter.

"Sit down, everyone, while I bring out some nibbles. As you can see, Jay is doing the BBQ, and he may be some time."

There was more laughing, and some good-humoured heckling of James by the other two men.

Jenny turned to Cassie and Anna. "Stella and Charles are on their way. Apparently Sophie fell asleep, and they had to wait for her to wake, so they're running a bit late."

"Oh they're bringing the kids? How lovely!"

Cassie turned to Anna, "I've mentioned Martha Bond,

haven't I, the most gorgeous little girl in my class? She's their eldest daughter and her sister, Sophie, is just three."

Anna nodded, and smiled, and let her eyes wander over the garden and the company, taking in the detail.

"So Anna, what is it you do?" Deidre asked.

"I'm a writer," said Anna.

Cassie was sure Deidre was only being polite. The jungle drums at school would have broadcast all Anna's details to everyone, long before this.

"Oh, how interesting. Have you written anything I would have heard of?"

"Everyone always asks that," said Anna, "but I doubt it."

"Anna's a closed book, when it comes to her work – excuse the pun!" Cassie put in. "I don't even know what sort of things she writes. She won't let me read anything – yet."

"But you make a living out of it?" asked Nicky.

"Just about," Anna laughed.

"You own a house in Chiswick," Jenny said, as she deposited a plate of canapés on the table. "That suggests you make more of a living than 'just about'. I think you're being too modest, Anna."

Anna smiled at Cassie, but there was an edge to her tone, when she said, "You've been gossiping, my love."

"No, I don't gossip. It's just that Jenny knows I moved into *your* house, and that it's in Chiswick."

"Chiswick eh?" said Greg, as he came up to grab some crisps. "I've done up a few places there. Lots of money in Chiswick."

"Greg's a builder, runs his own business," Nicky told Anna, to explain her husband's comments.

"Well, I do have a private income, courtesy of my very doting maternal grandfather, now deceased," announced Anna.

Cassie's eyes widened. This was the first she had heard of this.

"Hello all!" called Stella, as she rounded the corner of the house, with Charles and the girls in tow. Introductions were made, hands shaken and drinks dispensed. The two little girls fell upon the basket of toys, Jenny had put out for them. Despite not yet having any of her own, Jenny adored children, and loved to ensure their enjoyment.

Stella seemed more interested in Anna, and made a beeline to engage her in conversation.

"Cassie talks about you all the time, she's clearly madly in love with you. It's really good to meet you finally."

"And I hear you are one of the *Fab Four*, who frequented the hostelry together, once a month, but now gather here."

Stella laughed. "You should join us, one of these Fridays, and make it *The Famous Five*."

"I've never been invited," said Anna.

Cassie raised her eyebrows at the lie, but Anna but didn't notice.

"Well, you have now. I hear you're a writer, but you don't like to talk about it."

"Oh God, I'm notorious for it, it seems. How embarrassing!"

"Sorry. I guess you're a pretty private person and here we all are, talking about you behind your back. It's only because we all love Cassie so much, that we're intrigued about the person who has won her heart, and made her look so happy and beautiful."

Cassie blushed.

"Ok, I forgive you," Anna said, smiling, "but let's change the subject from me. What is it you and Charles do?"

"I'm a child psychotherapist, and Charles is a psychiatrist."

"Really? Where do you both work?"

"I work at CAMS in Hammersmith."

"CAMS?"

"Sorry, it stands for Child and Adolescent Mental Health Service. Charles works at Springfield Hospital in Tooting."

"Is my name being taken in vain?" asked Charles, peeling off from the group of men chatting with James around the BBQ, and heading toward them.

"Bat ears!" Stella chuckled. "Anna, meet my husband, Charles. Charles this is Anna."

"Delighted," said Charles, shaking Anna's hand. "So you're the partner that we have all heard about, but never seen. You're a bit like the Scarlet Pimpernel."

"Yes, I'm Cassie's partner and as you see, I'm here. You don't have to seek me out, here or there!"

"Didn't Cassie say you were at St Paul's school?" asked Stella.

"Yes, yes I was – on a scholarship."

Stella beamed, "I went to St Paul's too. What was your intake year?"

"1991. When I was thirteen."

"Oh my God, I went in 1993. We must have known each other. Were you still Anna Hardcastle back then?"

"Yes, but you would have been below me. I wouldn't

have taken much interest, would I, in someone two years younger than me?"

"Did you play any instruments or sports? Were you in any of the plays?"

"No, strictly limited talents, I'm afraid. What about you? What was your maiden name?"

"Stella Brigstock. Oh, I was a sickening all rounder," she laughed. "I was in the hockey team, the tennis team, the choir, and I also acted."

"Stella Brigstock? That does seem to ring a bell," said Anna.

"Which mistress was your mentor?"

Just then James announced that the first round of drumsticks and chicken wings was ready. Jenny called them all to the buffet table. Cassie, who had been talking to the little girls, now headed toward Anna.

"Excuse me," said Anna to Stella, moving toward Cassie.

They went to fill their plates and, as they moved away, and were momentarily on their own, Cassie asked in a low voice, "I saw you were talking to Stella and Charles. Did you like them?"

"Yes, they seem nice. I'm not too keen on psychiatrists and therapists, though."

"Why, what's wrong with them?"

"Creepy profession, if you ask me, poking about in people's heads."

"What are you two plotting? You look suspiciously like conspirators!" Deidre's husband, Brendan, joined them.

Cassie laughed, "Don't mind Brendan, Anna, he's a retired policeman, who still thinks he's on the Force."

Cassie had met the witty Irishman at many school events, and they had always enjoyed each other's company.

"What sort of policing did you do?" asked Anna.

"Child Protection work was what I ended up doing for a long time before I retired."

"I don't know how you did it, Brendan. I couldn't bear to work with that sort of stuff," said Cassie.

She turned to Anna.

"Brendan once told me about a mother who was sexually abusing her two young sons. Can you imagine? It beggars belief, doesn't it?"

Anna shook her head. "Awful."

"I think the fact that we couldn't have our own kiddies made it a bit easier somehow, as I didn't have to imagine all that stuff being done to one of our own."

"How do you fill your time now you're retired, Brendan?" asked Anna.

"I play golf, I garden, I'm in a barbershop quartet, and I write too. I'm trying to write an autobiography. It's true when people say they're busier than ever after they retire. Say, I could ask you for tips, couldn't I? I hear you're a professional writer."

"I shouldn't bother asking me for tips, I'm not a very good writer, you know."

"I doubt that somehow," Brendan snorted.

"So do I," Cassie laughed. "How far along are you with the book, Brendan?"

"I've got to my early years as a young constable, and I've just met Deidre."

"How romantic!" said Anna.

113

"It was, to be sure. Very romantic, indeed."

James was calling them to take the second round of food, sausages and burgers. There were vegetable skewers for Deidre and Stella, who were vegetarian and vegan respectively.

As people circulated, Cassie saw that Anna had plonked herself, with her plate, on the rug where Martha and Sophie were playing. She seemed to be in animated conversation with Sophie. Cassie was surprised and intrigued. She would not have expected Anna to be so into little children. She had given no hint of liking children, and yet here she was, engaging a three year old. Sophie seemed to be basking in the attention.

After a little while, Martha wandered off to her parents, but Sophie stayed chatting to Anna, and seemed to be showing her some toy. Cassie thought she would take advantage of Anna's preoccupation to nip upstairs to see Kit. She was sure it would be safe, if she washed her face and hands thoroughly, after petting him. After all, that's what she did before returning home to Anna, after their Friday nights here, when she petted Kit with impunity.

She passed Jenny, en route to the house, and asked which room Kit was in.

"The box room. He'll be delighted to see you. How do you think it's all going? Anna seems happy enough meeting everyone, don't you think?"

"Yes, it's better than I could have hoped for, with everyone getting on so well. Thanks so much to you and James for all your effort."

"Don't mention it, love, just enjoy yourself."

Kit mewed affectionately, when Cassie entered. He came to greet her, rolling over on his back, to be petted, and have his belly stroked. He certainly had not forgotten her.

Cassie picked him up, and nuzzled his head under her chin, as she stroked his back. He was purring so loudly. It made her realise how much she missed him in her life. She leant against the wall, and held him in her lap. He was not content with that, and stood on her chest, kneading her with his front paws, and butted his head against her face. She laughed and held him a little away from her face. What a shame Anna had this allergy. It would be so lovely to have him home.

After a little while, Cassie reluctantly wrenched herself away from Kit and made her way to the bathroom. She washed her hands and face thoroughly, so that Anna would not pick up any hairs.

As she came back into the garden, she saw Anna watching her walk from the French doors, across the lawn, towards her, where she sat with Jenny and Deidre. Stella and Charles were playing ball with the girls. Nicky was over with the men, who were standing, drinking, around the BBQ with James.

Anna's gaze was hostile. As Cassie approached, she raised her voice and said, "Welcome back, stranger. Where have you been all this time?"

Cassie faltered at the cold tone in Anna's voice, and the smile on Jenny's face faded, as she turned to look at Anna.

"Didn't Jenny say? I saw you playing with Sophie, so I thought I'd just slip upstairs, and say a quick hello to Kit."

"Quick? I thought you'd abandoned me, and didn't I ask

you not to pet that cat, whilst I was here?"

Anna tried for humour but it did not quite come off, and Cassie caught the look that passed between Deidre and Jenny.

"You did, but I couldn't resist. I've washed my hands and face thoroughly, and Kit sends his love."

Cassie made a more successful effort to hit a light note.

"He still loves you better than me then, despite all my best efforts?" Jenny said playfully, smiling at Cassie.

Anna stared hard at Cassie, as Deidre moved up the wicker sofa, to make room for Cassie to sit down.

For the rest of the afternoon, until the sun began to drop toward the horizon, the group settled into a circle, and chatted and laughed, taking turns to play with the two little girls. James continued to fill the glasses of those who wanted more and were not driving, whilst Jenny made pots of coffee for the rest of them. Anna continued to chat to the others, but her eyes avoided Cassie. Cassie knew, with a sinking heart, that things had taken a wrong turn, because of her visit to Kit.

It was Stella and Charles who signalled the end of the event, when they took their leave in order to take Martha and Sophie home to bed. The others took their cue from this first departure, and readied themselves to do the rounds of farewells, and hugs, and promises to do it again soon. Anna was fulsome with her "it's been lovely to meet you," and "thank you so much for inviting me to meet you all."

She even took Cassie's hand as they finally walked out of the garden. She quickly dropped it, however, once they were on the street heading to the car.

As Cassie started the engine, she turned to look at

Anna's stony profile.

"Goodness, whatever is the matter with you? What have I done?"

"You know very well what's upset me."

Cassie turned out of Jenny's street, and onto the main drag. "No, I don't."

"You bring me to an event, to meet all of *your* friends, then you up and leave me alone, while you go and drool over a bloody cat."

Anna had begun insistently rubbing her eyes and mouth.

"And why do you think I've kept my distance since? Does it not occur to you, that even one of that damned animal's hairs on you, can kick off a reaction in me, as it's doing now? Can you open your window please?"

She slid down her own window, and leant out, breathing deeply.

"Oh surely not. I was only with him a little while."

"You were gone ages, while I had to make inane conversation with those boring, fucking people. And what the hell do you think this is?" and she gestured to her chest and face, which looked fairly normal to Cassie, apart from the redness where she had been rubbing.

"It's a reaction to you contaminating me with that wretched cat of yours."

"I'm sorry, if that's what I've done. I didn't think it would affect you, just me seeing Kit. I'll have a shower, when we get in. You seemed to be really happy playing with Sophie, though."

Anna's mood changed, like the sun emerging from behind a cloud.

"I was, she's an attractive little thing, such lovely limbs, and those innocent, trusting eyes. Nevertheless, that doesn't mean you could just neglect me, in a situation where I barely know anyone. I just think it shows a complete lack of sensitivity and, to be honest, really selfish behaviour. I wouldn't treat you like that, if the situation was reversed, and you were in company where I knew everyone, and you knew no-one."

Cassie squashed the thought that this had never happened: she had not been introduced to anyone from Anna's life.

"Yes, you're right. Sorry, I have been thoughtless. You did ok, though, didn't you? You seemed to be chatting, and getting on with everybody. I was proud of you."

"I made that effort for you, Cassie, because I love you. Quite frankly, none of them are really my cup of tea. It was clearly important to you, for me to meet them, so I did my best."

"And thank you for that. I'm sure they all liked you."

Cassie remembered the look exchanged between Deidre and Jenny. She was not sure they all had liked Anna, but she hoped that they had.

When they finally arrived home, Cassie showered scrupulously, scrubbed her nails, and washed her hair twice. She put all her clothes in the washing machine, and slipped into one of the nightdresses that she knew Anna liked.

Anna was sitting up in bed, breathing shallowly, and sucking on an inhaler.

"I'm sorry, but I'm still struggling. Could you be an angel, and sleep in the spare room tonight? I don't want to keep you awake, and I need to be quiet and calm, until this settles down."

Cassie agreed, and took herself off to the single bed. She didn't know what she felt, amongst all the emotions at war within her. She felt churned-up, confused, upset, guilty and angry – all at the same time. Sleep was a long time coming.

Chapter 13

Easter Monday dawned bright and warm. Anna seemed excited, when she woke Cassie in the spare room with a mug of coffee.

"I'm fully recovered, and raring to go. Let's do something, on this beautiful day – just the two of us. What do you say? Let's treat ourselves. What do you fancy doing?"

Cassie struggled upright, fighting off the deep slumber, in which she had been enfolded. She warily took the proffered, steaming mug.

"Well, gosh, let me think. I'm still half asleep. I thought you said you had a deadline to meet, for that story you were commissioned for?"

"Oh, to hell with it! I'll crack on tomorrow. It's too nice a day to waste and, after all that socialising yesterday, I feel like having you all to myself for a few hours," and she stroked Cassie's thigh suggestively.

When Anna was on form, thought Cassie, there was no-one in the world who could make her feel more loved and desired.

"Why don't we take a boat up the Thames to Hampton Court, go round the maze and then have a long, lovely lunch on the river?"

"Perfect! You're a genius, Davies! That's what we'll do. First, though, I need you in my big bed, said the Wolf to Little Red Riding Hood," and she clicked her teeth at Cassie, and made a claw of her hand.

They both laughed, as Cassie put down her mug, and

drew Anna on top of her. After making love, they had just stepped in the shower together, when Cassie's mobile rang. Cassie wrapped a towel around herself, and walked back to the bedroom to pick it up. Her mother's face was illuminated.

"Shit," she said, and then, "hello, Mum. What a surprise."

"I'm sure it is, Cassandra. As you never ring me, I try not to disturb you too often."

"You're not disturbing me, Mum. Don't be silly. It's lovely to hear from you. How are you? How are things in L.A.?"

"Same as ever. No, the reason I'm ringing you, Cassandra, is that I have to come to London, to meet with a producer, who might be interested in my doing a film with him. I've taken the opportunity to contact the boys, and try and arrange a family get together, so I very much hope you can make it."

"A family get together?" Cassie asked, trying to disguise her surprise and incredulity. "Where? When?"

"Try not to be dense, Cassandra. With your family, of course – your two brothers, and their partners, both your nephews and, of course, your mother! We are all meeting at Sebastian and Henrietta's. It's scheduled for the Spring Bank holiday, at the end of May."

Cassie's head was spinning; this was all so sudden and unprecedented.

"You said 'their partners'? Do you mean Rafe has a partner?"

"Oh keep up, Cassandra, for heaven's sake. That just shows how little effort you make to stay in touch with your family. Of course Rafe has a partner; he and Jean-Paul have been together for months now. They're living together in Paris, for goodness sake."

Cassie sat down heavily on the bed. This was all too much.

"I've told them about your Anna. Sebastian was quite shocked, said he'd never have thought of you as gay, but, as I told him, it makes you far more interesting. Rafe's delighted, of course, that you and he have something in common, at last. We all can't wait to meet Anna, so you must bring her too. Rafe is bringing Jean-Paul, needless to say. It will be a jolly house party. I can't wait, I'm so excited. Who knows how long I have left on this earth, so I hope there will be no excuses from anyone."

Cassie bit her lip. Portia Portman was immortal. *A National Treasure*, as everyone said. *A legend in her lifetime.* Presumably the Elizabeth Davies, who still lived somewhere within the persona of Portia Portman, was not immortal. Nevertheless, she was only seventy, and she was in the rudest of health, as far as Cassie knew. She had been banging on about her death since Cassie was a little girl. Cassie thought that her mother had drunk so much, for so long, that now she was pickled.

"Well, goodness, you've quite taken my breath away. When was all this arranged? Am I the last one to know?"

"Now, don't go all sensitive and hurt on me, Cassandra. You're hardly one to talk about communicating. I was talking to Rafe, when he flew out with Jean-Paul after Christmas. They had come to visit me, so that I could meet his partner. It was their idea, actually, that we all get together.

Rafe wants Jean-Paul to meet all of his family, and dare I hope that you might feel the same about Anna? Then I had to make sure that Sebastian and Henrietta were free to put us all up, so it's only just been finalised. Here I am, ringing you up at the first opportunity."

"I don't know what to say, Mum. I'm sure we'd love to come, but I'll have to check diaries first. I have no idea what Anna's movements are at the end of May."

"She's a writer isn't she? Freelance? She shouldn't have any movements, therefore. She's her own boss."

"I'll still have to talk to her. I imagine it will be a bit daunting for her, to meet the whole clan, all at once, don't you think? I just hope she'll agree to it."

"Nonsense, it's not daunting at all. If she loves you, she'll be delighted to get to know your family."

"I'll talk to her, Mum, and get back to you. It will be lovely to see you anyway – and Sebastian and Rafe, of course. Oh and the rest of them. Lovely. It's a great idea. Look forward to it."

"Right, I'll wait to hear. You take care now."

"And you, Mum. Love you," but Portia had rung off.

It was odd, Cassie thought, how she called her mother 'Portia' in her head. Portia Portman had tried so hard to have Cassie stop calling her 'Mum'. Yet Cassie continued to call her 'Mum' to her face. It was only inside herself that it was 'Portia'.

Anna had donned a towelling robe, and was making eggs, and more coffee, when Cassie joined her in the kitchen.

"I missed showering with you, sweetie. Who was on the phone?"

"I missed it too. I've just jumped in again, and had a quick and lonely shower. That was my mother on the phone."

Cassie proceeded to relay the conversation to Anna.

"Well that's a bloody nerve, to be so high handed. Who does she think she is?" Anna exploded.

Cassie laughed, "She thinks – no, she knows – that she is *the* Portia Portman!"

"Portia Portman can go whistle, she's not summoning me, like I'm one of her flunkies."

"I don't blame you one bit. You see what I'm up against? I have to admit, I'd love you to meet my family, and them you. I quite understand your reaction, though. Let's not talk about it any more just now. I don't want anything to spoil our day together."

"You're absolutely right. Not another word. We'll have a leisurely breakfast, and be on our way."

Anna kissed the top of Cassie's head, as she bent to spoon scrambled eggs on to her plate.

They did have a wonderful time: Relaxed and loving and tactile, Anna was funny and warm, and interesting company, throughout the day. She looked radiant, flushed with the sun, her impossibly white teeth flashing, as she smiled and laughed the whole time. Cassie felt proud to be with her and knew why it was she had fallen so quickly and deeply in love with her. She felt accepted and approved of, in a way she never had growing up.

When they finally wandered home, arm in arm, in the golden dusk, Cassie wished the day would never end. Like a child, she did not want to let it go by falling asleep.

After making long and passionate love to one another,

124

however, she could not prevent her eyes from closing. Her entwined limbs grew heavy and slack, against her lover's.

The following morning, Anna was dressed for going out, when she kissed Cassie awake.

"Where are you off to?"

"Sweetie, there's that deadline. I'm afraid, with you on holiday, and in the house, I'm going to get distracted, and not concentrate on my work. I'll want to ravish you all day instead! I'm going to make an early start in the British Library. I've got some research still to do, anyway. Hopefully, by the time I return this evening, not only will my beautiful partner have cooked dinner, but I'll have finished this bloody story. You go back to sleep, and have a nice long rest. You teachers need to catch up on your beauty sleep, in the school holidays."

She kissed Cassie's forehead. Cassie groaned, and fell back under the duvet. Soon she was fast asleep once more.

The light was brighter when she awoke to the sound of the front door buzzer. She started up and looked at the clock. Ten twenty. Who could this be on a Tuesday morning, just after the Easter weekend? She stumbled across the bedroom, grabbed her dressing gown from behind the door, and padded barefoot downstairs to the front door. It opened to a smartly dressed woman, with a clipboard. Not a bloody market researcher, she cursed to herself.

"Yes?"

"Is Miss Hardwick in?"

"No, I'm sorry she's at work. Can I help?"

"And you are?"

Cassie bridled.

"I'm her partner, actually. Who might you be?"

"Oh, my apologies, I'm Virginia Cook. I'm from Barton, Barton and Trump."

"I beg your pardon? Who are Barton, Barton and Trump?"

"We're Estate Agents. Miss Hardwick is renting this property through us. I've come to do the annual spot check, as is our usual practice."

Cassie shook her head in confusion.

"I'm sorry, there must be some mistake. My partner, Miss Hardwick, she owns this property."

"Miss, er?"

"Miss Davies."

"Well, Miss Davies, I'm sorry, but the mistake must be yours. I can assure you that Miss Hardwick is a tenant of ours, and has been for the last three years. We know her well. This property is owned by a gentleman who lives in Dubai. The tenancy agreement stipulates that we can do an unannounced check, every year, and that is what I have come to do this morning."

Cassie stared vacantly at the woman for a moment and then said, with a shake of her head, "I'm so sorry, I... I must have got confused, how silly of me. I've just woken up – not thinking straight, I expect. No, please do come in, and do your inspection."

She stood aside, to let the woman and her large clipboard, into the narrow hallway.

"Can I get you a drink, a tea or coffee?"

"That would be lovely, thank you. Coffee, black, no sugar, please. All right if I start upstairs?"

"Be my guest," Cassie said, gesturing toward the staircase as she headed in to the kitchen.

Her head was swimming. If Anna did not own this house, then she had lied to Cassie – and others. What reason would she have to lie? Cassie robotically made the coffee, and took it up to the woman, who was ticking off boxes on the forms, clipped to her board.

"Thanks, that's lovely. Nearly done up here. It all looks fine so far."

"Is the house let furnished, or unfurnished? Miss Hardwick hasn't clarified that," Cassie asked.

The woman gave her a troubled, and searching, look.

"I'm not sure about the ethics of this, in terms of confidentiality, but, I'm sure it's ok to just say it's unfurnished," she said hesitantly, "so I'm just checking the state of the fabric of the house, and whether it's cleaned and cared for, and the garden is kept tidy."

She was looking at Cassie with pity.

"Oh right, I see. Good," and Cassie, flushing, turned on her heel, and crossed the landing to the box room.

Anna used this room as her study. It was where she did her writing. She always closed the door, when she entered or exited. Whilst she had never said Cassie should not enter the room, it was an unspoken agreement that this was her space. Cassie needed the computer, as she had left her laptop at school, as that was where she used it the most. She sat at Anna's desk, feeling uncomfortable and guilty. The desk was clear, apart from the computer and a pot of pens. Conscious she was invading Anna's well-guarded privacy, she nevertheless tried the desk drawers. They were locked.

She sat thoughtfully for a few minutes, staring straight ahead at the blank wall, then she switched on the machine. She went straight to the internet, and tried not to give in to the temptation to explore Anna's files. She googled *Anna Hardwick*. Trawling through the results, some actress of that name figured prominently, but it was not her Anna, and it looked nothing like her. There were no other *Anna Hardwicks* of any relevance.

She sat still, her hands resting in her lap, her calm pose belying the turmoil inside. She heard the estate agent go downstairs. If Anna used different *noms des plumes,* her own name might not be publicized. She sat forward and typed in *Paul Hardwick.* There were a great many people by that name, in all kinds of walks of life, but all were alive, or clearly not Anna's brother.

Then she came across the name, in an excerpt from a 1985 edition of *The Times* newspaper. *Grandson of billionaire businessman commits suicide.* She read on: *The body of Paul Hardwick, the grandson of the billionaire entrepreneur, and businessman, Sir Arthur Hardwick, was found yesterday, at the family chateau. The chateau is situated outside Gordes, in the Luberon region of Provence, in the South of France. He had apparently hanged himself, in his own bedroom. He was found by the family's housekeeper in the early morning. Paul was sixteen and a student. He is said to have left no note, and the reason he took his own life is not clear.*

A spokesperson for the family said, "Paul was a bright and talented young man, who was much loved by his family, and popular with his peers. He is said to have had no apparent problems, and had not shown any signs of disturbance or depression. He will be sadly missed. The family request that their privacy be respected at this painful time."

Paul Hardwick is survived by his grandmother and grandfather, Sir Arthur and Elsie Hardwick, 52 and 50; his mother, Carla Hardwick, 32, and his younger sister, Anna Hardwick, 14. Sir Arthur is best known for his hostile take-over of Nibex Foods in 1983.

"Hello? I've finished now," the voice called up the stairwell.

Cassie quickly went to the bannister and called down, "Ok, thanks. Could you see yourself out? Great. Bye then."

The front door clicked, and she hurried back to erase her browsing history, and shut down the computer. She had no idea what to think, or what to do, with what she had just read. Paul had not died in a road accident, so that was another lie Anna had told her. Worse, the article said she was fourteen when her brother died. That could not be right. That would make her forty-seven, not thirty-seven, as she had told everyone. Had she not said, she was just four, when Paul died? The journalist must have made a mistake.

There was no way she was in her forties.

Chapter 14

When the front door slammed, with a deafening crash, Cassie knew Anna had returned in a very different mood from that morning. Her stomach knotted. She came out of the sitting room, as Anna was shrugging off her coat, in the hall.

"Not a good day, sweetheart?"

"Fucking awful day, if you really want to know."

Anna brushed past Cassie, and marched into the kitchen. The fridge door banged open, and Cassie heard the wine bottle being uncorked, and wine glugging into a glass.

"I think I'll join you," she said, following Anna into the kitchen, and taking another glass from the cupboard.

"When did you last buy a bottle of wine?" Anna snapped.

Cassie stopped mid-pour, and stared at her.

"What are you talking about? You know it's usually me, who does the shopping. How can you say such a thing? What's the matter with you?"

Anna stared back at her, with venom on her face, then shrugged and turned on her heel.

Cassie put down the bottle, with a shaking hand and gripped the edge of the worktop. Anna's lightning changes of mood bewildered and frightened her. It was like living with Jekyll and Hyde. The aroma of roasting lamb wafting from the oven reminded her of the meal she had ready for them. She straightened up, took a deep breath, and walked to the sitting room door.

"I've done your favourite, babes, roast lamb, roast potatoes, and green beans, with red wine gravy. It's nearly ready. Are you hungry?"

"No," came the curt reply. Cassie hesitated and then went and sat beside Anna on the sofa. She put her hand on Anna's arm but had it shrugged off.

"Please talk to me. What's the matter? What's happened to make you act like this?" Anna looked at her, and her face softened.

"Oh don't mind me. Sorry I snapped. It's just been a very frustrating day. The writing didn't go well, and I couldn't find the material I was looking for. I'll be ok after a bit more of this," and she raised her wineglass.

Cassie breathed out, flooded with relief.

"Well, pour yourself another glass while I lay the table. You'll feel more like eating, when you've relaxed."

"You're too good to me, when I'm such a grump," said Anna, and she leant forward to kiss her.

When they were tucking in to their roast dinner, and Anna had cheered up, Cassie decided to risk it.

"Guess what happened today?" she asked brightly.

Anna stilled her cutlery and raised her eyebrows,

"What?"

"Barton, Barton, and Trump came round to do an inspection."

"Oh, what a bore for you."

"I was a bit surprised, 'cos I thought you'd told me it was your house. And didn't you let the St Anne's lot think it was yours – on Sunday – when Jenny said you owned a house in Chiswick?"

"What the fuck is this, the Spanish Inquisition? What right have you got to question me, you sanctimonious little bitch?"

"Anna, don't speak to me like that. I'm just confused; I thought you told me, when I moved in and wanted to contribute, that there was no mortgage on the house for me to contribute to?"

"There is no fucking mortgage, if I pay rent, is there? And I'll talk to you any bloody way I like, particularly when you start to interrogate me."

"But if there's no mortgage, I should be paying half the rent, shouldn't I?"

"Oh fuck off, you cretin. Do you think I want any of your poxy teacher's salary? I own a fucking chateau in the South of France, for Christ's sake. I don't give a shit what you think."

She put-on a simpering, child-like voice, mimicking and mocking Cassie's delivery, and added, "or how confused you are. Nor do I care what conclusions your retarded friends come to. It's of no consequence to me, do you understand? And your food is disgusting."

She lifted up her plate and flung its contents in Cassie's face. Cassie began to cry, and tried to scrape the food and gravy off her face. The front door slammed. When she could see again, she gazed helplessly at the mound of food that had fallen into her lap.

After she had cleaned up the mess, and sobbed herself dry, Cassie desperately wanted to talk to Flick. She felt too ashamed, however, to reveal what had happened. After Anna's response to the question of the status of the house, the idea of going anywhere near the subject of Anna's age, or the circumstances of her brother's death, was out of the question.

It was past midnight, when Anna returned. Cassie was lying awake in the spare room. Anna came in and turned on the main light. Cassie quickly shielded her eyes, but felt Anna sink down on to the bed. She grasped Cassie's hand.

"Darling, can you ever forgive me? I am so, so sorry. I have no idea what came over me. I had a really shitty day, and then your questioning – well, it was just too much, I just lost it. I can't apologise enough. I know I was totally out of order. I don't know what I can do to make it up to you. I just have this thing about being questioned – you know that. It makes me crazy. I just wish you'd remember that, and not do it. You're like a dog with a bone.

"It's all over nothing, anyway. When you moved in, you just assumed things, and I let you, because it didn't matter, it's just details. You know how private I am. I don't want to discuss my affairs with anyone – even you, my kind, beautiful, amazing lover. I am sorry about that, because you are my soul mate, my life, but it's just one of my quirks, and I'm not sure I can change this aspect of me. Please, please, say you forgive me," and she pushed out her lower lip in a parody of sadness.

This time Cassie could not laugh. Anna then began to kiss her, and slide her hand between Cassie's legs. Cassie caught her hand and twisted her face away.

"I do forgive you, but I'm still shocked and hurt and – well, frightened. Yes, I'm frightened of your outbursts. I'm not ready to make love yet. I need some time to feel better, and to feel close to you again. Every time you behave like this, another brick goes up in my wall. It takes time to remove it again. Let's sleep on it, and maybe make love in the morning, please, Anna?"

"I am so desperate Cass, I need you to want me, so that *I* can feel better," and Anna continued, forcing her fingers into Cassie. It hurt.

"Don't! Please don't, Anna. This isn't fair. I'm not in the mood."

Cassie tried to arch away from Anna's fingers, but Anna just pushed harder.

"Just relax and you'll enjoy it. If you truly forgive me, then show it," and she forced Cassie's lips apart with her tongue, and kissed her hard.

She took Cassie's hand and pushed it down between her own legs. When Cassie's hand was unresponsive, Anna straddled her thigh and commenced bumping and grinding her vagina against her leg, whilst still clamping her mouth round her lips. Cassie could taste, and smell, the whisky. Anna pinched and kneaded her nipples, and breasts, until Cassie let out muffled cries of pain. Eventually Anna climaxed, with a shudder, and rolled off her.

Cassie lay still. Tears silently coursed from the outer corners of her eyes, down her temples, and soaked into her hair, and into the pillow. She felt utterly violated, as if she had been raped. Could that have been rape?

"I love you," said Anna sleepily, her eyes closed. "No-one will ever love you, like I love you. You're all mine."

Soon her breathing slowed and deepened. She was asleep. Still Cassie lay unmoving, cold and rigid with shock and disgust. At last, she gingerly slid to the side of the bed. She felt bruised and sore. She took herself to the bathroom and, quietly closing the door, she turned on the shower, and stood under the scalding jets of water, for as long as she could bear.

She dried herself, and crept into the spare room, where she huddled under the duvet in a foetal position. The tears started afresh, until finally she cried herself to sleep.

She woke to find Anna, fully clothed, leaning over her, and tenderly stroking her hair. She stiffened.

"Hello, my darling. What are you doing in the spare room? Why did you leave me?"

Cassie pushed herself away from Anna's hand, into a sitting position, and drew the duvet close around her body.

"I didn't want to make love last night. It was too soon after you said all those horrid things to me, and threw the food in my face. I told you that, but you went ahead anyway. It felt awful, like a rape or something. I couldn't stay with you in the bed after that."

Anna stood at the side of the bed, and stared down at her. Her face had gone white.

"That is a terrible thing to say – 'like a rape'. I can't believe you could say that to me. We were making love, for Christ sake. How can you think of it like that? I don't know what to say, I'm so shocked."

"You must have known I didn't want it. I said so, and I wasn't able to respond at all, but you just went on regardless."

"My God, we had a row, and we were making up, by making love, or so I thought. Isn't that what lovers do? You've made it into something horrible and dirty. What's wrong with you? How can you twist something so wonderful into something so sick?"

Anna walked to the window, and stood rigidly, staring out, with her back to Cassie.

"You really have a problem, don't you? You're not going to make it my problem, though. You can paint yourself as the victim, if you like, but from where I'm sitting, it's the other way round. You can't forgive. You want to hold a grudge, so then you turn everything into a justification for doing just that. Maybe you really cannot come to terms with falling in love with a woman. Well you need to deal with it, and take a look at yourself. You can nurse your resentment on your own, because I'm out of here. I need some time to digest being called a rapist by my own lover."

By the time the front door slammed, Cassie was too nauseous and bewildered to move. She was so miserable, she could not even bring herself to telephone Flick. She turned over and pulled the duvet over her head. She wanted oblivion, respite. She needed a breathing space while the world stopped, and she would not have to think.

Eventually her wish was granted, and she fell deeply asleep, as if shocked into unconsciousness, despite the hours she had slept the previous night. She was awakened, sharply and rudely, by the doorbell being persistently rung, and the knocker being alternately banged.

Sluggishly, she struggled out of bed, pulled a robe around herself, and gingerly descended the stairs. She felt shaky and fragile, as if she might faint, or shatter into millions of atoms, and float into the stratosphere.

The opened door revealed a frantic looking Jenny.

"Jesus, Cass, you look terrible. I knew something was wrong. Don't you remember we were supposed to meet at Hammersmith tube, and go pick up Martha and Sophie to take them to the Zoo?"

Cassie squeezed her eyes shut and slapped her forehead with unnecessary force.

"Fuck, fuck, fuck! I'm so sorry Jen, it completely went out of my mind."

Jenny pushed her gently back into the hall and closed the door.

"Go into the kitchen and sit down while I make coffee. Don't worry, I phoned Stella and explained that something must have happened. Her neighbour's going to watch the girls until we get there. No rush, you need to come to, have a coffee, and something to eat, and tell me what the hell is going on. You're as white as a sheet, and you look as if you've been bawling your eyes out all night."

Jenny bustled about making coffee, and setting it before Cassie, and then started to beat some eggs.

Cassie felt mute.

"Ok, do you want to tell me now, or take your coffee, have a shower, dress, and prepare a face to meet the world? Then you can have some breakfast and we can talk after that?"

Cassie nodded, tried unsuccessfully to smile, and, taking her coffee mug, she trudged back upstairs.

Chapter 15

By the time Cassie came downstairs, looking and feeling much better, Jenny had a plate of scrambled eggs and a fresh pot of coffee on the table.

"Eat first, and then tell me what you are prepared to tell me."

They ate in silence.

Cassie's thoughts raced. She longed to tell Jenny everything, and yet, to do so would make everything too real. She would have to make decisions, and she was not sure she was ready for that. Maybe, she and Anna could work things out, and find a better place to be. It could be true that some of what was happening was her fault: She was pushing Anna to explain things, in a way she knew Anna hated. Perhaps she should bide her time and see how things would develop.

Eventually, Cassie could not take another mouthful, and put her fork down, amongst the half eaten eggs.

"It's just that we had an awful row, and things happened and were said, that shouldn't have been."

Despite herself, Cassie began to cry. Jenny put her cup down.

"Oh my God! Oh Cass, that's so shit! No wonder you looked like hell. Do you want to talk about it?"

"It's nothing really – a misunderstanding. I learnt that Anna is renting this house; that she doesn't own it, as I thought. I sort of accused her of lying to me, to all of us. She just said it was a detail, that it didn't matter; that I had got hold of the wrong end of the stick. It wasn't important enough for her to correct me. You know she's very private, and hates to be questioned. She got very angry and walked out."

Jenny was watching her closely, her face closed, and her eyes narrowed. Cassie could tell she was not buying this sanitised version of events.

"Yes, but she had every opportunity, when we were all going on about the prices in Chiswick, and how well she must be doing, to say, 'Well, no, actually, I'm just renting.' And didn't you say she told you she had no mortgage, so you could contribute by buying food and stuff? That's not just a misunderstanding on your part, is it? That's a deliberate lie on her part."

"I know. I'm trying to make sense of it. I want to understand it, to understand her, but clearly confronting her, in the way I did, is not the way to go. But look, I've caused you and Stella enough trouble already. I'm feeling much better now. We'd better make a move to pick-up these girls, and take them to the zoo?"

"I get the message, babe. We'll say no more, but remember, I'm always here for you if you want to talk."

Jenny leant over and hugged Cassie, before starting to clear the table. Cassie bit back more tears, and joined Jenny in stacking the dishwasher and washing-up the saucepan, before heading off to the tube.

Cassie was subdued on the journey to collect Martha and Sophie. Jenny tactfully left her to it, only making the occasional comment, about inconsequential matters. When they collected the girls from Stella's neighbour, however, Cassie had no choice but to become more responsive and upbeat, as the excited sisters chattered and questioned her and Jenny all the way to Regents Park.

The demands of the delighted Sophie, and insatiably curious Martha, as Jenny and Cassie took them from one set of animals to another, focused and distracted Cassie. Both Jenny and Cassie were able to laugh a good deal throughout the day, at the reactions and comments of the little girls.

"Will the lion eat us, Cassie?" Sophie asked, as they watched the big cat prowl around its enclosure.

"Don't be silly, Sophie, lions won't eat you," Martha said.

"Well, they always bite me," Sophie insisted.

"Sophie, don't fib! You've never seen a lion before!"

"Have too, Martha. I see lions all the time – and they bite me."

"Well, that lion can't get to us because of the big fence," Jenny said, tactfully.

By the end of the afternoon, Jenny and Cassie returned two very tired sisters to their mother. They stayed for a cup of coffee, and a catch-up, with Stella, before heading back to Hammersmith. At the roundabout, they hugged.

"Don't forget, I'm on the end of the phone if you want to talk, or you're welcome to come across to mine any time you want – no notice required."

Cassie squeezed her friend tightly.

"You're a star, Jen. What would I do without you?"

As they took their leave, Jenny went to catch the bus to Epsom, and Cassie walked up to Chiswick. As she headed up the high street, she allowed the tears, that she had been holding in all day, to fall unchecked. She did not care about the curious looks she elicited from passers-by.

She had dried her eyes by the time she walked through the garden gate of their house, but her heart was sinking, and her stomach was doing somersaults. She turned her key, and pushed open the front door, to find Anna in the hall, shrugging on her coat. There was a suitcase at her feet. When she saw Cassie, she came rushing over to embrace her, and immediately started crying.

"Oh Cassie, I didn't know where you were. I've been ringing you, only to discover your phone's on charge in the bedroom. I was just about to leave. It's my grandmother, Cass. She's dying. They don't think she'll last the night."

Cassie was bewildered.

"I didn't know you had a grandmother. Who is she? Where is she?"

Anna stood back and wiped her eyes.

"It's my mother's mother, Elsie, Elsie Hardwick. She's in the Royal Sussex County Hospital in Brighton. She's been living in a nursing home in Hove, for years before my grandfather died. She developed early onset Alzheimer's, whilst we were all still living in the chateau in France. I've always gone down to see her when I can, though she doesn't know me any more, hasn't for years. I have to go to see her before she dies.

"She was a simple woman, the eldest of five children. Her father was a fisherman in Hull. She met my grandfather there, but she never coped with his money or success, and she was never happy in France. I have very fond memories of her, though, she was so loving. I hope I'm in time."

Cassie thought how little she knew about Anna's life or her movements.

"Of course, you must go. Would you like me to come with you?"

"No darling, that's kind of you, but I'd rather do this on my own."

"Does your mother know?"

"Yes, I've rung her, but she won't be able to get here in time, I don't think. She was going to see if she could get a flight from Avignon today, or tomorrow."

"Will she come here?"

"Oh God, no. We wouldn't last five minutes in each other's company. There's no love lost between us. She's never forgiven me for being Grandfather's favourite, replacing her in his affections. And, of course, he left me the chateau, and most of his money. She has a small allowance from his Trust Fund, but nothing like I got. She'll stay in a hotel. Look I have to go. I'll ring you as soon as I can, to let you know what's happening. I love you and I'm sorry we rowed."

"Me too. We'll talk again. You go now."

Cassie hugged her, and waved her off at the front door. She wandered into the kitchen, deep in thought, and, opening the fridge, retrieved a half-full bottle of Chardonnay, and poured herself a glass. She sat at the kitchen table. Why had Anna never mentioned this grandmother of hers? When did she last go down to see her? They had been living together for eight months now, and Cassie had known nothing of this woman. What else did she not know?

Clutching her glass, Cassie went upstairs and opened the door to Anna's study. She leant against the door jamb, and stared at the bare desk, and its locked drawers. What was in them? Where did Anna keep the key? She crossed to the bedroom, and put her glass down on her bedside table. She sat on the side of the bed, but immediately stood again, and crossed to Anna's side. She opened the drawer of the bedside cabinet, and rummaged through the contents. No key. She looked in the cupboard, underneath the drawer. She walked to the chest of drawers and riffled through the contents. She opened Anna's wardrobe, and, with a feverish determination, checked through pockets and handbags, ran her hand over the top shelf. Still nothing.

She looked through the suitcases, that Anna kept under the bed. Empty. She hurried back to the study, and lifted the corners of the carpet. She slid her hands quickly across the top of the door jamb, and the wooden pelmet above the window. She felt beneath the desk top, for anything taped to it. Again, no key.

"Stop this, Cassandra," she told herself firmly, exhaling slowly.

Collecting her glass, she returned to the kitchen to prepare her supper. She should not be snooping on her partner. She felt ashamed of herself. This was no way to conduct a relationship. She determined that she would not allow herself to think like this again, let alone act on the thoughts.

Chapter16

Elsie did die that night. She had been unconscious when Anna arrived on the ward, and she never regained consciousness. Cassie received a tearful call from Anna, the following morning. Her mother was arriving at Heathrow, that evening, and Anna was returning to meet her at the airport.

Cassie offered to go in her stead, but again Anna said she would deal with it herself. She would go with her mother straight back to Brighton, as that is where the funeral would be held. She would see her installed in a hotel, stay the night, and return home the following day. The funeral would not be for another week, and she said she could not stand being around her mother all that time. She did agree to Cassie attending the funeral, however, and meeting her mother there.

The Easter holidays were over, and Cassie was back at school. She needed to see the Head, to negotiate a day's leave, but Mavis was more than supportive. So it was, that the following Friday, Cassie found herself sitting beside Anna on the 10.20 train, from Victoria to Brighton, on a warm, May day. When the train pulled into Brighton station, on time at 11.17, the hailed a taxi for Woodvale crematorium, on the Lewes Road. They would be meeting Anna's mother there, in time for the 11.45 service.

"You mark my words, she will have booked a flight straight back to France, today. There'll be no wake, or hanging about."

"I hope I get the chance to talk to her. Couldn't we go for lunch, or something, afterwards?"

"I'll suggest it, but don't hold your breath. She's somewhat of a recluse, my mother. She hasn't been back to the UK in over a decade."

"Not even to see her mother, holed-up in a nursing home here?"

"She hated her mother. She was a Daddy's girl."

"Goodness! Will anybody else from your family be there?"

"I have no other family, sweetie. There will probably be some representative from the home, and that will be about it, I should think."

"How sad."

"Gran wouldn't care. She and my grandfather moved down from Hull to London, when they married. Elsie was eighteen then. Neither of them had much to do with their families after that, and once my grandfather had clawed his way up from barrow boy to department store owner, he cut all ties with their Northern roots. Eventually they moved to France, when my mother was still small."

"Gosh. You've never told me any of this before."

"Why would I? It's all history, and totally irrelevant to us. It's only come up now, 'cos poor old Gran's gone."

"But haven't you ever wanted to track down your extended family – your grandmother's family, your grandfather's family?"

"No, what are they to me? I told you about Elsie's family, and my grandfather was the youngest of ten kids. His father was a fisherman too, I think. They were desperately poor and uneducated, from all accounts. My grandfather outgrew his families. I'd have nothing in common with their relatives, even if I met them, but I have absolutely no interest in doing so. At least my mother and I agree on that much."

"You said your grandfather outgrew his families. What about your grandmother?"

Anna laughed scornfully. "You didn't know Grandfather, Cass. He was a force of nature, not to be opposed. Everyone in our family was controlled by Grandfather, including my poor Gran. That's why we all bear my grandfather's name, not our poor Australian father's name."

Cassie was silent. The Hardwick family sounded so ruthless, and tragic, and Anna's poor father seemed to have been erased from history.

The taxi drew into the Crematorium, and Cassie saw a woman standing by the door to the chapel. She was unmistakably Anna's mother. They shared the same slender frame, fine features and auburn hair. In confirmation, Anna raised her hand to the woman in greeting. They paid the driver and strolled over to join Carla Hardwick.

"This is Cassie, Carla. Cassie, this is my mother."

"Pleased to meet you, Cassie," Carla said, proffering her hand to shake. Up close, Carla looked older, more tired and lined, but well-preserved, and still striking. She wore a sleeveless, close-fitting, linen dress, elbow-length black gloves, and discreet jet jewellery. Cassie guessed she must be in her mid to late sixties. She looked the epitome of French chic, though, of course, she was not French by birth. Cassie shook her hand.

"I'm very pleased to meet you, Mrs Hardwick, but I

wish it was in happier circumstances."

"Oh do call me Carla, Mrs Hardwick sounds so stuffy. It's not really so sad, you know. My mother had a good innings, given her dementia. I think her death comes as a blessed release to her, and to us."

"Shall we go in?" asked Anna. There was an edge of irritation in her voice.

Carla and Cassie followed her into the chapel. As Anna had predicted, there was only one solitary person, already seated. She came over to introduce herself as Deborah Walters, Manager of Sunnybanks Nursing Home, and to give her condolences. The perfunctory and arid service then commenced. Eventually the coffin slid through the curtain, and the mourners were released into the sunshine.

"Cassie wondered if we should have lunch?" Anna said.

"Well, I have to go straight to Heathrow, for an early evening flight, but I suppose, if we found somewhere near the station, I would have time for a quick lunch."

Deborah put in, "I have to get back to Sunnybanks, but I have to drive that way back. Why don't I give you a lift to the station?"

"Are you sure? That would be great," replied Anna.

They piled into Deborah's car, and made polite, stilted conversation, until they alighted opposite the station. They wandered down Queens Road, and found a likely looking pub that served gastro food. Anna went to the bar, to order some wine and collect the menus. Carla and Cassie settled themselves around a table in the window.

"How long have you and Anna been living together?" Carla asked.

"It's coming up for nine months, but Anna's so private. Do you know, I didn't know about Elsie until she died? To this day, Anna still hasn't let me read anything she's written. Have you read any of her stuff?"

"Read what? Sorry, I don't know what you're talking about."

"Well, Anna's a writer, isn't she? Didn't you know?"

"First I've heard of it, sweetie. I thought she was living on my father's money. There was enough left to her for her not to have to work for the rest of her life, more than he left me, that's for sure. Still I suppose she earned it, but so did I."

Carla sounded bitter and resentful. Cassie's head was reeling.

"Earned it?" she asked faintly.

"Oh, yes. Didn't Anna tell you?"

"Didn't Anna tell her what?" Anna plonked a tray in front of them. It contained three menus, glasses, and a bottle of white wine, in an ice bucket. Anna commenced to pour.

"That you earned your grandfather's fortune," said Carla, "and the chateau."

Both women were staring at each other with undisguised hostility.

"I should shut my mouth, if I were you," said Anna to her mother, a threat hanging in her words.

"So, I hear you're a writer now. What do you write, Anna? I'm intrigued. Would I have read anything you've written?"

Anna rounded on Cassie. "So you couldn't wait to gossip about me to this bitch, could you? What else have you told her?"

"We were just chatting," Cassie protested feebly, her

148

stomach knotting.

"Temper, temper, Anna!" Carla sneered, "You haven't changed much, have you, baby girl?"

She turned to Cassie.

"You'll have to watch yourself, Cassie. Anna has a terrible temper, and she's been known to be violent too, you know. She once threw a chair at my head. I feared for my life on that occasion, I can tell you."

"Anyone who has been as bad a mother as you have been, Carla, deserves to be murdered. When have you ever been there for me, when I've needed you, or acted like a mother to me?"

Carla's eyes narrowed, and she hissed, "Well you made damn sure there was always *someone* to look after little, old, Anna, didn't you?"

Anna tilted her glass, and threw its contents into Carla's face.

Cassie gasped, and, at the other tables, heads turned toward them. Anna and Carla both stood. Carla took out a handkerchief and wiped her face.

"I'm leaving now. I never want to see you again, Anna. I hope that's clear. Goodbye, Cassie and good luck, because you'll need it," and with that, she turned on her heel and left.

"Excuse me," Anna mumbled, heading for the lavatories.

Cassie sat unmoving, still in shock at the whole horrific scene. She had no idea what had just taken place, nor why it had happened. She wanted to go home. She wanted to be with Jenny or Flick. She wanted normality.

After a while, Anna came back. She slid wordlessly into her seat. She looked as if she had been crying. Cassie watched her anxiously. Anna drained her glass and then refilled it. She glanced across at Cassie's glass and recharged that as well.

"Do you want to order?" she asked without looking at her.

"No, I couldn't eat anything now. Are you ok?"

"I'm fine, but I can't eat either, though. I'm sorry you had to witness all that, but you see why I hardly ever talk to my mother. We hate each other."

Cassie didn't know what to say. She slid her hand across the table, and put it over Anna's hand, and squeezed.

"Are you mad with me?"

"No, sweetie, it's not you, it's her. Sorry, if I snapped at you. That's what she does to me, she drives me crazy. It will suit me down to the ground never to have to see her again, and now that Gran's dead, there'll be no reason to, if I don't want to."

Still Cassie could think of nothing to say.

"Come on, Cass, let's go home."

They finished their wine, and set off for the station. Neither spoke a word. Once on the train to Victoria, Anna slept, and Cassie stared out at the passing countryside, her mind racing with thoughts and questions.

Chapter 17

That evening, Cassie was due to go to Jenny's house to see Kit, Stella, and Nicola. After the day she had had, she was desperate to go, but Anna was still upset, and wanted her to be with her. So, she stayed in, and they had an early night. Anna wanted to make love. Cassie did not feel remotely aroused, but she went through the motions, for Anna's sake, and tried to hide her lack of interest. When it was over, Anna curled herself into Cassie.

"You know I love you so much, Cass. You are my safe harbour, especially after a day like today, having yet another show-down with my cow of a mother. I don't know what I'd do without you. Kill myself, I guess."

"Anna, don't say things like that, even in jest. It's not funny."

"I'm not intending to be funny, my love, I mean it. I don't think I could live without you, now."

"If you love me so much, Annie, why do you shut me out so much? Like about your grandmother, or your inheritance, or your writing?"

"I don't mean to shut you out, my darling, it's just the habit of a lifetime, to guard my privacy. It was the only way I could protect myself, when I was growing up. I learnt not to trust anyone. You've seen what she's like, my bitch mother. Elsie was weak, and cowed by my grandfather, and by my mother, but she was the only one showed me any love and affection, apart from Paul, of course, before he died."

Cassie felt a rush of love and tenderness for this complex,

difficult woman.

"But I thought your mother said, you were your grandfather's favourite?"

There was a long pause, and then Anna said quietly, "Yes, but that was different."

"What did she mean when she said that you always made sure there was one person who could take care of you? Why did that make you throw your wine at her?"

Cassie felt Anna stiffen in her arms. She pulled away and looked in Cassie's eyes.

"She meant my grandfather. She and he had always been very close. She was the only child, and he doted on her. He loved Paul, of course, but when I was born I became his favourite. She hated me for that. She was jealous of me, and my relationship with him. She treated me as if I had deliberately stolen him away from her. I was just a child, but she didn't love and protect me. She treated me like a rival who had bested her."

"Oh how awful, Anna. I can see now why, what she said, angered and upset you so. Did no-one else love you, as you grew up? Did you love anyone? You've never talked to me about other relationships, even though I've told you all about mine."

"What can I say? When I left France and was sent to school in England I was fourteen. It was after Paul died. I had some crushes on girls at St Paul's, but I really didn't have any real relationships until University. There was a man then that I was in love with. It lasted about two years. After that, there have been some men and some women, but no-one who has been as special as you. I've been quite promiscuous in my time darling, I'm sorry to say."

Anna, curled Cassie's hair between her fingers.

"I did have a longer, more serious relationship, a few years back, with a woman called Lucy, but it didn't work out."

"How long were you with her? Did you live together?"

"We were together about three years, but only lived together for eighteen months, and that's what fucked it, really. She became so possessive and controlling. She got increasingly violent, first verbally, and then physically, and was always putting me down. She was so unpredictable and, at times, frightening. I couldn't stand it. I had to get out, in the end, for my sanity's sake! My self-esteem was left in shreds."

"Oh, Anna, I'm so sorry! That sounds terrible. Did she live here?"

"No, it was before I came here. I moved in with her at her place. Big mistake. No, sweetie, nobody has been here before you, and nobody will ever be here again. Only you, Cassie Davies, my lover, my love," and Anna leaned over to kiss Cassie, at first gently, and then more passionately.

This time, Cassie found herself responding and, pretty soon, she was panting, and begging Anna to make love again. Anna obliged.

The next morning, they stayed in bed late. Passions were running high again, for both of them, and Cassie wondered how she ever could have doubted their relationship. Yes, Anna could be difficult and mercurial at times, but she was also passionate and exciting, and, essentially, loving.

"Darling, don't forget it's my family get together at the

end of May. Will you be able to bear it?"

"You bore with my bitch mother, I'm sure I'll cope with your bitch mother, and siblings!"

They burst out laughing and, falling into each other's arms, they rolled around the bed, tickling each other.

One more weekend passed without them seeing another soul, or talking to anyone else. Monday rolled around all too quickly. Cassie was glad to catch up with Jenny, however, and she told her all about the funeral, and the scene with Anna's mother.

"God, it sounds a nightmare. There's never a dull moment with Anna is there?"

Cassie laughed, but she was not sure that Jenny had meant the remark as a compliment.

"How was the girls' night on Friday?"

"Yeah, good. Since you weren't coming, there was no need for Stella or Nicky to see Kit, so we went to the pub after school. It made a nice change. Stella says the girls haven't stopped going on about our trip to the zoo. They keep asking when we're going to take them out again."

"Ah, how lovely. Bless 'em. We must do it again. Perhaps in the summer holidays? They're such lovely kids."

"They are," agreed Jenny, but she looked wistful.

"Any news on that front, Jen?"

"We're been referred for IVF. The investigations have found nothing wrong with either of us, that would stop us getting pregnant, so they just don't know."

"Still, that's good news all round isn't it? Nothing obviously wrong, and the chance of IVF doing the trick?"

"I suppose so. Making love to order has been a bit of a

154

strain on both of us, but especially on poor, old James. I see that you are glowing again, though, so that's a good sign."

To her consternation, Cassie felt herself blush. Jenny burst out laughing.

"Oh Cass, you kill me, you're so easily discomfited. I didn't mean to embarrass you, girl."

"Oh, don't mind me, Jen."

Jenny leant over and hugged her. "I do love you, you daft 'apeth."

The bell rang for the start of lessons, so the friends reluctantly took their leave, and headed off for their respective classrooms.

They caught up at lunch, and Jenny talked some more about how she and James were feeling about the IVF – desperate and anxious, and excited and hopeful – all at the same time. Cassie told Jenny of her apprehension at the upcoming meeting with her family and Anna. Jenny related Kit's latest amusing, and endearing antics. They laughed and reminisced about their day out with Martha and Sophie. Both were careful not to mention the state Cassie had been in that morning, when Jenny had turned up, nor the reasons for it.

When Cassie arrived home that night, Anna had a *coq au vin* simmering on the hob, and the table laid. A green salad was in the centre. There was a bottle of red wine breathing on the worktop.

"Wow! What's the occasion?"

"No occasion, I just wanted to do something nice for you, to show you how much I love you and how happy you make me."

"You're spoiling me."

"And why not? You're always spoiling me – far more than I spoil you – so I wanted you to know how much I appreciate you."

Anna came over and took Cassie in her arms. They started to kiss, and both of them were responsive, and beginning to become aroused. Anna pushed Cassie gently away,

"You're not spoiling my meal, you siren, you! First I feed you, *then* I fuck you!"

Cassie burst out laughing and they both moved to eat. Cassie poured the wine and Anna ladled out the chicken, and brought some hot crusty bread from the oven.

As they both tucked in Anna said, "About this weekend with your family, can you find out if your brother has any cats. It might be a problem, if so; you know I can't be too careful. If they do have cats, I suppose we could stay in a guest house nearby, and just meet them at a local restaurant, rather than staying in their place. What are they called again, your brother and sister-in-law?"

"Sebastian and Henrietta. The thing is, it's supposed to be a sort of house-party set-up, from Friday to the Bank Holiday Monday, so I don't think they'll be going out to restaurants, as such."

Anna groaned. "God, I'm not looking forward to it. I hope you don't mind me feeling like that, babes?"

"Of course, not. I quite understand, love. You know I'm not looking forward to it much either, but I will enjoy them meeting you."

"I bet they'll hate me."

"They won't hate you. They'll just patronise you, and

despise you. Just as they do me!"

They both giggled, and smiled into each other's eyes. Anna raised her wineglass.

"Here's to you and me against the world, my love – families included! We won't let the bastards grind us down."

"I'll drink to that," and Cassie took a swallow of the excellent Malbec Anna had bought for the occasion.

"You know what, though, I think I'll give Seb a ring, after dinner, and get the lowdown about the weekend, and check out the cat situation. What do you think?"

"Thanks babe, for taking care of me, about this. Yes, I think that's a good plan, and it will set my mind at rest."

After clearing up together, Cassie went into the sitting-room to make her call, whilst Anna set up the ironing board in the kitchen.

Sebastian and Henrietta's landline rang for quite a while, before going to answer phone. Cassie did not bother to leave a message, instead she tried her brother's mobile. It went to voicemail. She thought of trying again later, but she wanted to know what to tell Anna, so she tried Henrietta's mobile.

"Hello?"

"Oh Hi! Is that Henrietta?"

"Yes."

"Ah, Henrietta, it's Cassie here, Seb's sister? I tried your landline, and Seb's mobile, but couldn't get through."

"Oh, Cassandra! My goodness, the Ghost of Christmas Past! What a long time since you and I have spoken! Well, yes, I'm at the gym, not at home, and Sebastian is still at work. What can I do for you?"

"Is it a good time to talk now, if you're at the gym?"

"I obviously don't want a two hour heart to heart, at the moment, Cassandra, but if we can deal with this briefly, then please go ahead."

Cassie winced. "I just wanted some details about the Spring Bank Holiday weekend get together at yours. Just so that Anna and I know what's happening, and what to plan for, and pack, as it were."

As it were? What on earth was that about? She never said *as it were.* She was morphing into Henrietta.

"It will just be a weekend house party, just family, and a few friends round on one of the days, the usual thing. Your mother is hoping everyone will arrive Friday night, and leave after lunch on Monday. That's fine by us, but, obviously, if any of you can't make the whole of the weekend, that's fine too. We'll just work around things. Is that ok, Cassandra?"

"It sounds marvellous, Henrietta, and it's so good of you to be doing this for all of us, when I know you're so busy with work, and the boys and everything. Can we bring anything?"

"No, don't be silly, but let us know nearer the time when you expect to arrive and leave – day, time – that sort of thing. The boys will be home, of course, for the Bank Holiday, so it will be lovely for everyone to be able to see them won't it?"

"Oh yes!" lied Cassandra, though, she had not known that they were not at home all the time. The last time she had seen them, she had found them to be precocious and smug. They seemed to have inherited their parents' sense of entitlement and superiority.

"Good. Well, if that's all, Cassandra, I shall return to my treadmill." Henrietta attempted a light-hearted laugh.

"Just one more thing, Henrietta."

Cassie caught the sound of a suppressed sigh at the other end.

"I can't remember, do you have any pets – any dogs or cats, or whatever? It's just that Anna is frightfully allergic to cats."

Frightfully? Another Henrietta-ism.

"I'm surprised you've forgotten, Cassandra," said Henrietta, with ice in her voice, "your youngest nephew is also allergic to cats *and* dogs, so, no, we do not have any pets."

"Oh, of course, yes, how silly of me."

How silly of me! Cassie screwed-up her face in shame.

"Well, it's been lovely talking to you again, Henrietta."

No, it had not, she thought.

"We look forward to seeing you next weekend and I'll let you know exactly when we're arriving and leaving. Enjoy the rest of your evening, on the treadmill."

Cassie silently doubled-up with embarrassment. Had she actually said that?

"Bye, Cassandra."

The connection ended. Cassie was still bent over, biting the knuckle of her left hand, whilst the right continued to grip the phone. What an idiot she was. Henrietta always managed to make her feel like a gauche, stupid, little girl – but then – so did the rest of her family.

Cassie eventually went back into the kitchen, to tell Anna that there were no pets. Their rueful faces, as she shared the news, made them laugh, as they realised they had both been hoping for a reason not to go.

159

Chapter 18

Anna and Cassie agreed that they would make their excuses for the Friday night of the Bank Holiday weekend, claiming Anna had a prior engagement for a publishing do at *The Savoy*. That way, they could arrive in time for lunch, on the Saturday, and only have to spend two nights, instead of three, at the gathering.

Cassie was told by Sebastian, when she rang him to tell him, that everyone else was arriving on Friday, including Portia, Rafe and Jean-Paul. She could tell by the irritation in his voice, that, already, they were the black sheep of the gathering.

"It is so typical of you, Cassandra, to complicate matters, but I quite understand that Anna has more important things to do."

Cassie bit her lip, at Sebastian's cool tone.

"Anna's publisher only let her know about this function last week. She told him she had a prior engagement, but he stressed, for the success of her current book, she needed to be seen there, and have the chance to network. It was a difficult decision and Anna sends her apologies, Seb."

Cassie was amazed, and rather ashamed, by the fluency of her lying.

"I see. We'll look forward to hearing all about this important book then, and Anna's illustrious writing career."

Cassie's heart sank. "Oh no, you see, Anna is very private about her writing. She doesn't like to talk about it at all – to anyone – not even me."

"Curiouser and curiouser," Sebastian replied.

After the phone call, Cassie was dreading the visit, even more than she had before. When Saturday rolled around, it was with a sense of foreboding, that Cassie drove them onto the eastbound North Circular.

"This is fun," laughed Anna, as they hit a stationary queue of traffic, before the turn off for the M11.

"I'm afraid that nothing about this weekend is going to be fun, mark my words. I'm dreading it."

Anna placed her hand over Cassie's, which was resting on the gear stick.

"Don't forget, my love, this time you have me with you. I won't let anyone hurt you."

Over two hours later, they drove up the sweeping, gravel driveway to Sebastian's seventeenth century manor house, nestled on the outskirts of Clare. They had barely drawn level with the four cars, already parked in front of the house, when Sebastian and Henrietta appeared, arm in arm, framed in the large front door, like royalty.

"Heard your wheels on the old gravel. Jolly good ETA, Cassandra. Almost spot on to the minute! I am surprised!" Sebastian boomed to Cassie, before bounding down the stone steps.

He gave her a hug, and held out his hand to Anna.

"Delighted to meet you, Anna Hardwick. I'm Sebastian, of course, Cassandra's brother, and this is my wife, Henrietta."

Henrietta had followed Sebastian more slowly, down the stone steps and now, stepping onto the gravel, she extended her hand to shake Anna's, and then turned to kiss Cassie on her cheek.

"Welcome, both of you, to our home. You've timed it perfectly, we're just having aperitifs in the drawing room, before luncheon is served. No, Cassandra, leave the luggage. Sebastian will bring it in. Come and join the others. Everyone's dying to see you both."

As they entered the chintzy, pink and green room, four of the five figures seated around the room rose to greet them. Her nephews, Marcus and Giles, stood to attention with self-conscious gallantry, and diffident half smiles. A stocky, hirsute man, whom Cassie guessed was Jean-Paul, made a mock bow to them. Portia, of course, remained seated. Cassie, without even looking, could feel her mother's eyes raking over her, and sizing-up Anna. The fourth male, Rafe, crossed the room quickly, to hug Cassie and shake Anna's hand.

He looked different from how she remembered him, from their last meeting. He had grown his hair, and now sported a beard. He was leaner than she remembered and, all in all, seemed a younger and more raffish version of himself.

As he hugged her, he said, "My God, Cassandra, I don't think I've ever seen you looking so *soigneé*."

"Thank you, Rafe. I'm sure I'd be delighted if only I knew what it meant!"

Portia, from the corner of the chaise longue, gave a histrionic sigh, and, Sebastian, who had just entered the room, tutted.

Jean-Paul chuckled and said, "*Je suis désolé*, Cassandra, but it is my fault your brother is being so Gallic. I am a bad influence on him. He means you are looking elegant, well-groomed and smart, and indeed you are – both of you."

He beamed at Anna. "Ah, *la belle dame sans mercie, non?* You are indeed a heart breaker, *mademoiselle.*"

"Welcome," said Rafe, extending his hand to Anna. "My partner's right. I must say my sister has shown unexpectedly good taste in picking you, or allowing herself to be picked by you. You are very beautiful, Anna, and I suspect you are the reason she is looking so radiant."

Cassie saw that Anna was positively glowing with all this praise.

"Well introduce me properly to *your* reason for looking better than I've ever seen you look," laughed Cassie, looking across at Jean-Paul.

Portia was smiling magnanimously at being side-lined by her progeny. She positively twinkled at Cassie and Anna, as introductions were made.

"Anna, Cassandra, meet the love of my life, Jean-Paul Lenoir."

"*Enchanté,*" cried the lover, bounding across to kiss Cassie on both cheeks. "*Et tu, la belle ma'mselle*, Anna," he added, turning to kiss Anna in the same extravagant manner.

"Charmed, I'm sure," laughed Anna ironically.

"Anna," announced Sebastian, "this is our mother, Elizabeth Davies, more well known as Portia Portman, of whom I'm sure you will have heard," and he gestured dramatically to the striking woman, who still remained seated on the chaise longue, holding court.

Anna obeyed the prompt, and paid obeisance to the matriarch, by going over to her to shake hands. Portia remained seated, and extended a bejewelled hand.

"Delighted to meet you at last, Anna. Welcome to our little family. Cassandra, come and give your mother a kiss."

Cassandra did as she was bid.

"What would you girls like to drink?" asked Henrietta.

"I'll have a gin and tonic, please," said Cassie.

"The same for me," Anna said.

Sebastian continued his hosting duties. "Anna, this is Marcus, our eldest son and Giles, his younger brother. Boys, say hello to your aunt, and her partner, Anna Hardwick."

The boys, after standing up, when Cassie and Anna had entered the room, had sat back down next to their grandmother. They now leapt to their feet again, and parroted, almost in unison, "Hello Aunt Cassandra, hello Anna."

Cassie thought how robotic they seemed. They had inherited Henrietta's pale skin and lank, dark hair.

"Giles has just joined Marcus, as a boarder at Dulwich College," Sebastian continued proudly.

Ah, that's why Henrietta had said they would be at home this weekend, Cassie realised. She thought about her own pupils and the difference between them and her privileged nephews.

"Do you still have that damn cat, Cassandra?" Portia interrupted.

She turned to Anna and said, "I've been telling her, Anna, that she would turn into some mad, old, spinster school-teacher, surrounded by cats and smelling of piss."

"Anna is allergic to cats, so Kit had to go. My friend took him. I had to ring Henrietta, before we came here, to check she didn't have cats."

She could have bitten her tongue out! She had laid

herself open again!

Of course, Portia did not miss the opportunity. "What on earth is the matter with you, Cassandra? Surely you should remember that Giles is allergic to everything? Fancy having to telephone poor Henrietta with such a question! Really! Well, thank goodness you've got rid of that creature of yours. They are revolting animals, always killing poor little birds, and mammals."

"I must say, I agree with you there, Portia," said Anna.

Cassie looked at her, incredulity and hurt written all over her face. Why would she say that?

"Shall we go in to luncheon?" put in Henrietta. "Bring your drinks through, everyone, if you haven't yet finished."

They all trooped into the red and mahogany dining room, which was Henrietta's idea of stately home living, but just felt oppressive and claustrophobic to Cassie. There were place names to indicate where they would sit. Anna had predictably been put between Portia and Sebastian. All the better to interrogate her, thought Cassie. She was between Jean-Paul and Marcus. She had taken a liking to Jean-Paul.

As Sebastian poured the wine and they helped themselves to the salad, bread and cold cuts, Anna asked, "And what is it you all do? Obviously, I know what Portia does but, you, Sebastian?"

"I'm first violinist at the Royal Philharmonic Orchestra, and I also lecture at the University in Cambridge. Henrietta is a partner in a GP practice in Haverhill. Rafe?"

"Ah yes, well I'm a jobbing journalist for my sins, Anna."

"He's a well-regarded foreign correspondent, actually," Jean-Paul scolded, smiling at Rafe.

"And he is a well-regarded film director in French cinema," added Rafe, gazing fondly at his lover.

"Shouldn't it be us, asking searching questions of you, Anna?" Portia asked, with an unctuous charm. "For instance, how long have you been a writer? Have you ever worked at anything else? What have you written? What is your *nom de plume*, as I confess I googled Anna Hardwick and couldn't find anything?"

Cassie watched two small red spots appear on her lover's cheeks, and her heart sank, knowing that Anna was becoming enraged.

"As Sir Cliff Richard said, when rudely questioned about his sexuality, 'that ain't nobody's business but mine.'"

Anna smiled a saccharine smile, and took a sip of wine. Cassie stifled the gasp that was rising in her chest, and Portia's lips tightened.

"My, you are an enigma, wrapped in a mystery, aren't you, Anna Hardwick?"

Sebastian cleared his throat, and tried for a jocularity that was not quite convincing. "Cassandra, and what about you? Are you still wasting what talents you have, teaching little oiks, in the inner city?"

It was Cassie's turn to feel rage.

"I would hardly call Hammersmith, the inner city, Seb, and nor can my pupils, who are all from diverse backgrounds, be called 'oiks'. But, yes I am still teaching and enjoying it."

"And very talented she is at it, too," added Anna, and Cassie shot her a grateful look, though her thought was that Anna could not possibly know anything about her as a teacher.

"You would earn more, teaching in the private sector, wouldn't you?" asked Henrietta.

"I don't know," said Cassie, "but I wouldn't want to do that."

She did not add that she probably would not earn more in the private sector, nor that she did not believe in privately educating children, with the unjust two-tier system it led to, that only perpetuated inequality in society. She wanted nothing more, at this moment, than to take her leave from this family of hers, where she had never really felt she belonged.

"You're not still in that ghastly little bedsit in Shepherds Bush, are you?" Portia asked.

"No, I told you, I'm living with Anna."

"Did you? Oh, I don't remember. I can't keep up with you all," and Portia waved her hand dismissively past her ear.

"Where?" asked Jean-Paul.

This time Anna answered. "In Chiswick. We have a house there we share."

Cassie noted that, this time, Anna did not claim it as hers.

"Property prices are quite high in Chiswick, I understand," fished Henrietta.

"Mm," murmured Anna, forking some salmon into her mouth.

There was a silence, in which could be heard the sounds of mastication and swallowing. As the silence went on, an awkwardness descended on the table. Cassie surmised that the questioning of all the others had taken place the previous evening, so she and Anna were the only ones left in the limelight.

As if to prove her right, Portia suddenly launched at Anna.

"Did you go to University Anna? You know, of course, Cassandra refused to sit the entrance exam for Oxford or Cambridge, despite all our advice and encouragement, didn't she boys? Insisted on that silly Bachelor of Education from some nondescript new University. She could have done so much better for herself."

"Yes, I did. I went to Bristol, as it happens, but I do think a University education is over-rated these days. At least Cass did something useful and vocational, unlike my English degree."

Cassie again felt a rush of gratitude and love for Anna. She had promised she would not let Cass's family hurt her, and, here she was, trying to stand up for her. Sebastian and Henrietta visibly blanched at this pronouncement of Anna's. They exchanged a shocked look, and both glanced anxiously at their sons, as if this heretical notion might corrupt their young minds.

It was a relief all round, when Jean-Paul turned the conversation round to Portia's reason for being in the UK. They discussed the likelihood of her being cast in the lead of a new British drama. Portia warmed to her theme, with the spotlight being upon her, and everyone else began to breathe again, and to relax just a little.

Chapter 19

After dessert and coffee, it was agreed everyone should have time out, to read or rest in their rooms, go for a walk, or explore the gardens. They were to meet in the conservatory for drinks at six o'clock before driving to the restaurant in Clare, that had been booked for 7.30pm. Anna and Cassie were able to retire to their room to unpack and freshen up.

It was a light and spacious double room, with a small ensuite bathroom. It overlooked the lawn and orchard to the rear of the house. As they entered, and closed the door behind them, Anna exploded.

"Your bloody family! You weren't wrong, were you? They're a nightmare. Your mother's a bitch, and fucking Sebastian and Henrietta are up their own aspirant arses."

Cassie smiled, despite herself, at Anna's outburst, as she put her pyjamas under the pillow, and placed her dressing gown on the bed.

"And as for those nephews of yours, they're like Little Lord Fauntleroys, with pokers up their backsides."

"I know, babes, but they're all the family I have, I'm afraid."

"No, they are not, Cassie! I'm your family now. You don't need those bastards. You don't need any of them, now we have each other. How can you say such things, 'they're all the family I have'? Don't you know how much that hurts me? I don't feel you love me in the way I love you. I don't need anyone else but you. You clearly don't feel the same."

Cassie felt the blood drain from her head. She could not

face one of their scenes again, and not with all her family around. She tried desperately to smooth things over quickly.

"Oh baby, you know how much I love you. I didn't mean anything by what I said – just that they *are* my family. You know I love you and need you, as much, if not more, than you need me."

She put her arms around Anna but was flung off.

"Don't try and get around me, you disloyal bitch. There I was, supporting you against your horrible family, and you spit in my face."

"Please Anna, don't do this. Not now, not here."

"Not now, not here," Anna whined, in a parody of Cassie. "You take the biscuit, you do, Cassandra Davies. You cause a row between us, and then go all pathetic on me – trying to make me the villain."

Anna's voice was rising to a shout.

"Hush! Please, please, Anna, don't let the others hear us rowing."

"Listen to yourself – 'please, please, Anna.' You make me sick. You're such a hypocrite. There's no point in whining now, when you've spoiled the whole day."

Cassie thought frantically how she could stop this escalation: should she disappear into the ensuite, to let Anna calm down, or maybe she could go downstairs? Anna was pacing up and down, and becoming more agitated by the minute. Cassie did not know how to reach her, and she was afraid. When Anna became like this, she seemed like another person – or herself, but no longer in her right mind.

"I knew it was a mistake to meet your family, to come here. I only did it to please you, and be there for you, as you clearly find them all so difficult. But what do I get for my pains? You turn on me and side with them."

"I'm not siding with them, Anna. I only said that they were my family. That doesn't mean that I don't love you. It doesn't mean that I put them before you. Can we please stop this now? We have to go out to dinner with everyone tonight. It will be awful if we're at loggerheads."

"Well, who's fault is that? And don't patronize me with your 'can we please stop this now'! I'm not one of your bloody kids. I don't want to go out for dinner with you, or your fucking family. I don't want to be with you, and I don't want to be here. I'm going to get a taxi to the nearest station from this God-forsaken hole, and you can go fuck yourself, once and for all."

Cassie slumped on the bed, and started to weep. How could their relationship be so wonderful, one minute, and such a painful nightmare the next? Did Anna want her to beg? She would beg, if that was what it took to get back *her* Anna, and regain their closeness. She couldn't bear the idea of Anna walking out and leaving her to the smug pity and *schadenfreude* of her family. She would be shown up to be the loser they so clearly felt she was. They had all found Anna beautiful and interesting, and had clearly thought she was too good for Cassie.

"Anna, please, don't do this. I need you."

"How much? How much do you need me, Cassandra? Enough to turn your back on your fucking, vicious family, and declare your loyalty to me? Do you need me that much?"

Anna had come up close, and put her hand around Cassie's throat. She was not squeezing or hurting, but the

171

pressure was enough to keep Cassie still, vigilant and frightened.

"Of course. There's no question that you are the most important thing in my life."

"Then prove it."

"What do you mean?"

"Show me how important I am to you. Seduce me. Go down on me. Bring me off, like I've never climaxed before. Beg me to let you. Go on, make me succumb to you."

Cassie felt embarrassed and unwilling, yet she knew that if she wanted her loving Anna back, she was being given a way, and she needed to do what was asked of her. It was demeaning and humiliating, going through the motions of abasing herself to Anna, who, throughout, was rejecting and unresponsive. Yet Cassie could tell from her breathing that she was aroused. When Cassie tried to kiss or touch her, Anna twisted Cassie's nipples or bit her lips. When Cassie tried to touch Anna's clitoris, Anna painfully forced her fingers into Cassie's vagina. As Cassie tried to go down on her, as instructed, Anna held her head, by tightly clutching a handful of her hair. She rammed Cassie's face rhythmically between her legs, until Cassie felt nothing more than an object. She may as well have been a vibrator or a dildo.

When Anna reached orgasm, it was with loud moaning and shrieks, that Cassie was sure were heard all over the house, and perhaps they were meant to be. Anna rolled toward Cassie, and started kissing her passionately.

"My darling Cass, that's better. You are wonderful. I don't deserve you, I really don't. I'm so sorry if I got a little stressed, and gave you a hard time earlier. It's just that I love you so much, that I get jealous and insecure. Especially in this situation, being judged by your family. I just need to be reassured that we're ok, that you love me, and need me, as much as I need you. Please say that you forgive me, that we're ok again."

In response, Cassie stroked Anna's hair, because she could not trust herself to speak. She felt sick and dirty, like a discarded condom. There was nothing she could say, at present, that would not betray her feelings. She wondered how much of their argument and Anna's noise during sex, had been heard by the others. She wondered if that was what Anna had wanted.

As soon as she could, she excused herself to go and shower. As she dressed, she considered saying she would go downstairs to wait for Anna, but in the circumstances, she felt that would be taken as an incendiary move. Instead, she sat on the basket chair by the window, whilst Anna went to shower, and stared out at the trees and the fields, that stretched to the horizon. Could she make this relationship work? Did she want to?

Anna was in a good mood, when she came out of the bathroom. She looked stunning in a close-fitting, emerald green, jersey dress, with sparkling green, drop earrings. She had swept her auburn hair into a chignon.

"Oh Anna!" Cassie could not help but blurt out, "you look absolutely beautiful."

"Thank you my darling. You too look lovely."

Cassie regarded the black crepe trousers, and white, silk shirt she wore, and shrugged.

"Don't do that, sweetie. Learn to take a compliment.

You have to challenge this poor self-image of yours. Come on, let's knock them dead."

Cassie was dreading facing everyone, not knowing who would have heard what, but it was now ten after six and they had to go down.

As they entered the conservatory, all eyes turned to them.

"Ah, the lovers, at last," Jean-Paul giggled, and was immediately dug in the ribs by Rafe. The men were wearing identical, white, linen suits.

"So, you two have made up, have you?" Portia drawled, pursing her lips, and giving both of them a hard stare. "I must say, I don't think any of us wanted to overhear your lovers' quarrel."

Cassie thought she might just sink through the floor, as she felt the deep blush spread up from her chest to her face.

"Apologies all," Anna said, breezily, *"the path of true love* and all that, but we're sorry if we embarrassed anyone, aren't we Cass? We especially apologise to our generous hosts, if we have not been the guests we should have been. Ours is, indeed, a passionate relationship, *n'est pas, ma cherie?"*

She winked at Jean-Paul, and flashed a dazzling smile at Sebastian and Henrietta. Cassie wanted to die, as she wondered how much of Anna's vitriol, toward her family and herself, had been overheard.

"Think nothing of it," said Sebastian, with a tight smile, "Glass of champagne, Cassandra, Anna?"

"Wonderful!" Anna gushed.

"Thank you, Seb," Cassie murmured.

She was aware of Henrietta, staring studiously into her

champagne flute, and Marcus and Giles being, apparently, riveted by their phones. She had never felt so humiliated in her life, and could not believe Anna's insouciance. It was a relief to everyone, or so it seemed to Cassie, when the driver of the minibus, hired to take them to the restaurant, rang the doorbell.

At the large round table, where they were seated, Anna was charming and loquacious throughout the meal. Cassie struggled to swallow her food, and could hardly bring herself to meet anyone's eyes. She dreaded the thought of the whole of Sunday, and Monday morning, stretching ahead of her, before she could make her escape. She wondered if it was possible to hate the very same person that you loved.

Chapter 20

On the Sunday, Sebastian and Henrietta had thrown a bit of a do: it had been something half way between a BBQ and a garden party. They had invited the great and the good from half of Suffolk, or so it appeared to Cassie, as she had watched the stream of vehicles, roll up the drive. The event was a welcome respite from the time the family had spent, together.

Portia had revelled in the sycophancy, and the adulation, she was accorded, as the famous, film-star mother of Sebastian. She had, after all, magnanimously deigned to rub shoulders with the inhabitants of this rural backwater.

Anna, too, had waged a charm offensive: numerous people had remarked, to one or other of the family, how delightful Anna was, and what a striking, and well-suited couple, Cassie and she appeared to be. Watching her mother and Anna at work, Cassie was struck, for the first time, by the similarities between them.

The weekend had finally come to an end. Anna had continued to be loving to Cassie, and engaging and funny with everyone else. Cassie's family had seemed to warm to her, though Cassie failed to be as pleased about this, as she felt she should.

Bags packed, Anna and Cassie went downstairs, on the Monday morning, for the farewell, late, brunch.

"Let's make a run for it now," whispered Anna.

Cassie, despite her low mood, laughed.

"I'd love to," she agreed.

"In here, you two," called Henrietta from the conservatory.

As they entered, Cassie saw that everyone was gathered around the large, glass and wicker, dining table.

"*Bonjour, ma'mselles!*" Jean-Paul cried.

"Good morning," the others chorused.

"Well, you're quite the sluggards, this morning, you two," exclaimed Portia, "are we nursing hangovers?"

"No, we are not." Cassie was indignant.

"What about you, Portia?" laughed Anna, "Have your nightcaps left you with a headache this morning?"

Portia had drunk a few stiff brandies before bed.

"Oh, no, Anna. We old broads can handle our booze," Portia replied tartly.

"Giles, pass the orange juice to Anna and Aunt Cassie," Sebastian instructed.

"Now then, everyone has had cereal or grapefruit. Anna, Cassie, do help yourselves, if you want either. Otherwise you can join the others from the hotplate. There's the full English, or kedgeree, whichever you prefer. Tea and coffee in the flasks, over there, and I'll just bring in more toast," said Henrietta, heading in the direction of the kitchen.

Everyone milled around, filling their cups and plates, until all – including Henrietta – were finally seated, back around the table.

Rafe raised his glass of Bucks Fizz. "I want to make a toast to Seb, and his lovely wife, for what has been a splendid weekend. You have been wonderful hosts, and it has been really great to have had all the family together, like this. Well done."

They all raised glasses or cups and toasted Sebastian and Henrietta with a chorus of "hear, hear!" and "well done!"

"We have really enjoyed it too, haven't we darling?" Sebastian smirked at his wife, pink with pleasure.

"Yes, indeed we have, and it's been lovely to meet Jean-Paul and Anna, so thanks to Portia for suggesting such a get together, in the first place. We hope her talks with the producer go well, so that we might have her back working in the UK, for a while, all the better to spend time with her children and grandchildren."

Henrietta raised a toast to Portia, that the others echoed. Portia inclined her head in gracious acknowledgement.

"Well, of course, I am the matriarch, so that's my role – to ensure we stick together, as a family. Now, Jean-Paul, you make sure my son drinks less, and takes more exercise and, Anna, you smarten my daughter up, make her a little more glamorous, like yourself. Giles, Marcus, you boys both work hard at school now, and make your old grandmother proud."

It was with huge relief, that Cassie embraced her family farewell, as she and Anna stood on the front steps. They loaded themselves, and their luggage, into the car, and, waving a final goodbye, set off for home.

Anna, predictably, was soon sound asleep, and only woke as Cassie was coming onto the North Circular.

"I'm exhausted," she announced. "I'm so worn out from socialising with your horrible family that I need some solitude. You won't mind, sweetie, will you, if I go to my club and sleep there tonight?"

Shocked, Cassie turned an incredulous face toward her.

"What club?"

"The University Women's Club."

"I've never heard of it!"

"Well, darling, it's only been established for over 120 years, so it's quite understandable you might not have heard of it!"

"Don't talk to me like that, Anna! Where is it?"

"It's in Mayfair, sweetie. I tell you what, why don't you drop me at a tube station somewhere along the North Circular – say Hanger Lane. It's on the Central line, and it'll take me to Bond Street. It'll save me coming all the way to Chiswick, and then having to go back into town."

Cassie felt bewildered and upset. She was passing over Staples Corner, so they had little time to talk this over, even if she knew what to say. She drove in silence. As she reached the gyratory, the lights changed to red. Anna reached for her bag in the back seat, leaned over to kiss Cassie's cheek, and jumped out of the car.

As she slammed the door shut, she called out, "Now I may stay over, or I may not, depending on how I feel, but you're not to worry. You relax and unwind, before you have to return to the grindstone tomorrow."

The lights changed, and Cassie had to drive. She looked in her rear-view mirror, to see Anna striding toward the underpass.

When she had returned the Car Club vehicle, and finally walked into the house, she went and slumped in the kitchen. She felt catatonic. She could neither move nor think. She did not know how long she had sat there, but it had grown dark, when she was brought back to herself, by the sound of the doorbell ringing. When she roused herself to move, she realised she was icy cold, and stiff as a corpse.

She opened the door to a white and shaking Joan Carter.

"Joan? You look terrible, what's wrong? Come in, come."

She ushered the old woman into the kitchen, and put on the kettle, and a fan heater.

"You look like you could do with a cuppa. Sit by the heater, while I make it."

"Where's Anna?"

"Sorry, Joan, Anna's not home right now, and I'm not sure when she'll be back."

"Oh no!" the old woman wailed. "It's Tiddles, you see. I need her to take care of him for a few days. My sister's been taken into Birmingham City Hospital. She's had a heart attack. I've got to go up there straight away."

"I'm so sorry to hear that, Joan. Anna is very allergic to cats, so she can't help, but I could go in twice a day to feed Tiddles, if you'd like."

Cassie placed a mug of tea before Joan, and sat down opposite her with her own mug.

"But Anna always takes care of him. She always has. Tiddles knows Anna. He trusts her. I've never heard anything about an allergy."

Cassie felt the blood drain down her body.

"How many times has Anna looked after him?"

"Oh, lots of times. My sister and I used to go to Butlin's every summer, until Dot got too ill. Ever since Anna moved in, she's looked after him. Says she loves cats. Must be at least three or four times now, maybe more."

"Has she got a key to your house?"

"Yes, it makes me feel safer knowing she has a key. I don't know where she keeps it, though. Tiddles has been fed tonight, but Anna knows where everything is kept, so maybe she can start feeding him in the morning."

She sipped greedily at her tea.

"I needed that. Thank you, Cassie. Tell Anna, I'll ring her as soon as I know what's what with Dot, and how long I'll have to stay."

Joan gulped down the last of her tea, and stood up.

"That's better, now I have to get my skates on. Goodbye, my dear. Tell Anna, I'm really grateful."

Cassie saw Joan out, then she shut the door slowly, and stood with her hand still on the latch, deep in thought.

Chapter 21

That night, Cassie lay sleepless, tossing and turning in the bed. She wanted to talk to Flick, or to Jenny, but she could not bring herself to share this with them. They would think she was a fool not to confront Anna with what Joan had said, and her belief that Anna had been lying to her. But why would Anna lie about having an allergy to cats? The answer slotted straight into her mind: a plausible reason to get Cassie's beloved Kit out of the way.

She was sure Jenny and Flick would judge her for not confronting Anna at once. The truth was, she was afraid of the reaction she would get, if she challenged Anna. Yet, she also knew she would have to confront her, otherwise the doubts questions would consume her.

She rose at 7am, with a dry and gritty mouth, having eventually dozed, but only fitfully, once the sky had begun to lighten. She had to find the key to feed Joan's poor cat. She had no idea when Anna would return. She showered, dressed, and put on some make-up. She looked washed out, with dark circles under her eyes, which the make-up did nothing to improve.

Having made herself a coffee, she hunted for a Yale key – any Yale key. She found a couple in the drawer of the kitchen table, and one was hanging on the back of the larder door. She took the three keys to Joan's front door, and tried them one by one. The third one worked, and she gave a sigh of relief. She went into the kitchen and saw that the back door had a cat flap, so no litter tray was needed. Joan had said that Anna knew where everything was, but she would just have to look around until she found what was required. Tiddles came through the cat flap, and started threading himself through Cassie's ankles. So much for needing to know the person who was to feed him, she thought. Cats were notorious for their cupboard love. His bowls were on a mat next to the kitchen sink cupboard, and Cassie quickly located the tins of cat food, and packets of dried food, on the floor of the larder. She fed Tiddles quickly and left to return next door.

She put Joan's key on the kitchen table, and scribbled a note to Anna to say what had happened to Joan's sister, and how Joan had asked them to look after the cat, and that she had fed him this morning. She did not say that Joan had specifically asked for Anna to help.

Cassie hurried off to school, her head full of confused thoughts and questions. She did not catch up with Jenny until lunchtime, when her friend flopped down beside her in the staff room.

"Caught you at last! God, Cass, you look like shit! Was the family visit that ghastly?"

"It was, Jenny. Pretty shit, all in all. Anna and I had a row the first day, to kick it all off. My mother was ghastly and my big brother was his usual up-his-backside self. Henrietta is a pain, but she's a good hostess. Rafe and his lover were alright. I think, in the end, they liked Anna but, boy, was I glad to leave yesterday!"

"You poor thing. Are you and Anna ok now, after the row, and the family shit ?"

"Yes, but she was so exhausted, and pissed off with the

whole thing, that she took herself off to her club last night."

"What? You are kidding me, aren't you? Her *club?* Am I in a P.G.Wodehouse novel? Did you know she had a *club?*" asked Jenny, astonishment written all over her.

"No, to tell you the truth. You could have knocked me down with a feather."

"Well, that takes the biscuit, that does! What the hell did she think she was doing, swanning off and leaving you all alone? Didn't she think you needed some moral support, and time together, after going through a weekend with your lot, meeting her for the first time, and vice versa?"

"You know Anna, she's a law unto herself."

"Cassie, I really worry about you. You have to assert yourself more with Anna."

"I know you're right. I should." Jenny squeezed Cassie's hand.

"Do you want to go for a drink after work?"

Cassie blinked back the tears, that Jenny's affectionate gesture had elicited.

"It's a lovely thought, but I think, in the circumstances, I had better get back to see if she's returned."

"Why don't you ring her?"

"I've tried, but her phone is switched off."

"That's a bummer but, remember, James and I are there for you any time."

It seemed a long school day to Cassie and, when she eventually let herself through the front door, it was to find that Anna was still not home. The key and the note remained on the kitchen table. Cassie wondered if Anna *had* returned but left again. She screwed up the note and threw it in the bin.

Taking the key, she went next door to see to Tiddles. When she returned, after taking some time to stroke and pet the mewling creature, Anna was seated at the kitchen table with a glass of white wine in front of her.

"Where have you been?" she cried, jumping up, and coming to embrace Cassie. "I've missed you, baby. Have you missed me?"

She held Cassie away from her, and scanned her face. "You're not cross with your little Anna, are you?" she pouted.

"I've been next door to feed Tiddles. Joan came last night, to ask for you to do it, as her sister has had a heart attack, and she had to rush off to Birmingham."

Anna's face went blank, but Cassie thought her eyes had hardened.

"Why would she ask me, when she knows of my allergy?"

For a moment, Cassie felt non-plussed.

"She said she didn't know anything about an allergy. She said you'd looked after Tiddles every year since you've lived here."

Anna turned abruptly on her heel, and returned to her wine and her kitchen chair.

"That woman is obviously going senile. Of course, I'd never have been able to look after her fucking cat. She's obviously confusing me with Susan, who does sometimes look after Tiddles for Joan."

"But I thought you said Joan was always at loggerheads with Susan?"

Anna slammed her fist down on the table. The glass and wine bottle shook, and Cassie jumped.

"It's one thing to have a demented neighbour, but it's

quite another to have my partner believe said neighbour's ramblings, and start interrogating me. What is it? You think I made up my allergy, do you, Cassandra? Who the fuck *are* you? Who the fuck do you think *I* am? Do we know each other at all? Why do you think I would lie to you about this?"

Cassie was shaking now, in the face of Anna's rage, but she remembered Jenny's advice, that she should be more assertive. She took a deep breath and blurted out, "I thought that, maybe, you didn't want me to bring my cat into your house, so you found an excuse."

Anna stared at her with cold hatred. Slowly she rose from the table, and moved toward the door. Cassie went to put her arm out to her.

"I'm sorry, Anna. I'm sorry."

Anna suddenly whirled around, "You fucking bitch!" she growled, as she pushed Cassie hard. Cassie fell backwards against the wall. Her feet went from under her and she slid down to the floor. Anna was suddenly on top of her, with her hands around her neck. She was pushing Cassie flat on her back, and at the same time tightening her grip on her windpipe, until Cassie was struggling to breathe. She tried to kick her legs, or slide away sideways, but she was powerless to dislodge Anna. Anna was straddling her, her knees either side of Cassie's waist, her red face looming over her. Cassie felt her head swell, as her heart tried to hammer its way out of her chest.

She was dying.

Chapter 22

Cassie opened her eyes. At first, she had no idea where she was, and then she realised she was lying on the kitchen floor, with a cushion under her head, and a sobbing Anna sitting beside her, stroking her hair back from her brow.

"Oh, Cassie, my darling Cassie. Thank God! Thank God, you're all right. I am so, so sorry. Can you ever forgive me? Please say you forgive me."

Cassie remembered the attack, the feeling of dying, the malevolence in Anna's face, as it hung above her own. Her throat felt sore, her mouth was dry. She could say nothing. She could feel nothing. Anna was babbling, "I promise you, this will never happen again. I will never lay hands on you again. I'll get help for my anger. I will, you'll see. I can't lose you. I can't live without you. I'll kill myself if you leave me. Please say you will forgive me, Cassie. Please, please, my love."

Cassie turned her head, to see Anna's blotched face and red eyes, tears streaming unchecked down her cheeks. What did she feel for this woman? She felt only tiredness. Exhaustion. She wanted to sleep, and not wake up.

Anna was still talking, "I'm begging here, baby. I'm begging you, on bended knee, please say you forgive me, that you love me. I'll do anything, anything at all. I'll do whatever you want. Do you know, before I came home I'd decided to show you one of my latest novels? I felt it was time I let you in to that part of my life. I've even brought a copy with me, inscribed for you. I went to my publishers to pick it up, as I didn't have any more here. Can I give it to you, darling? Will you read it? Will you accept it as a profound apology, as a peace offering, and a token of my love for you, my trust in you? I know I can't ask for your trust or love, right now. I know my behaviour has forfeited that, but in time do you think you can forgive me, learn to trust me again, learn to love me again, do you? Cassie?"

"I think I need to go to bed. I'm sorry," Cassie croaked.

"Of course, my sweet. Let me help you up. I'll put you to bed. I'll bring you my book, and something to eat and drink, yes? I'll sleep in the spare room tonight so you can rest up."

Cassie wanted her to shut up, to go away, but she let herself be helped to her shaky feet, and up the stairs. Anna wanted to undress her, but Cassie shook her head. Anna left her and went back downstairs. By the time Cassie had stripped and fallen into bed, Anna returned with a tray on which was a paperback book, a bowl of soup, a glass of water, and a brandy.

"Can I get you anything else?" Anna asked, sounding like a scolded child.

Cassie shook her head, and tried to smile.

"Can I kiss you goodnight?"

Cassie stiffened, and the little smile she had managed, slipped.

"I understand, Cass. We'll talk tomorrow, darling. Sleep well," and she crept out, closing the door quietly behind her.

I think I'm in shock, thought Cassie, as she became aware of her bruised and aching muscles. She felt drained, but too traumatised to want to sleep. She could not face the soup, but she sipped delicately at the brandy. She turned over the book. The title was *White Socks and Pederasts,* and the author was called Madeline Malan. The book cover showed a child's legs, encased in white, knee-length socks. She turned the book over. There was no picture, or biography, of the author, just some blurb about the book:

Akila came to France from Algeria as a six-year-old. She was already being sexually abused by her father, and older brother, and it was not long before they were pimping her out to other men. Akila had watched her own mother be abused and crushed by the men in her family, including Akila's maternal grandfather, and she was not about to let that happen to her. This is a harrowing, but uplifting, story of the triumph of the human spirit over terrible circumstances, by a previously unpublished, female writer, who wishes to remain anonymous.

That could not be true, she thought. Anna must have been published before. She had said 'my latest novel.' It must be a marketing ploy. She commenced to read. It was well written, the characters were compelling, the dialogue convincing, and the story unfolded with good pacing, and some suspense. Anna could write!

Despite the barricades that had sprung up around her, Cassie felt a thrill of pride. Her lover was a writer who could write! She read until she could keep her eyes open no longer. She found just enough energy to lean her arm across to the lamp switch, before falling into a deep but troubled sleep, that was punctuated throughout the night by different, yet terrifying, scenes of violence: as Cassie's hands were squeezing Anna's neck, she watched her face and tongue turn black.

She awoke, shocked and panting. The light from the window was the pearly gloom of dawn. She arose quietly, and set about showering, dressing, and preparing herself for the world. Peering into her magnifying, make-up mirror, she saw, to her horror, that there were thumb-shaped bruises on her neck. She plastered on the concealing cream, that she kept for the occasional break-out.

After the events of yesterday, she felt she had to see to Tiddles herself, as if acknowledging that Joan had been mistaken about Anna's involvement with the cat. When she had finished with the cat, she left early for school. She walked briskly through the sunny morning, trying to clear her head enough to make sense of what had happened between her and Anna, and how she felt about it.

She had not reached school before her phone rang. She peered at the screen, and saw that it was Anna. She let it go to voicemail. Shortly afterwards her phone pinged. It was a text:

I'm so devastated to have missed you. I'm desolate. I need to talk to you, and you're not picking up. Can't you talk to me? I'm not sure I can get through the day like this. Please text me. Tell me you can, in time, forgive me. I can't say what I will do if I don't hear from you. I will want to die, Cass, if you stop loving me.

Cassie felt backed against a wall. She stopped to text a reply: *Anna it's fine. We'll talk when I get home. I've seen to Tiddles, so he'll be ok until I get back. Go and have a nice day, and take your mind off things. I'll see you tonight.*

And she added, *xx.*

Cassie avoided Jenny as long as she could, as she could not trust herself to dissemble to such a close friend. Jenny was on playground duty, so Cassie made herself very busy in the staff room during morning break. She rushed out at lunchtime, on the pretext of having an errand to run, and found she had to see the Head, about an urgent matter, during the afternoon break.

She was in the classroom, clearing up at the end of the day, when Jenny came in.

"Cassandra Davies, you have been avoiding me all day, don't think I didn't notice. What the hell is going on?"

"What do you mean? Nothing is going on, I've just been frantically busy all day. How are you, lovely?"

Jenny came over, and stared at her.

"Cassie, what the fuck are those marks on your neck?"

To her knowledge, Cassie had never heard Jenny utter such a profanity. She had forgotten, during the day, to touch-up the concealer, on the bruises on her neck. Jenny was now looking at them intently.

Cassie coloured. "Love bites?" she faltered, with an attempt at humour.

"Did she do this?" Jenny spat.

"It was a mistake. It was sex play, but we got carried away. You know, flirting with asphyxia – or is it hypoxia?"

Cassie vaguely remembered reading something about this. Jenny was staring at her with horror and – yes – disgust. Cassie froze. What was she doing? What was more shameful – claiming to indulge in perverse sexual activities, or admitting that her lover had tried to strangle her?

She started to cry. "Yes, ok, I lied. It wasn't sex play. She lost it and put her hands around my throat. She promises to get help for anger management. She's desperate for me to forgive her, and she promises it will never happen again.

Please don't judge her, Jen – or me. We're trying to work it out."

Jenny was pale, and sank down onto the chair that was beside Cassie's desk. She shook her head silently, and stared at the floor. At last she looked up and gripped Cassie's arm.

"Cassie, for Christ sakes, this is dangerous. *She* is dangerous. Do you really need her in your life? Is it worth it?"

Cassie was incapable of speech, as the tears continued to pour down her face.

Jenny went on, "You've become more and more closed. You are more and more – I don't know – timid, cowed. I almost don't recognise the Cass I knew and loved. Do you honestly think this woman is good for you? Is she really making you happy?"

Cassie's tears fell even faster, but her throat was closed up and she could say nothing, even if she had known what to say. With her head bent over her lap, she saw, in her peripheral vision, Jenny shake her head.

"I won't say any more now, Cass. Just remember, I love you. We all love you. If you ever want to talk, you know I'm here for you. Come over soon, and see Kit. He'd love to see you. I promise I won't talk about Anna, if you don't want me to."

Cassie tried unsuccessfully to smile, but Jenny stood, and came to give her an enveloping hug.

"Take care of yourself," she said, as she released her, and walked out of the door.

Cassie sat immobile in the darkening classroom, her mind and body numb, until the sound of Mr Jenkins, the caretaker, roused her. She rose stiffly and left for home. She went first to see to Tiddles, delaying the moment she had to face Anna. When she let herself in, Anna emerged from the kitchen. She had obviously been crying, and for most of the day, if her red face, and swollen eyes, were any indication. She said nothing, but came and threw herself against Cassie, putting her arms tightly around her waist. They stood in silence, locked together, until Anna drew away and said, "I've got a stir-fry ready, and a bottle of Prosecco. Hungry?"

Cassie nodded, though she did not feel she could stomach even a mouthful of food.

They were both subdued as they ate, and when Cassie said that she was so tired, she thought she would go straight to bed, Anna nodded and began to clear up.

Cassie took off her make-up, and cleaned her teeth. She was just settling into bed when there was a hesitant knock on the bedroom door.

"Can I sleep here with you tonight?" Anna asked, like a frightened, little girl.

"Of course."

They lay quietly, Anna curled against Cassie. She spoke in a whisper.

"I've always known I have rage inside of me, but what I did to you has shocked and frightened me so much, I've made an appointment for next Friday, to see a counsellor, who specialises in anger management issues. Whether you can forgive me or not, I need to do this for myself, too."

Cassie said nothing.

Anna went on, "Cassie, my darling, I don't know what I would do without you. If I lose you, I will just die, and that's not a figure of speech. I will kill myself."

She said it simply and with such conviction that Cassie believed her. All she could do was stroke Anna's hair until, after an aeon of silence, wile they listened to their own, and the other's breathing, they both finally fell asleep.

By the following week, Anna had stopped tip-toeing around Cassie quite so much, and they were both relieved. Cassie continued to see to Tiddles, in an unspoken pact between them, to preserve the fact, or fiction, of Anna's severe allergy. Cassie, however, could not stop herself grieving afresh for Kit. She wondered if it had all been an elaborate charade, for Anna to avoid accepting into her home a cat that was not hers. A darker thought was hastily dismissed: that Anna had faked her allergy in order to separate Cassie from something she loved, and, which she had, in those early days, prioritised over her lover. Perhaps that had threatened Anna.

Joan came back, with tales of her sister's brush with death, and miraculous recovery. Much fuss was made of Tiddles, and effusive thanks given to Anna and Cassie. None of them went anywhere near the question of Anna's allergy, and previous care of the cat: for Anna and Cassie, it was a minefield, and for Joan, it was off her self-absorbed radar.

Chapter 23

The following day, as Cassie was in her empty classroom, packing-up her things, Flick rang.

"Where have you been, you bugger, it's been ages?"

Cassie laughed, "And lovely to hear from you too, darling!"

"So how are things going, with the lover? Didn't you say she was going to meet your family? How did it go?"

"All in all, it went better than I thought it would. We had a bit of a row at the start, but it was ok after that."

"Seems a bit of a habit with Anna, to start off with a quarrel, if your visit to me was anything to go by. How's it going generally?"

"Ok, most of the time. Actually, she's just given me one of her books to read, so that's a bit of a breakthrough. I've started to read it, and it's really good, Flick, which I'm really relieved about. Wouldn't it have been awful, if I'd thought it was crap?"

"God, yes! What's it called? Is it under her name or has she got a *nom de plume*?"

"It's called *White Socks and Pederasts.*"

"Jesus!"

"I know, it's a bit strong, isn't it? She's called Madeline Malan."

"What an uninspiring name! What does it say about the author on the book cover?"

"That she wishes to remain anonymous."

"Weird, eh? Why so mysterious?"

"Well, you know how private she is. I get the impression that she uses different names for different types of books."

"I'll have to read it, I'm intrigued. No doubt I can get it off Amazon."

"I suppose so. Anna said she got her copy from her publishers – in London somewhere, no doubt."

"Who's the publisher?"

"Oh, I don't know. I forgot to look."

"Doesn't matter, I'll find it."

They talked on, exchanging their news, and Cassie told her more about how her family had been.

"Plus ça change, plus ça même," was all Flick would say.

Things between Cassie and Anna returned to normal in the following weeks. Anna had said the counselling was helpful in understanding her rage, and getting it more under control and, indeed, there had not been any more outbursts, or unpleasantness. She told Cassie that the Counsellor felt, that it did not help, if Cassie constantly challenged Anna about things. It made her feel that Cassie distrusted her, and did not really love her, and that set off her demons from childhood, when she had felt her mother did not trust, or value her.

Cassie felt somehow blamed, as if it was her insensitivity that had pushed Anna into acting out her violence. She wanted to dismiss this as untrue, but she was left feeling uneasy. Perhaps Anna was right. Maybe she did not trust, and love, Anna as much as she should – as much as Anna, obviously, loved and trusted her.

It was a few weeks later, that Flick caught her again at

the end of the school day.

"Hello, my love," Cassie said, seeing Flick's picture appear on her screen.

"Hello, *cariad*. How's things?"

"Good, yes. Did you read Anna's book yet?"

"That's why I'm ringing. I did read it, and I was impressed. So much so that I put it forward to my Book Club."

"Oh yes? That's brilliant. Did you tell them you knew the author? What did they think of it?"

"No, I didn't tell them about knowing Anna. I didn't want to prejudice their reactions in any way."

"And?"

"Most of them liked it, or, if they didn't like the book itself, they still rated the writing. Then I told them the author was the girlfriend of a very good friend of mine, though I didn't say what her name was. One of our members is a Senior Lecturer in English, at Swansea University, and she's having a novel published at the moment. She liked the book a lot, and mentioned it to her publisher, when they had a meeting about her own book. He told her that he'd heard on the grapevine about the author, who is published by one of his competitors. Apparently she is French-Algerian herself, although she's lived in Britain for years. She wanted anonymity because, it's said that the novel is a thinly veiled autobiography. She was abused herself, and pimped out by her father and brother."

"What? How can that be? He's got to be mistaken."

"That's what Bethan said. She told him I had met the author, who is British. He said either I was mistaken, or the person, claiming the book as hers, was lying."

Cassie's head was spinning. How could this be?

"Cass? I'm really sorry. I've thought long and hard about this, but I felt you really needed to know."

"I can't believe it, though. I think there must be some mistake. Why would Anna do this? If she really isn't the author, why would she take the risk of lying?"

"I've asked myself the same question. Perhaps she just wanted to impress you. Perhaps she's just a fantasist. Either way, if you think about it, it makes sense. You claim as your own a book written by an anonymous author. Who is going to know? I googled the pen-name, and all that came up was her name as the author of this book, absolutely nothing else – no picture, no details about her – zilch – so it's a closed circle."

Cassie's thoughts wouldn't go in a straight line: she couldn't think, she couldn't compute. She thought of Anna last night, pleasuring her, kissing her, adoring her. She had fondled the hair on Anna's head, as her lover had brought her to orgasm with her muscular tongue. She thought how lucky they were, to have found such love and passion with one another.

"Flick, I don't know what to say, it's too ridiculous."

"Cassie, what the fuck is the matter with you girl? What will it take for you to start to question yourself about this woman? P'raps a corpse, and her standing over it with a smoking gun?"

Cassie's heart sank. Flick was angry with her and, more importantly, disappointed.

"I am going to talk to her. I'm going to tell her about this, and see how she reacts, and what she says. Then I'll know what to do. I know you have my best interests at heart, and I love you for it. I'm glad you felt you could tell me about this – I'm going to sort this out with her, honestly."

Even as she said it, her heart sank at the thought of discussing this with Anna.

"Well, *cariad,* I really think you have to. You can't have a successful relationship, with issues like this between you, like great, fat, elephants in the room."

Cassie thought of all the other issues that lay between them. They talked on, but Cassie's mind was already racing ahead.

That evening, Anna's mood, as she greeted Cassie with a wave of her hand, and a set face, was clearly spiky. Cassie's stomach dropped. This was   not the time to risk inflaming her further.

"How was your day?" she ventured.

"Just bloody awful, if you want to know. I haven't been able to write a line all day, and I've got a deadline coming up. The fucking phone hasn't stopped ringing, with offers to reclaim PPI payments, double-glazing promotions, or do I want to take part in a competition to win a Spanish villa. My fucking mother has sent me a bill, for some repairs to the chateau, and I've lost the connection from my computer to the printer."

"Oh sweetheart, I'm sorry. Let me pour us a glass of wine."

"I don't want a fucking glass of wine. Is that your answer to everything? For Christ's sake, Cassandra, you'll end up an alcoholic at this rate."

"Anna, that's not fair."

"Don't whine, Cassandra. It's really unattractive, you know. I haven't had time to cook, with everything that's gone on today. Do you want to cook, or shall we get a takeaway?"

"I'll cook, babe. What do you fancy?"

"Oh, I don't bloody know, just use your initiative, if you have any. I'm going to have a bath."

Anna slammed out of the kitchen, leaving a shaken Cassie to look in the freezer, for their dinner. She decided on spaghetti Bolognese, and defrosted some mince. With a slightly shaky hand, she poured herself a glass of wine, and set about chopping an onion. She felt she might cry, and not because of the onion.

The table was set, the sauce bubbling gently, and the pasta almost *al dente*, when Anna wafted into the kitchen, smelling of Chanel No 5. She came up behind Cassie, and slid her arms around her waist, her body cupping Cassie's.

"So sorry I was a grump earlier, baby. It really has been a shit day and I was in a foul mood, but I really shouldn't have taken it out on you. Can you forgive me?"

She nuzzled Cassie's neck. In answer, Cassie twisted around and kissed her.

"I'll have that glass of wine now," Anna laughed.

Everything had changed in an instant and they both tucked into their meal, exchanging news, joking, and laughing. Later, when they were sitting side by side, in front of the fire, in the sitting room, Cassie risked approaching the thing, that was sitting at the back of her mind, gnawing away at her.

"Anna, you know I told you I had really enjoyed *White Socks and Pederasts?*"

200

"Yes, I was really chuffed," said Anna, taking a sip of her wine.

"Well, I was so proud and impressed, I told Flick to read it."

"Oh, Cassie, no! You should not have done that. You know I don't like to publicise my work to people who know me. I only wanted to share that with you. It was a gesture on my part to show you how much I love and trust you, not for the likes of Flick."

"I'm so sorry. I didn't mean to upset you. It was just that I was so excited at having read something of yours. I thought it was really good, and I was so proud of you, I wanted to show you off. Flick and I always recommend books to each other, and talk about ones we've enjoyed reading. She was the obvious person to crow to."

"Don't tell me – she doesn't like me, so she said she didn't like the book. Am I right?"

"No, not that. She took it to her book club. I think they all rated it, so much so, that one member, whose own novel is about to come out, talked to her publisher about it."

"What the fuck for?"

"Just out of interest, I think, because she thought it was good."

"So?"

"Well, apparently, he told her he knew who the author was, but the person he told her about wasn't you. He said it was some French-Algerian woman, who wanted to remain anonymous, because the story is based on her own experiences – apparently. I told Flick there must be some mistake, but I just wanted to let you know, see what you

201

think has happened."

Anna was still. She leant forward and placed her glass carefully on the coffee table. There was silence, and Cassie began to feel scared.

"Anna?" she said.

"You fucking bitch," Anna whispered, not looking at her, "I share something really important with you, something that I usually don't share with anyone, as you very well know, and then you go behind my back, without speaking to me about it, and tell your fucking precious Flick. You know she didn't like me. You know she's jealous of your relationship with me, that she wants you all for herself, and yet you betray me to her like this."

"Anna, it's not..."

Cassie tried to protest but Anna, still not looking at her, raised her voice and talked over her.

"And clearly, you're only telling me now because you believe what that bitch has said. You believe that it's not my book, but someone else's. You're telling me, just so that I can try and convince you that I'm not the liar, you and your friends already think I am. You fucking little cunt! You disloyal, mistrustful, unbelievable, little piece of shit!"

Then she did turn to Cassie and, with lightning speed, she raised a bent arm behind her, made a fist, and punched it, with full force, into the side of Cassie's jaw. A nuclear flash of light went off in Cassie's head, as she fell sideways off the couch, slammed into the edge of the coffee table, and crumpled to the floor, her wine glass splintering under her.

Chapter 24

"Don't try to move, Cassandra, it's ok. I'm Gary and this is Sue. We're paramedics. Anna called us because you fell and hit your head, and knocked yourself out. We're just putting a collar on you. It will hold your head and neck still, until we can take you to hospital and get you checked out, just in case you've done any damage. Probably not, but better safe than sorry."

Cassie opened her eyes. Two people in green were kneeling beside her, peering into her face, and doing something with her head. She must be lying on the floor of the sitting room, judging by the carpet under their legs. Her head hurt and, on the left side of her face, she felt as if her teeth and jaw were being hammered into her brain. The 'collar' was more like a big, foam box that encircled her head and limited her vision. It felt both claustrophobic and comforting, but it made the pulses of pain in her face more intense. Gary was running his hands over her, asking her if this hurt, or that hurt.

"Just my head and face," she croaked.

She felt a sharp pain in her abdomen. Her hand involuntarily went toward it.

"It's ok, Cassandra," said the other one, whose name Cassie had now forgotten.

She gently put Cassie's hand back by her side and then lifted Cassie's jumper.

"It's just bits of glass from the wine glass. It must have broken beneath you when you fell. It's only a couple of shards. We're just going to tweezer them out and put a temporary dressing on until you can be checked properly in A & E."

As the woman bent over, Cassie saw Anna behind her. She was sitting bolt upright on the edge of the sofa. Her face was white, and she stared at Cassie as the tears fell, silently and unheeded, down her cheeks. The knuckles of her hands, clenched over her knees, were as white and naked as bone. Cassie dropped her eyes. She remembered now. She remembered the punch that knocked her sideways off the sofa. Was that why her teeth and jaw ached so?

"Now then, young lady, let's get you on a stretcher," Gary said.

"Are you coming in the ambulance with her?" the other one asked Anna.

"Yes, please." Anna stood shakily. "Is that alright, Cass?"

"Ok," whispered Cassie.

The two paramedics, one either side of Cassie, expertly and efficiently slid her onto the stretcher that they had lain beside her. They carried her out to the ambulance, with Anna bringing up the rear. Once safely installed by both of them, Gary said, "Sue will look after you Cassandra. You're in good hands. I'll drive us to Charring Cross Hospital."

Sue sat at Cassie's head, and Anna was seated on the bench opposite.

"What do you remember, my lovely?" asked Sue, stroking Cassie's hair back from her forehead.

Cassie frowned slightly and felt Anna's eyes on her.

"Not much."

"We'd both had quite a bit of wine. As I said," Anna

interjected. "I'd gone to the bathroom, when I heard this almighty crash. I ran down to the sitting room to find her on the floor. I can only imagine she tripped over the sofa, fell onto the coffee table, and knocked herself out."

Cassie could not see Anna, over the foam box surrounding her head, but she heard the nervousness in her voice, and the unspoken plea, that Cassie not say that she had been punched.

"Mm," Sue murmured, "except she has a swelling on one side of her head and pain and bruising on the other side. I can't see how she'd have managed to knock both sides of her head if, she'd tripped."

Anna said nothing. Cassie was shocked, hurt and dismayed that, for all Anna's protestations, and her attendance at therapy, she had still become violent with her again. Nevertheless, she did not want this to be made public, for both their sakes.

"I think I might have banged my head against the door, before falling on the coffee table and hitting the other side of my face. I'm not sure," she croaked.

"Can you remember how much you had to drink?" Sue asked, looking at both of them in turn.

Anna said, "A bottle between us with dinner, and then we both went on drinking. I'm not sure how much, but it was quite a lot for us, I think."

Sue glanced at her watch. Cassie imagined she was thinking that it was still early in the evening for them to have drunk that much. She might, however, have merely been checking the time.

The ambulance stopped, and Gary opened the doors. He

and Sue lifted her out, and she was quickly wheeled into A & E and straight into a curtained cubicle. Gary and Sue briefed the attending doctor, about Cassie's injuries, vitals, and the hypothesised version of how she came to hurt herself. Anna was waiting outside the cubicle. Cassie, as she had been lifted out of the ambulance, had seen the stricken look and the greenish hue of Anna's face.

There seemed to be no end of procedures, people and activity, around Cassie, and she suddenly felt very tired, and desperate to be alone. She was made to track fingers, with her eyes, suffer lights being shone in her pupils, a plastic peg being put on her finger and a cannula stuck in her arm. Pins were poked in her feet, and blood pressure readings done.

At one point the doctor asked, "Was there a fight or an assault, or any sort of altercation this evening, Miss Davies?"

"No, of course not," said Cassie, a little too rapidly.

The Doctor looked at her intently.

"Sure?"

She swallowed and gave a nod. He said no more.

She was wheeled to Radiology for an X-ray of the side of her face and then for a CT scan. At last she could be released from her foam box. There was a great deal of hanging around, waiting, and then being wheeled back and forth. Eventually she was back in A & E, and she was left alone for a while in a different curtained cubicle. Anna was shown in by one of the nurses, and came to sit by the bed. She grasped Cassie's hand, and opened her mouth to speak, but Cassie held her hand up, and closed her eyes. Anna fell silent, but she continued to hold Cassie's hand.

After a long interval, during which Cassie dozed off, the

same doctor and a nurse returned.

"The bad news is that you do have a fracture of the jaw."

Anna gasped loudly, and tightened her grip on Cassie's hand. The doctor glanced at her and then turned back to Cassie.

"The good news is that it a small, hairline fracture, so no treatment is required except for rest, pain killers and eating soft food that doesn't require chewing – and not talking too much! What work do you do?"

"I'm a primary school teacher."

"Ah, well, in that case, I would advise that you take some time off. Now, as for the blow to the head, which you think might have been caused by bouncing off a door, or the table, we think you might have a mild concussion. We'd like to keep you in overnight, for observation, just to be on the safe side. Is that ok?"

Cassie nodded. It will be a relief, she thought.

"You go on home, Anna. You've had to wait long enough, you must be tired," Cassie said.

"No, I want to stay, but I might need to go and fetch you some stuff from home, first."

"We're waiting for a bed on one of the wards, so it probably would be better if you went home," the doctor said.

"I won't need anything," Cassie added, "I can sleep in a hospital gown, and I can wait until I get home tomorrow, to shower and clean my teeth."

"Ok," Anna said, a little uncertainly, "I'll say goodnight then. What about letting work know? Do you want me to ring them in the morning?"

"No, it's fine. You brought my bag, didn't you? I'll text

207

Jenny later, and ask her to tell school."

Anna's face crumpled and she began to cry. "Oh God! Cass, I'm so sorry."

"What have you got to be sorry about? It's fine," Cassie said quickly, watching the doctor's face turn to scrutinise Anna.

Anna bent down and kissed Cassie's cheek, as if they were just friends, or flat-mates.

"Give me a ring tomorrow and let me know what's happening, and whether you want me to come in with anything, or come to fetch you home."

"Ok, thanks. See you tomorrow, then."

After Anna left, the light was turned down in the cubicle, and Cassie finally relaxed and, as she did so, the tears began to flow. What was she going to do? Thinking of that, she was reminded she had to phone Jenny. It was already past ten. There would be no point in texting, because Jenny would only ring back to find out the details. She tapped on Jenny's number, and steeled herself to tell her where she was.

"Hello?"

"Jen, it's Cassie. Sorry to ring so late, but I'm not going to make it to work tomorrow. Can you tell Mavis for me?"

"Of course, darling. What's the matter?"

"You're not going to believe it, but I fell and knocked myself out," said Cassie, trying for a lightness she did not feel.

"What?"

"I'm in Charring Cross Hospital. They want to keep me in overnight for observation, to rule out a bit of concussion."

"How did it happen, Cassie?"

"I'm ashamed to say, I had a bit too much wine, tripped,

and fell hard onto the coffee table and knocked myself out."

She had decided against mentioning her fractured jaw. Hopefully, she could get away with resting, and eating soft foods, without having to tell anyone the full account of her injuries.

There was a silence and then Jenny said, "You're right, Cassie, I don't believe a word of it – not after the state you were in when we went to the zoo, or those finger marks on your neck. What really happened Cass?"

Cassie felt her throat constrict. She squeezed her eyelids shut to stop the tears. She longed to unburden herself, but she knew Jenny would tell her she had to leave Anna, and charge her with assault. Cassie knew she could not do either – at least not right now. After all, she had known how much it would hurt and anger Anna, to be questioned about her writing, but she had gone ahead anyway, because of what Flick had said. It was true what Anna had said – she was more loyal to her friends, than she was to Anna. Yet she knew better than anyone how vulnerable Anna was, and how much she needed Cassie.

"No, Jen, it's as I said, I was a bit pissed and I tripped. It was just an accident – nothing to do with Anna this time," she added ruefully.

There was a sigh from Jenny and then she said, "How long do you think you'll need to be off, Cass, and is there anything I can do?"

"I don't suppose I'll be in for the rest of the week but I'll need to see what they say tomorrow. Best if Mavis reckons on me returning on Monday but tell her I'll ring her if I hear anything to change that."

"Is Anna with you?"

"Yes, she was," Cassie said, with a cheerfulness she did not feel, "but they told her to go home when all the checks were done and they said I was fine. They're waiting for a bed on a ward for me, just overnight, just to make sure everything's fine, then I can go home tomorrow."

"Oh, I see. Is *she* ok?"

"Yeah, you know, a bit shaken-up, like me. She heard me fall. She was upstairs. Must have been a bit of a shock finding me unconscious. She had to call the ambulance."

"Yes, I'm sure."

"Well, Jen, sorry to land this with you. Catch up soon?"

"Let me know what happens and how you are. Keep in touch, Cass, and remember, I'm here for you any time."

"Thanks, babe. Night-night now."

Cassie rang off before her voice broke with the emotions she was choking back.

The nurse who had come to tell her they were taking her up to the ward found her sobbing her heart out.

Chapter 25

Cassie was discharged a day later, with instructions to rest a great deal, to eat liquidised, or soft food, and to avoid exertion or stress. They gave her a list of symptoms to watch out for, lest complications set in, with instructions to present herself at A & E, if she started to suffer from any of them.

Anna had taken a taxi to the hospital, and left it waiting outside, while she came up to the ward, to collect Cassie, and carry her overnight bag downstairs. She kissed Cassie on the cheek, and smiled hesitantly.

"How are you feeling, babe?"

"Ok," said Cassie, who did not want to talk. She wanted only to get home, and go to bed. She had had time to think whilst in hospital, as she had barely slept. She still cared about Anna, but Jenny was right, she was not making Cassie happy any more, and the violence was escalating. First, she had to recover and feel stronger again, but she had resolved to leave Anna, and find somewhere else to live. She would not say anything about her decision at the moment, but soon she would have to find the courage to tell her.

They were silent in the taxi, although Anna had grasped Cassie's hand, and Cassie had not had the heart to pull away. When Anna opened the front door, and they entered the hall, Cassie said she would go straight to bed.

"I'll go in the spare room, so I can rest undisturbed."

Anna nodded, but her face hardened.

Cassie slid gingerly into bed, and lay staring at the ceiling. Her face and jaw ached. She felt anxious and miserable, and was aware of a feeling of longing, like homesickness. It was as if she wanted to go home, or run to her mother – yet in truth, she felt she had never had a place to call home, nor a mother who could comfort her. She missed the Anna she loved – had loved – no, *did* love. Yes! She realised that, despite it all, she still loved Anna. How could that be? She felt lonely without her, and wanted things to be back as they were. Tears slid sideways down her temples, into her hair and pillow. She felt too exhausted and grief-stricken to move. There was only silence. She did not know if Anna was still downstairs, or had left the house. She would go to her soon, but first she had to rest for a little.

She awoke and it was dark. She felt completely disorientated. It came back to her, that she had come home from the hospital, with Anna, and had gone to bed, but that was after lunch. She must have slept for hours. She switched on the lamp, and peered at the bedside clock. It was 9.45pm! She felt light-headed and faint. She needed to eat something.

Where was Anna? She looked at her phone, which she had switched to silent, when she had come to bed. There were missed calls, and texts, from Flick, from Jenny, and from Mavis, but nothing from Anna. She called her name, but there was no answer, and calling hurt her jaw. She manoeuvred herself out of bed with some difficulty, feeling as if she had gone ten rounds with Tyson Fury. She padded across to their bedroom. It was empty, as was the bathroom. She went downstairs. All was in darkness and there was no sign of Anna. She wondered where she could be at this time of night. Perhaps she had gone to see a film, or meet with one of her writer friends?

Cassie winced at the thought of writers, and the row and the violence that had been triggered by Flick's accusation. Perhaps Cassie should have just trusted Anna, and not passed on what Flick had been told. No wonder Anna had been so hurt and angry. Suddenly, Cassie felt desperate to see her, to have them make up and say sorry to one another.

She took a yoghurt out of the fridge, and a teaspoon from the drawer, and went back upstairs to try Anna's mobile. When she hit the call button, there was a pause, and then the sound of ringing from across the hallway. What? Cassie realised Anna, and her phone, must be in the study. There had been no light showing from beneath the door, so she had not thought to look in there. She clicked off the call, and crossed the landing.

When she opened the study door, the room was indeed dark. She switched on the light and saw her. She was lying on the carpet, eyes closed and face white. Beside her stood a bottle of vodka, with a few inches left in the bottom, and four, empty, paracetamol blister packs.

Cassie knelt beside her, and tried to wake her, calling her name, and shaking her shoulders violently. She could not rouse her. She put her hand to Anna's chest, and could just about feel the shallow rise and fall. She dashed back to the bedroom for her mobile and, with shaking hands, she dialled 999.

For the second time that week, an ambulance was dispatched to the house. By the time the paramedics arrived, Cassie had dressed hurriedly and sat by Anna. She had gathered the empty packets of paracetamol, to give to the hospital staff, but the paramedics took them from her. They needed to know when she had taken them. Cassie told them she had been asleep, but it must have been some time after 2pm, when she had gone to bed.

"Coming up to eight hours," said one to the other, and they quickly put both Anna and Cassie in the ambulance. When they arrived at A & E, sirens still blaring, they and Anna were hurried into a side ward and Cassie was asked to wait outside.

Oh God, don't let her die. Oh God, don't let her die, Cassie chanted silently, over and over. She hardly knew what she was saying – or to whom.

She had sat numbly for almost an hour, when an impossibly young woman, who claimed to be the registrar treating Anna, came into the waiting area to find her.

"Hi, I'm Karen. You're the patient's flatmate, I understand?"

"I'm her partner, Cassie Davies."

"Oh sorry. Are you ok, Cassie? Your speech is a bit – indistinct?"

"Yes, I'm sorry. I recently fractured my jaw. It's still sore, and I can't really open my mouth properly."

The woman gave Cassie a strange look, before continuing, "Well, we are giving Anna the antidote to paracetamol which, hopefully, will prevent serious liver damage. It's just eight hours since she took the overdose, so there's a good chance she'll be ok. She's still not fully conscious, and we'll need to give her another two infusions of the drug, over the next 24 hours. Then she'll be tested again for any damage. It's likely to be another day or so before we can consider her discharge, and even then she'll have to have a psychiatric evaluation first. I understand she left no note?"

Cassie shook her head.

"I really think it best if you go home tonight, Cassie. There's nothing you can do here, and we can't give you any more information than I've already told you. You can ring in the morning, to see whether you can visit with her tomorrow."

Cassie nodded dumbly. She felt close to tears.

"Can't I see her before I go?"

"You can peek in, but she's hooked up to all sorts."

The registrar led the way to the side room and opened the door. Anna lay pale and prone, attached to a drip stand, and with an oxygen mask over her face. Her eyes were closed. Cassie swallowed and placed a kiss on Anna's forehead, before thanking Karen and hurrying out to ring an taxi.

When Cassie finally arrived home, it was almost midnight. She desperately wanted to talk to someone – anyone, but it was too late to ring someone at this time of night, even Flick or Jenny. She was starving. She heated up some tomato soup, and dropped morsels of crustless bread into it, to soften further, until she could spoon the pap into her half-opened mouth. She swallowed it down easily, without having to chew. As her hunger abated, she was able to think more clearly. Should she have realised how close to the edge Anna had been, having realized how much damage she had caused to Cassie and to their relationship? They had to learn to be kinder to each other if their relationship was to last, she thought.

She climbed the stairs wearily and prepared herself to turn in. She lay in their double bed, and smoothed her hand over the empty space, where Anna usually slept.

She was awoken by the ringing of her phone. Sunlight was streaming through the window. The bedside clock showed 8.30am.

"Hello?"

"Cassie, at last! I was getting worried about you. It's Jenny. What's going on? I tried you all day yesterday. I even rang the hospital, and they told me you'd been discharged yesterday lunchtime."

"Oh Jen, it's awful. I came home yesterday and went straight to bed. I didn't wake until the evening, and I couldn't find Anna. When I did, she was unconscious in her study. She'd taken an overdose. She's still in Charing Cross."

"My God! That's awful, Cass. What a shock! Is she going to be all right?"

"She took a load of paracetamol and vodka, so they're worried about liver damage. They're giving her some antidote, and I have to ring today and find out how she's doing. I didn't even know there was an antidote you could use with paracetamol!"

"What made her do it, Cass? Have you any idea?"

"I don't know, Jen. I didn't notice anything different."

Cassie could not tell Jenny what she felt was the real reason, without revealing that Anna had attacked her and broken her jaw.

"Well, I hope she recovers fully. But how are you? That's what I was ringing for, because I was worried about *you*. And, actually, Cass, your voice sounds really peculiar. What's the matter?"

"I'm fine, not concussed, so it's all good. I think, though, that I might have cracked a tooth, when I fell. I've got awful toothache, which is making me keep my mouth half closed. I'll have to go to the dentist. I was hoping to be back in work Monday, if Anna is home, and ok by then, but I might not be able to return this Monday."

"I'm in school now, but do you want me to come over at the end of the day?"

Cassie thought about the bruises on her face and said quickly, "No, it would be lovely to see you, and thank you for the offer, but I don't know what will be happening. I'll probably be at the hospital, or bringing Anna home."

"Are you sure there's nothing I can do to help?"

"Thank you, my love, but it's fine, really. We'll catch up soon. Kit ok?"

"He's fine. He's taken to jumping on the bed every morning, and yowling, until James or I get up to feed him!"

"Sorry about that. You're spoiling him!"

"He's adorable." Jenny laughed, "We love him to pieces. Now you take it easy. If you need anything, or want to talk, just give me a bell. I'll tell Mavis I got hold of you, and that you're home, and will be back, hopefully next week. She was worried about you, too, and tried to ring you yesterday as well."

"Yeah, I saw her missed call. I was going to ring you, and her, this morning."

"I beat you to it!" Jenny laughed again. "I'd better get on, so you take care of yourself now. Give my regards, and best wishes, to Anna."

"She probably won't want anyone else to know that she attempted suicide."

"Oh, Gosh, you're right. Stupid me! So don't give her my regards, and best wishes! Speak to you soon. Bye, darling."

"Goodbye," Cassie echoed.

After she rang off, Cassie showered and dressed, and then telephoned the hospital. She was told which ward Anna had been moved to, and when she could visit her. They said she was doing well, and it was likely that she could be discharged tomorrow.

Cassie made herself a sloppy bowl of Weetabix and, when she still felt hungry after clearing the bowl, she scrambled some eggs, to a very soft consistency, and finished off those as well. After a good sleep, and having eaten well, she felt almost back to her normal self, apart from some residual soreness.

When she eventually walked into Anna's ward later that morning, carrying a bag of stuff for her, Cassie found her sitting up in a chair beside her bed, in a hospital gown, topped with the cardigan she had been wearing when she was admitted the previous night. She looked delicate and pale, but very beautiful. Cassie hurried over, and they embraced fiercely for a long time, without a word spoken by either of them. When at last Cassie released her, and pulled over another chair, she saw that Anna was crying, big, fat silent tears.

"Oh Cass, I am so sorry, so sorry for everything – for hurting you – for taking the overdose – for everything."

Cassie leaned forward, and grasped Anna's hand.

Anna went on, "I felt so wretched. I thought I had lost you, that you would never forgive me. I didn't want to live if you didn't want me any more, but I'm still so sorry to have put you through all of this. I was out of my mind. Can you ever forgive me?"

Tears continued to course down her face, and Cassie felt like crying herself.

"It's all forgotten, sweetheart. We'll start over, as if none of this has happened. We're going to look after each other, and be kind to one another, until all of this feels like just a bad dream."

Anna leaned in to lay her head on Cassie's shoulder. Cassie stroked Anna's hair back from her brow, and kissed her forehead.

"What are the doctors saying?" she asked eventually.

Anna sat up. "Thank God, my liver seems fine. I have to see the psychiatrist this afternoon, who will decide if I'm fit to go home. If it's agreed, I could be out of here later. I can't wait to be back with you, just the two of us. How are *you* feeling? How's your head and your jaw?"

She started to weep again.

"It's fine, just a little soreness, but getting better all the time. We'll get over this, darling, you'll see."

Anna nodded but she looked so forlorn, that Cassie's heart ached for her, and she too could not wait for them to be together again. Whatever the difficulties, she believed they were meant to be together, because when it was right, it was so right.

Chapter 26

The psychiatrist agreed that Anna could be discharged. Cassie went back to the hospital to fetch her that evening.

"I told him I was in therapy, and that I would tell the therapist about my overdose. He asked for his details, and is going to write to him as well, so I'll be well supervised, little one!" she joked.

They were both being very tender and calm with one another, in acknowledgement that there were wounds that needed to heal. That night, they lay in one another's arms and made gentle, slow love, before falling asleep, entwined together again.

In the days and weeks that followed, Anna needed almost constant reassurance that Cassie had forgiven her, that she loved her, that she was not planning to leave her. She would break down weeping, asserting that if she lost Cassie, there would be nothing left for her. She would not want to live. Cassie still felt love for her – and pity – but she was beginning to find it stressful, to keep reassuring her lover, and reiterating the same soothing phrases. Anna also wanted to make love constantly, and, if Cassie gave any indication that she was not so keen, Anna would become very low, and shut down. She would barely speak for hours. Cassie was worried that she would try to kill herself again. She felt as if she were walking on ice, that threatened to give way under her at any moment. It was a relief to go to work and joke with Jenny and her colleagues.

She resumed the monthly, Friday night get-togethers with Jenny, Stella and Nicola. Each time, she asked Anna to join them, as she could tell Anna resented these evenings, yet she would always refuse, ramping up Cassie's guilt.

On one occasion Cassie had mentioned that Stella had turned up for one of their Fridays, after a holiday in Greece, with her husband, to celebrate their wedding anniversary. They had left the girls with their grandparents. Stella, who tanned easily, was deeply bronzed, and wearing a white dress. She joked that they had all been green with envy, because she looked so stunning. Anna had turned on her furiously and spat, "Anyone would think you had the hots for her, talking like that. You want to fuck her, don't you?"

Cassie had tried to make a joke of it: she had put her arms around Anna, and told her she was the only woman, for whom she had the hots. In the face of Anna's rage, however, she knew that she had felt frightened again.

Cassie had also resumed her weekly telephone talks with Flick, ringing her from school at the end of the day. She had told Flick about Anna's furious rebuttal of the suggestion that she was not the author of *White Socks and Pederasts*. She left out all mention of the attack, of course.

"Well, that's bloody odd, isn't it?" Flick had said, "Praps that publishing guy got it wrong."

Cassie also did not tell Flick, that she was now *persona non grata* with Anna, that her name could not be mentioned without a hurt look, and a tightening of lips. So, Cassie did not mention Flick any more to Anna, and she tried not to talk about Anna to Flick. She was learning to compartmentalise her life, in a way she would once not have believed possible.

It was the end of the summer term, and Cassie was on her way to meet the others for their last Friday outing, until after the summer holidays, given that one or other of them would be away for every Friday in August. It was a beautiful evening and they had decided to meet at a riverside pub, where they could sit outside in the sunshine. Cassie was looking forward to it.

As it was the end of term, Mavis and Deidre were joining the usual four musketeers, and it promised to be a good night. Cassie felt a surge of happiness to be away from Anna for the evening, and to be in the company of her uncomplicated friends. They made her feel good about herself, in a way she had not felt for a long time. As she registered this thought, she was immediately struck by a body blow of guilt. How could she feel this way about Anna? How could she be so callous? Anna was right, she was not capable of loving Anna, in the way Anna loved her.

The poor girl was so vulnerable at the moment, she must try to be a better partner to her. If she turned back now, Anna would be over the moon. She hesitated, torn in half by conflicting feelings. In the end her need for light-hearted company won out and she continued on her way to the pub, and her carefree evening with her friends and colleagues.

The others had arrived, by the time she entered the Garden, and she was greeted by waves and cheers, as she made her way over to their table. Hugs and kisses were dispensed all round, and Jenny handed her a glass of Prosecco, from the bottle that was already half-empty, sitting on the table, in its ice-bucket.

"You're late," Jenny laughed, "We'd almost given up on

you. We're a little ahead of you on the Prosecco stakes. You've got a bit of catching-up to do, you lightweight!"

Jenny sounded a little squiffy already, Cassie thought, smiling to herself. No doubt, James was coming to collect her.

"You couldn't persuade that woman of yours to join us then?" Stella asked, grinning.

"No, you know Anna, not exactly the most sociable butterfly!" Cassie replied, with a somewhat forced lightness.

Stella turned to Mavis and Deidre, as some banter was exchanged.

Jenny took the opportunity to ask quietly, "How is she?"

"Oh, you know, getting there," Cassie said evasively. She did not want to get into it.

"How are you, my darling? I don't seem to have caught up with you in ages," asked Nicola.

"I'm good, Nicky. How are things with you?"

"Not too bad. Can't complain."

The wine flowed, and the women chatted, and laughed, and joked. At some point, Stella started to talk about her Spanish au pair, who seemed to be having some sort of breakdown, and needed to be flown home at the end of the week.

"I don't want to sound like a middle-class bitch," she laughed, "though, of course, that's what I most certainly am, but I really wish she could have scheduled her breakdown for any other time than the start of the summer holidays."

The women laughed.

Mavis asked, "What will you do about child care now?"

"Well, we'll have to try and get another au pair, but it all

223

takes time. Charles and I have full clinics until August, when we're all off to Cyprus. I have no idea what we can do. Charles's mother is spending July at a writing retreat in Corfu, and my Mum and Dad are back-packing around South America."

"Well, I would help, as you know, but I'm doing this OU summer school," said Jenny.

"Oh, I didn't mean I was thinking any of you could help. Oh God, how embarrassing! I was just sharing, not trying to guilt-trip any of you into volunteering."

They laughed at Stella's discomfiture.

"Actually, Stell, we *could* help, Anna and I," Cassie said. "You know how well Anna got on with Sophie, at Jen's party, and I adore Martha. I think she's quite fond of me, too. We're not going away, or doing anything in the near future, so we would be delighted to have the girls, until you can sort something out."

"You are an angel, Cassie Davies, and that's for sure!" Deidre cried, in her Northern Irish brogue.

"I couldn't possibly impose on you two like that," Stella protested, as a blush crept up from her chest.

"Honestly, Stell, if you can trust us with your precious girls, we'd be delighted to do it. I don't even have to ask Anna, because she has never stopped talking about what a delightful, and beautiful, little girl Sophie is. It will give us both something to do, organizing outings and sightseeing, for them. We'd enjoy it tremendously. What do you say?"

"Oh God, Cassie, this is so amazing. I can't thank you enough. Our problem solved at a stroke! Let me discuss it with Charles and the girls, and ring you tomorrow evening. Is that ok?"

"Absolutely fine. I'll talk to Anna tonight, but I know she'll be delighted to do it. If all of you are happy, we just need to work out the logistics."

By the time they all made their farewells outside the pub later that evening, Cassie was happier than she could remember feeling in a long time. It had been a lovely evening, and she had felt surrounded by love and friendship. It was good to have offered help to Stella, and she was excited at the prospect of her and Anna taking on a project together.

When she arrived home, Anna was watching TV, a glass of wine in front of her on the coffee table. Cassie went to join her on the sofa and kissed her cheek.

"How was your evening?" Anna asked, and Cassie proceeded to tell her about Stella's predicament, and her suggestion that they could help.

"Well, it would be quite a commitment, Cass, and we don't know for how long, but, yeah – I can see it might be fun."

Cassie hugged Anna.

"I knew you would agree! Thank you darling. I hope Charles, and the girls are happy with it, then we can start planning what we will do with them. It will be like playing at being parents!"

Anna smiled at her boisterous enthusiasm, but her eyes had darkened. Turning off the TV, she said, "Let's go to bed."

Chapter 27

It was all agreed, and the following week, Stella dropped off Martha and Sophie at Anna's house at 8.30am. Both Anna and Cassie were up, and dressed, and awaiting their charges. They had decided to stay at home this first day, so that Martha and Sophie could familiarise themselves with the house, and with the two women who would be looking after them daily for the next few weeks.

"They've had breakfast," Stella told them.

They had been briefed on the little girls' routines, and their likes and dislikes. They would really only eat fish fingers and chips, or chicken goujons with smiley potato cakes for lunch. They liked yoghurt or ginger biscuits for snacks, and drank water and apple juice only. They could watch a little TV in the mornings, and after lunch. They were only allowed sweets on Saturdays, and they did not like ice-cream or chocolate. Sophie sometimes still had a nap after lunch, but she was beginning not to want or need one. She was reliably clean and dry.

"Could you imagine that there could be any children in this world who don't like ice-cream or chocolate?" Anna had marvelled.

Both girls were a little shy, that first morning, and Cassie put on CBeebies for them, so they could settle in more easily.

"She's such a beautiful child, Sophie, isn't she?" asked Anna.

"I think they're both beautiful."

"Yes, but Martha's beginning to get that leggy look, that six and seven year olds have, whilst Sophie is still deliciously plump, and innocent looking."

Cassie thought it was a strange comment, but brushed the thought aside, and continued making their breakfast. She turned to Anna, who was seated at the table, flicking through the morning newspaper.

"Could you ask the girls if they want a piece of toast with us?"

Anna went into the sitting room and returned, shaking her head.

"They say they're still full up from breakfast," she smiled. "What shall we do with them this morning?"

"I thought we could take them to the High Street, and let them choose some paper and paints and stuff, and maybe a story book each?"

"That's a good idea. We could all so some painting later, in the back garden maybe?"

"In the sun. Lovely."

They smiled at each other. This was going to be fun.

As the week went on, both little girls grew more comfortable with Cassie and Anna. They became more talkative, and boisterous. Martha clearly favoured Cassie, and she her, but Cassie was touched by the care and attention Anna lavished on Sophie, and how Sophie warmed to her. Stella said the girls talked of nothing else, but what they had done with Cassie and Anna each day, and what Cassie had said, or what Anna had said.

"To tell the truth I'm getting quite jealous," she joked, as she handed over the girls' bags to Anna and Cassie, on their doorstep. The sisters had already scampered in to turn on their TV programme. Anna and Cassie laughed.

"We're loving having them," said Cassie.

"And we're getting to see places we would never have gone to on our own, aren't we Cass?" Anna added.

"Who would have thought Legoland could be so fascinating, Stella!" Cassie laughed.

In the second week of looking after the children, Stella asked if they could take Martha to her swimming lesson on the Thursday. They were all going to go. They would take Sophie for a drink, and a piece of cake, at the café above the pool. They could all watch Martha have her session with her coach. At the last minute, however, Anna said she thought Sophie was tired. She thought that it would be better if she stayed at home with her, and they watched a little television, or she read to her. Sophie seemed full of beans, to Cassie, but as the little girl eagerly agreed to Anna's suggestion, Cassie asked Martha if she was happy for just the two of them to go to the swimming pool.

"I'd like that," Martha smiled.

Cassie had hired a car, whilst they were looking after the girls, so they could more easily take them out and about. She and Martha left the house, and walked to the parked car. Cassie buckled Martha into the back seat, and started the engine, to set off for Brentford leisure centre.

She had just reached the Chiswick roundabout when Martha cried out, "Oh, Cassie, I've just checked my bag and my goggles aren't in there. Sophie was playing with them earlier, and I thought she'd put them back, but she must have left them on the lawn. I can't swim without my goggles; my eyes get all red and sore. Oh, I'm so sorry, Cassie."

She sounded as if she was about to burst into tears.

"It's ok, Martha, it's not a problem. I'll just go go all the way around the roundabout, and head back to the house. We've plenty of time, but it won't matter, anyway, if you're a little late starting the lesson. Are you sure she was playing with them out the back garden?"

"Yes, she was pretending to be Batman, and she said the goggles were his mask."

Cassie smiled as she headed back down Chiswick High Street. She pulled up in front of the house.

"Well, you stay buckled-up in the car while I run in and get them. I won't be two ticks. She switched off the engine and ran up the path. Turning the key in the lock, she quickly looked into the sitting room, to tell Anna and Sophie what she was doing.

For a moment she could not take in what she was seeing. She stood frozen on the threshold, trying to comprehend the scene before her. Anna's face was stricken, and she hastily scrambled to her feet. Sophie's face was red and tear-stained. She was lying on her back, her legs opened and splayed, and her knickers round one ankle, her vagina red and wet.

"Anna, what the fuck have you done?" Cassie eventually cried, moving immediately to Sophie, who was holding out her arms, and crying loudly now.

"It's not what it looks like, Cass, I was just..."

Cassie saw, with horror, Anna's bloodied fingers.

"Shut up!" she shouted, cutting her off, and she scooped up Sophie, and headed for the door. She was trembling, as she tried to buckle the still sobbing child into the second car seat.

"What's the matter, Sophe? What's happened? Cassie, what's wrong with Sophie?" Martha herself started weeping, in her shock and fright.

Cassie did not know what to do, or what to say. Her mind was a tsunami of thoughts. She abruptly left the car, and threw up violently in the gutter.

Wiping her mouth, she returned to the driving seat, and gripping the steering wheel, she took some deep breaths.

"Sophie has been hurt, Martha. We will have to forget the swimming lesson for today, and take you both home."

"But Mummy and Daddy won't be back yet. We can't get in. What's wrong with her? What's wrong with you Sophe?"

Sophie hiccupped, "I don't like Anna."

"We're not going to talk any more, just now, girls. Ok? We're not going to ask Sophie anything yet, Martha. We need to see your mummy and daddy first."

She pulled into a side road, and parked the car. She was shaking so much, she could hardly punch in Stella's number. Her secretary answered. Stella was not available, she was with a patient. Cassie explained who she was, and that there was an emergency with Sophie. She said she was taking the children to Stella's house. She needed Stella to get there as soon as possible.

Both children were silent and pale, as Cassie drove to their house and parked-up outside.

"Wait here, sweethearts, I'm just going to make a quick phone call," she told them.

She stepped out of the car, far enough away to be out of earshot, and telephoned James Moore. She was not expecting to be able to get hold of him but, but, by some miracle, he was in the office.

"Cassie, what can I do for you?" he asked, brightly.

She told him what had happened. There was silence on the other end and then he said, "Let Stella and Charles know everything, and let them decide what to do next. If they decide to report this, the Safeguarding team will need to be informed, and they will want to interview everyone, and maybe have Sophie examined. Best not to let them question her too much, before the team is called in, if that's the case. If they prefer, they can ring me direct and I'll refer it on to the appropriate team. Stella and Charles are pretty clued-up, doing the work they do, on the therapeutic aspect of this. They'll know what to do to help Sophie. You'll not want to go home, I imagine?"

"Oh God, no!" Cassie shouted, nausea washing over her at the thought of seeing Anna again.

"You must come and stay with us. Jen will be back tomorrow from the OU course, but I'll speak to her tonight."

Cassie was crying now.

"Cassie, you are in shock. This is horrible. You are going to need friends around you. If you want me to pick you up from Stella's house, I am happy to do that."

"I have this hire car."

"I don't think you should be driving, Cass. Ring me when you've spoken to Stella and Charles, and I'll come straight round."

As she clicked off the call, Stella's car screeched into the driveway.

"What's happened?" she called, as she rushed to wrench

open the back door of the car. Martha and Sophie had unbuckled themselves, and they now threw themselves at their mother, both bursting into tears.

"Let's talk inside, not in front of the children," Cassie warned. "I don't think Sophie is physically much hurt, but we need to talk before you speak to her."

Stella's eyed widened but she said nothing. She opened the front door, and ushered everyone inside.

"Martha, I want you and Sophie to put on *Frozen* while Cassie talks to me in the kitchen. Is that all right?"

Martha nodded and took her little sister's hand. Sophie had visibly brightened, at the mention of her favourite film.

"I'll be right there, in a few moments, ok poppets?"

The girls nodded, and Stella closed the sitting-room door on them, and led the way down the hall to the kitchen. She shut that door behind them also. Cassie felt terrible, and could barely look at Stella's expectant face. She felt tarnished by association. She told her briefly what had happened, and what she had seen. Stella clapped her hand over her mouth, and tears spilled over her hand.

"How could you let this happen, Cassie? Why did you leave her alone with that monster?"

Cassie flinched, and felt close to tears herself.

"Oh, Stella do you think I would be with her, if I had had any inkling that she was capable of something like this? I thought she was just genuinely fond of Sophie, and Sophie adored her – until this. I don't think anything can have happened before, she's never been alone with Sophie, as far as I can remember. We've all been together in the house, or on outings."

"Of course. I'm so sorry, Cass. It's just such a shock, I can't think straight. I want Charles here. I'm going to ring him."

"I phoned James for advice, as I was out of my mind with panic. He will come and get me, when I ring him, but he said, if you and Charles decide to report this, you can ring him direct, and he'll sort it. If you want to do it yourselves, contact the Safeguarding team. They will probably want to interview Sophie, and maybe have her examined."

"Oh God! Dear God!" Stella groaned.

She took her mobile into the garden, to try and speak to Charles. Cassie put the kettle on to make them a cup of tea.

"He was in the office, thank God! He's ringing James for him to make the referral immediately, then he's coming straight home."

"Here's a cup of tea, Stell."

"Thanks. Let's go and sit with the girls, till their Daddy gets here."

"Shall I get them a drink and a snack?"

"Would you? There's some apple juice in the fridge, and some cup cakes in the tin by the bread-bin."

"You go to them, I'll bring it in," Cassie said. She was glad to have something to do. She was still trembling, and she could not get out of her head the scene that had greeted her, when she had rushed in on Anna.

Chapter 28

The rest of that traumatic day would be etched on Cassie's memory, until the day she died. She wanted the ground to swallow her up, especially when Charles arrived home, giving her an inscrutable look, as he said "Hi," before going to kiss Stella, and hug his daughters. Sophie was beside herself to have Daddy home so early, as well as Mummy. Martha, however, looked anxious at this unusual turn of events, confirming for her, that something was very wrong.

James had rung Charles back to say that he would be coming by, as soon as he could, to pick up Cassie. Now that Charles was home, Stella took the opportunity to take Martha upstairs to talk to her. She told Cassie later, that she had told her daughter, in the simplest way possible, that Anna had touched Sophie in a way that was wrong. Martha had been shocked, but was visibly happier when she came downstairs, now that she knew what it was that was wrong, and had been making all the grown-ups act in such a weird way.

It was agreed that Cassie would take Martha to the local park, to play on the swings, while Charles and Stella talked to Sophie.

As they set off, Martha asked, "Was Anna very naughty, Cassie?"

"Yes, I'm afraid she was, sweetie."

"What will happen now?"

Cassie did not know. What would happen now?

"Well, I will have to find somewhere else to live because

I don't want to be with someone who could be naughty like this. I suppose the police will have to decide what will happen to her."

"Will she go to prison, Cassie?"

"I don't know, Martha. She might have to go to prison, or she might have to do lots of work for free, to show she's sorry."

"Oh," said Martha, and Cassie thought, *Oh God!*

When they finally returned home, Sophie was asleep, curled up on her father's lap.

"Let's get you fed, Martha. Sophie's had her supper already, but yours is in the oven. Pizza and chips, is that all right, sweetheart?"

"Yes, thanks, Mummy. I'm hungry. I need ketchup on my chips."

"Come through to the kitchen then, and I'll dish it up for you."

"Look, I'm sure you want to be alone as a family. I'll take myself off, and let James know where I'll be," Cassie said.

"Don't be silly, Cass," said Stella. "This has all been as horrible for you, as for us. You can't go back to her, of course, so stay and have a drink with us, until James comes. I'll just get Martha her supper."

She took Martha into the kitchen.

Charles said, "James said he would go back with you to get your things, so you didn't have to see the bitch, on your own. You'll move out, of course?"

"Oh God, yes! I couldn't possibly go on being with her, after this."

"Just let me get my hands on her. There wouldn't be

235

much left of her," growled Charles.

"Is everything – you know – ok?" Cassie ventured quietly, rolling her eyes toward Sophie.

"She's fine," he murmured, "a little bruising and abrasions, and we helped her talk through what happened."

Cassie's face contorted in pain and disgust, and she closed her eyes, as she fought to control the scream that wanted to issue forth.

Stella returned. "Glass of wine, Cassie, Charles?"

"I'll have a whisky, and make it a double," said Charles, grimacing at his wife.

"Actually, could I have a whisky too?" asked Cassie. She had never felt more in need of a really stiff drink.

"Good idea. We'll all have one," said Stella, heading for the drinks cabinet.

Charles's phone rang.

"It's James," he said, clicking it on.

Both Stella and Cassie stopped, and watched him, as he nodded and grunted into the phone.

"Well, someone had better track her down pronto, or I'll go out looking for her myself," and he laughed bitterly, at something James said in reply. "Ok, see you in a bit," and he clicked off.

They looked at him expectantly.

"James has contacted the Safeguarding team. They will be in touch. He went round to tell her she has been reported, but she's done a runner, or at least she's not there. Neighbour said she saw her go out, just after you left with the girls. Nosey neighbour, eh?"

"That'll be next door, Joan Carter," Cassie nodded.

"Well, the police put out a 'wanted for questioning notice', or whatever they call it, and asked the neighbour to contact them if she returns."

"Maybe she's gone to her club," mused Cassie.

"Tell James, so he can pass it on, and have them check it out," Charles replied.

Stella handed them both a tumbler, with a generous measure of whisky in each.

"I'll carry Sophie up to bed, before I drink mine," Charles said, as he tenderly cradled his sleeping daughter in his arms, and left the room.

Stella looked at Cassie, and hesitated before beginning to speak. "Don't blame yourself, Cassie. I'm sorry about what I said earlier. You couldn't have known. I didn't take to Anna from the off, but none of us could have dreamt she was capable of this."

Cassie burst into tears, sobbing so loudly, that an alarmed Martha ran in from the kitchen.

"What's the matter with Cassie, Mummy?"

"She's just upset about what Anna did to Sophie, darling. She feels bad that it was her friend who hurt your little sister."

Martha came over to Cassie, and put her arms around her neck, which only made Cassie cry harder.

"Don't be upset, Cassie. It's not your fault. You've always been kind to me and Sophe."

"That's right, sweetie, she has, hasn't she? Now kiss Cassie goodnight, and I'll take you up for a bath. We'll leave Cassie to feel better, ok?"

Cassie hugged the little girl, and Stella led her out of the room.

Cassie was just drying her eyes, when the doorbell rang, and she heard Charles run down the stairs, and open the door. She heard James's voice. They stood in the hall, for a while, talking, in low voices, before they both came through, to join her in the sitting room.

James came straight over to give her a hug. "How are you doing, Cass?"

"I'm ok, but I feel awful for all your concern. I'm not the one harmed here, it's the Bond family who need our concern."

"You're just as much of a victim of that bloody woman, Cass," James snapped. "Jen was spitting blood when I told her. She said, 'I always knew that bitch would end up crucifying Cassie.'"

Cassie's eyes widened.

Charles said, "I think we all felt there was something off about her, but we wanted it to be ok for you, so we tried to ignore the signs. Recently we were all becoming more concerned, though, weren't we James?"

"Jenny wanted to stage an intervention," said James. "We should have listened to her, shouldn't we, Charles?"

Charles nodded. Cassie felt sick. So, her friends had been talking about her and Anna, behind her back? How stupid had she been? Had she known this woman at all? Clearly not.

"Look, you must be exhausted, Cassie. Let's get you to Chiswick, to pack your stuff up. Then I'll drive you back to our place. Jenny will be home by the time we get there. She's dying to see you, and is worried sick about you. We won't disturb Stella's bedtime routine with Martha. Just give her our love, and we'll talk soon."

"Ok, mate," Charles said, clapping James on the shoulder, and turning to give Cassie a quick hug.

"Stell and I are glad you'll be in safe hands tonight, Cass."

Cassie bit her lip, to try and stop further tears. She did not deserve this much kindness, she who had brought this viper into their midst.

James ushered her into his car, and told her that Jenny would bring her back tomorrow, to return the hire car.

Chapter 29

James took Cassie's key, and let them into the Chiswick house. He searched it first, whilst she remained in the hall.

"No-one here," he called from upstairs. Cassie pulled her two suitcases from the cupboard under the stairs, and went upstairs. She threw clothes and toiletries, jewellery and shoes, books and device, into them, any which way. She wanted to get out of there as quickly as possible.

"Where would she keep her paperwork and stuff, Cass?" asked James, hovering in the bedroom doorway. "There may be something in them that will give us a clue where she's gone."

"Probably in her study – that's the box room – but she keeps it all locked."

"I bet she does. She has a lot to hide. Are you happy if I unlock it? I obviously can't do this officially, as I have no search warrant, but you could, because of needing to trace her?"

By the time she had packed as much as she could, James had several black bin liners, filled with the contents of Anna's desk and filing cabinet. She took a last look at the house, and pulled the front door shut. They drove in silence to Epsom, each lost in their own thoughts. As they drew up outside the house, Jenny threw open the front door, and came running down the path, to fling her arms around Cassie.

"It's so good to see you. I am so, so, sorry about what has happened. You must be devastated."

Cassie nodded dumbly, tears already pricking at her eyes,

her throat hurting.

They all unpacked the car. James dumped the bin liners in the hall, and took Cassie's cases up to the spare room. Jenny ushered Cassie into the dining room, where the table was laid for supper, for the three of them. Kit came bounding in, mewing a hello, and promptly leapt into Cassie's lap. It was wonderful to see him again, and pet him with impunity. Jenny smiled at the pair of them, and poured her and Cassie a glass of wine each. She went to fetch the pot of *coq au vin* from the oven. James joined them and Cassie was surprised to realise how hungry she was.

As they ate, Jenny told them all about the course she had been on, and James filled his wife in on what had been happening while she was away. Finally, Jenny asked Cassie if she would like to talk about what had happened. Cassie told them both in more detail about their time with the little girls, what they had done with them, and the events leading up her ringing James.

"Where do you think she might have gone?" Jenny asked.

"Cassie mentioned this club of hers, but I telephoned and she's not there," James said.

Cassie looked at him with surprise.

"While you were packing," he explained, and she nodded.

"I wonder if she has fled to France, to her mother," Cassie said.

"Do you have her mother's address or telephone number?" Jenny asked.

"No, but I picked up some letters and cards of hers,

before we left the house. I don't know if there's anything in there."

"I'll go and get the lemon cheesecake. Why don't you have a look through them, while I'm doing that. James, hon, can you open another bottle?"

They went into the kitchen, and Cassie started sifting through the wadge of stuff she had stuffed in her handbag. There were some postcards and birthday cards, from various people that Cassie had never heard of, and some from Anna's mother, but there was no address. The she unfolded a letter. Bingo! The letter was hand-written, but was on headed notepaper, with the printed address, and telephone number of the chateau, across the top of the page. It was signed *Carla Hardwick,* not *Mum,* or even *Mother,* as if the woman was writing to a stranger.

Cassie scanned the content. It was a short note informing Anna that the family solicitor, who did not have an up-to-date address for her, wanted her to contact him to discuss her trust fund. The letter was dated three years ago, about the time Anna had moved to the Chiswick house. Cassie looked at the envelope. It was addressed to Anna, care of her London club.

"Any luck?" asked Jenny, bringing in the cheesecake. James came in also, and refilled their glasses.

"Yes, I've found a note from her mother, and it has the address, and telephone number, of the their chateau in the South of France."

"Maybe you should ring her, tell her what's happened, and ask if she knows where Anna is, or might be," said James.

"Do you think I should tell her about Sophie?

242

They're not very close, almost estranged, really."

"Why not? She might have to know soon anyway, if they find Anna and charge her," he replied.

"Won't she be devastated?" Cassie asked.

"Perhaps she knows more than you think she does about your mystery woman," Jenny added, darkly.

Cassie flushed. How awful to have been so blind and stupid, as to have brought this woman into all their lives, she thought.

After supper, Jenny and James said they would retire to the sitting room, and leave Cassie to use the telephone in their bedroom. That way, she would have some privacy to make the call to Carla Hardwick. Cassie took a large swallow of wine. She felt acutely anxious. The telephone rang, and rang, and Cassie was just about to put the receiver down when a woman's voice said, "*Bonsoir?*"

"Is that Carla Hardwick?"

"*Mais, non.* Who eez this, *s'il vous plaît?* I will get 'er."

"It's Cassandra Davies. It's about Anna Hardwick."

There was no response, and Cassie could only imagine the woman had gone to fetch Anna's mother.

After what seemed an eternity she heard, "Hello, this is Carla Hardwick."

"Oh, hello. It's Cassandra, Mrs Hardwick, Cassandra Davies, Anna's – er – girlfriend. Do you remember me? We met at your mother's funeral."

"Yes, of course I remember you. How can I help you?"

"I wondered if Anna is with you, or if you have heard from her?"

"No and no. Why? Should I have?"

"This is rather difficult. Something rather awful happened today, and Anna's disappeared."

"Disappeared? What happened?"

Cassie's stomach knotted itself even tighter. She tried to clear her throat, which seemed to be going into spasm.

"We – that is, Anna and I – have been looking after a friend's little girls. I walked in on Anna unexpectedly today, when she was alone with the youngest little girl, who is just three, and Anna was in the middle of sexually abusing the child."

There was a sharp intake of breath, on the other end of the line.

"I took the little girl home immediately to her parents, but Anna has not been seen since. Obviously, it's concerning, as the police are also looking for her."

"Well, I'm sorry to hear that, but she's not here, and I haven't heard, of course..." Carla Hardwick snorted, "Anna and I are dead to one another already. It was to her, not to me, that my father left the chateau and most of his money. I don't think that's very fair, do you? Not that she cares a fig about me, and I don't care a fig about her."

Cassie gasped, at the callous way Carla Hardwick had written-off her daughter.

Mrs Hardwick went on, "I have no interest in hearing about her or her whereabouts," and she put the phone down.

Cassie stared for a moment at the receiver in her hand before replacing it on the cradle. She was trembling. Slowly she went downstairs to join Jenny and James. They looked at her with concern, as she sank into the sofa.

"Bloody Hell, Cass, you're as white as a sheet," said

James.

"What is it?" Jenny urged.

Cassie relayed the conversation. It was their turn to look shocked.

"What kind of a family are they?" Jenny whispered, as if to herself.

"Well, it certainly makes sense of her behaviour, doesn't it? What kind of a monster is this mother?" added James.

"I almost feel pity for her," murmured Cassie.

"Yes, but not as much pity as I feel for Sophie and for the Bonds," snapped Jenny.

"No, of course not. There is no excuse," Cassie added hastily.

"How old did you say Anna was? Or rather, how old did *Anna* say she was?" James asked.

"Thirty-four, when we met, but she's thirty-five now. Her birthday was in March. March 1st."

James took from his pocket a passport, and laid it on the coffee table in front of Cassie. She picked it up, and opened it. There was a picture of Anna, looking much younger. She looked at the date of birth. March 1st, 1973. She stared at it , trying to compute it.

"Forty-five, Cass. That makes her forty-five," James said gently.

"He showed it to me while you were upstairs," said Jenny. "It makes you wonder what else she's lied about, Cass, doesn't it?"

When Cassie finally fell into bed, at the end of the evening, she thought she would fall into a heavy, dreamless sleep, so emotionally and physically exhausted was she. Sleep eluded her, however, and she tossed and turned, trying to process a world which had suddenly sunk into an abyss beneath her feet.

Chapter 30

After James left for work, Jenny went to wake an exhausted Cassie. She carried a strong cup of coffee, which she placed on the bedside table.

"Stella rang last night, after you'd gone to bed. We told her about Anna's passport, and what her mother had said. She was gob-smacked. She'd rung to say that, if you don't want to carry on looking after the girls, she would quite understand, but she would be more than happy for you to continue. At her house, rather than the Chiswick house, obviously. She's really concerned that you might be feeling responsible and guilty. She says that there is absolutely no need for that, and she has the utmost faith in you."

Jenny went to pull the heavy curtains open, to let in the morning sunshine.

She went on, "She's going to stay home with the girls today, and so is Charles, so they can spend some time, all together."

Jenny came and sat on the edge of the bed.

"If you are happy to carry on, I could take you over there, tomorrow morning. You could come back here at the end of the day, in your hire car. She said to take your time, think it over, and do whatever feels right for you. She'd like one of us to ring her this evening, however, to let her know what you decide, so she can make other arrangements, if necessary.

"You didn't sleep much, did you? I heard you tossing and turning, then later, much later, I heard you creeping down the stairs."

"Oh, I'm sorry if I disturbed you," said Cassie, hauling herself up, and reaching for the mug.

Jenny shook her head, "I didn't sleep so well myself. Nothing to do with you. It's all been so shocking hasn't it, with revelation after revelation? James thinks you should go through her papers today. See if you can get a clearer picture, and maybe get a clue as to where she might have gone. I'd be happy to do that with you, if you feel it would help to have company."

"That's great, Jen. Yes, I think it would and, as for Stella and the girls, I would love to continue. It would feel like a chance to atone, for my part in what has happened to Sophie. I'll text her once I'm up. When I came up to bed I tried to call Anna last night. Her phone just goes to voicemail."

"She must be so ashamed. At least, I hope she is. Probably doesn't want to be found yet – if at all. Now, you take your time getting up. Have a nice long bath, or have a steam bath, and a shower, in our new cabinet! We're really posh now, aren't we! I'll make us a bit of breakfast, when you come down. Scrambled eggs, ok?"

"Smashing, and thanks for everything, Jenny, and to James."

"No probs. You'd do the same for us."

She blew Cassie a kiss as she went out of the room.

Cassie thought about Anna's papers. She was not sure how much more she could take of shattered assumptions and beliefs. She knew, though, she had to know the truth – the whole truth – about this woman who had come close to ruining her life.

After having their breakfast on the terrace, in the

morning sunshine, Jenny and Cassie dragged James's bin-liners onto the lawn. They settled themselves in recliners, and started to sift through the mounds of papers. Kit came and curled up at Cassie's feet.

A few moments later, Cassie exclaimed, "She's had a full face-lift! It's dated 2014," and she waved a receipt aloft. "No wonder she got away with claiming she was ten years younger than she really was! It wasn't cheap, either, fourteen thousand quid!"

"Never!" Jenny gasped, "what a fake, but a rich fake."

They fell silent again, each sifting through the papers and files at their feet.

"There's a lot of rejection letters from publishers, and literary agents," said Jenny, after they had both been busy for some time.

"I wonder if she ever did get anything published," Cassie said, thinking of Flick's assumption that Anna had lied about writing that book. "See if you can find a manuscript."

After a while, Jenny triumphantly held up a battered bunch of printed pages, held together by metal-ended, string tags. The title page read, *Mr Right by Anna Paul.*

"Paul was her dead brother's name," said Cassie, "so it could be her. Read some of it out."

Jenny flicked over the title page and started from Chapter One:

Sadie Stephens provocatively tossed her beautiful silky blonde hair back from her lovely face then smiled as sexily as Cleopatra at the gorgeous hunk in a white coat who had just masterfully entered the ward. Sadie gazed lustfully at his piercing blue eyes that were like lasers and his jet-black hair

*and he was tanned and muscular and Sadie suddenly felt her
knickers getting very wet with lust. And she said huskily,
"I'm Nurse Stephens." And he gave her a wolfish dazzling
smile and she saw his brilliant white teeth. He throatily
introduced himself as Dr Wright. Oh, he is most definitely
my Mr Right Sadie thought and I will have him. His
amazing eyes raked sensually over her shapely body and he
licked his lips hungrily. Her lips pouted out redly with
desire…*

"Enough!" Cassie cried, "Ugh! It's disgusting – and she
can't write for toffee!"

"It's just soft porn, isn't it?"

"And bad porn, at that. I dread to think how it goes
on. No wonder she has so many rejection slips."

"So she was just pretending to be a writer?"

"Seems so, doesn't it? It must have been what she
originally wanted to be, but she failed. The manuscript
looks pretty old," Cassie agreed. "Look at this," and she
passed the pile of type-written papers, she had just unearthed,
to Jenny.

She watched as her friend flicked through them. Jenny's
eyes widened, and her mouth fell open in astonishment. She
looked up at Cassie.

"What on earth?" she asked, an expression of disbelief
on her face.

"I know," said Cassie, "nothing but pages and pages of
obscenities, four-letter words, typed over and over again, line
after line. So that was her writing: nothing but the rantings of
a mad pervert. How can I have been so blind, Jen?" she

wailed. Jenny came over and hugged her.

"Cass, you loved her. She was clever and manipulative. We were all taken in at first."

"Yes, *at first*. I went on making excuses for her, though, didn't I, long after I should have known better?"

"Cassie, you have to stop beating yourself up. She's done enough damage, and hurt you for too long, for you to add to it, by indulging in all this self-recrimination. She's already changed you enough."

"What do you mean?"

"Oh, Cass! We've all been so worried about you. You've become a shadow of the kind, fun, gregarious girl we knew. We rarely saw you, and when we did, you were quiet, distant, low and always so nervous, especially around her."

"Oh, God!" Cassie groaned.

"Come on, put it all away, now. I'll go and make us a coffee. We can leave this for another time."

"No, I have to finish this, Jen. I'll carry on, while you make the coffee."

When Jenny returned with a tray of coffee, she found Cassie staring into space, holding a yellowed letter in her hand. She was paler than Jenny had ever seen her.

"Cass, whatever is it? What have you found?"

Wordlessly, Cassie handed the paper over to Jenny, who read:

Dear Anna,

If you are reading this, I will have found the courage to kill myself, and I will already be dead. I'm so sorry to leave you like this, because I love you, my little sister. You are the only thing I

251

do love in this shitty world, so I am so sorry to be causing you any more pain, but I cannot see another way out. I don't think Grandfather or Mother will have to ask why. They know the secret, but you may not know. I will spell it out for you, as you have a right to know. I suspect, however, (but I hope I'm wrong) that you might already know, all too well.

I wanted to trace our father, the mysterious Australian, David Rothwell. I wanted to know why he had refused to be put on our birth certificates, and why he had left, and never contacted us again. I drew a blank, however. The only David Rothwells I could find, were of the wrong age or ethnicity. I asked Mother more questions but she was evasive and weird. I became more suspicious and, as I thought about it, small memories, odd comments and observations, that I had forgotten or dismissed, began to fall into place.

My first step, in testing out my growing conviction of the truth, was to send my own DNA off for testing. I won't go into all the scientific data, but you know what a geek I am! Suffice it to say that, in the DNA of the products of incest there are, what are called, 'runs of homozygosity.' 'Runs of homozygosity' are stretches in the genome where identical DNA was inherited from each parent. If you inbreed, you're gonna have a greater number of longer runs of homozygosity in your genome than if you don't. You don't need the parents' DNA to test for this marker of in-breeding. My test came back confirming these runs in abundance. I confronted them both. Mother only cried, but Grandfather admitted it, almost as if he was proud of it. Then he told me that he had been abused by his own father and older brother, as if this was some kind of excuse! No wonder they bundled off poor, old Grandma, as soon as they could, to rot in an English old people's home. He said he loved his grandchildren/children! Mother got angry. She said how he had raped her from the age of three, had used her up, and then thrown her on the scrap heap, when he had another three year old to start fucking. She shouted that she knew he'd left everything in his will to 'her', and nothing to herself. She sounded so angry and bitter about this 'her' that I didn't think it could be you she meant. I really, really pray she didn't mean he started on you, Anna. If it is you, get out. Get out as fast as you can, anyway you can, and don't look back. I can't live with knowing I am the product of incest. I cannot live with these monsters another day. I will be better off dead. I think you would be too, and, if I wasn't such a coward, I'd take you with me. I'm so sorry I couldn't have protected you. I've been a shit brother.

I am so sorry. Don't hate me.

All my love,

Paul

The two women stared at each other. Finally, Jenny said, "My God, Cass, it just keeps getting worse and worse, doesn't it? What a sick, sick family!"

Cassie shook her head in disbelief. "Anna's had to live with this all her life. No wonder she is what she is."

"I can't believe it. It's like a horror film, or something, isn't it?"

Jenny handed back the letter, and poured their coffee.

"I hope there are no more revelations in these sacks," she added.

Cassie stroked Kit, who had jumped onto her lap, and thought of everything she had learnt about Anna, in the last twenty-four hours. She wondered where she was now, and what she was thinking, and feeling. She remembered the last words Anna had spoken, 'it's not what it looks like'. What on earth had she thought she could claim to have been doing to Sophie, except abusing her?

Chapter 31

The following morning, Jenny took Cassie to Stella's house, and the three women huddled over coffees on the terrace, while Martha and Sophie played in the paddling pool on the back lawn.

"My God, it beggars belief," Stella cried, after they had told her what the paperwork had revealed. "I see some things in my job, as you can imagine, but this takes the biscuit."

Cassie was going to say that it made it more understandable that Anna had done what she had done. She bit her lip, just in time.

"Frankly," said Jenny, "I don't care a toss, what happened to her. Not all abused children end-up as abusers. People have a choice. She is just a wrong 'un!"

"Still no news of her?" Stella asked Cassie, who shook her head.

"Her phone just goes to answerphone."

"Do you think she would top herself?" Jenny asked.

Cassie nodded. They were silent.

After Stella left for work, Jenny stayed for a while, helping Cassie entertain the girls. When she took her leave, as Cassie was making the girls lunch, she said, "After supper tonight, if you feel up to it, we could finish going through her papers together. James is playing squash, and going for a pint with a colleague."

"Ok. It would be good to get it over and done with."

They hugged, and Jenny kissed the girls and left.

As she drove back to Jenny's that evening, Cassie

thought about Anna, and where she could be. What must she be going through? It was crazy, she knew, but she still cared about her, and even missed her. She was worried that Anna might do something to herself. She had been imagining all sorts of lurid scenarios. It would be a relief to know, one way or another.

Jenny and she had a light supper and settled down, with a glass of wine, to go through the rest of the papers. It was not long, before Jenny handed Cassie a letter she had been looking at. Cassie read:

Dear Anna,

When you read this I will have packed and gone. You have became increasingly possessive and controlling. You are always putting me down. Your violence to me, first verbally, and now — more and more — physically, is escalating. You are so unpredictable and, at times, frightening. I can't stand it any more. I have to get out, for my sanity's sake! You have left my self-esteem in tatters. I loved you so much, Anna, but you have killed that love.

Goodbye,

Lucy

Cassie stared at Jenny in astonishment.

"These words are almost exactly the ones Anna used to me about Lucy! It's as if she just quoted them verbatim but referring them to her, not herself."

"There's no address or surname, so you couldn't trace her, I suppose. It sounds as if Anna has a pattern of being abusive, in relationships, doesn't it? You've had a lucky escape, Cass."

Cassie nodded, her eyes filling with tears. Was there no end to it?

They heard the front door close, and James walked in.

"You're early, love. I didn't expect you for ages yet," said Jenny.

"They've found Anna's body."

"What?" cried Jenny, and Cassie's hand flew to her mouth to stifle the scream that was rising from her.

"The guys knew I was involved in the case, so one of them contacted me. A dog-walker stumbled on her in dense undergrowth in Richmond Park. She only found her because the dog kept barking over the body. Anna had ID on her, so Kingston Police contacted Chiswick. They think it was an overdose, but we'll have to wait for the post-mortem now."

James went on, "They think she had been there a day or so, given the state of the body."

Cassie was crying freely now. She felt a surge of desolation, thinking of her poor, beautiful Anna, lying cold and stiff and alone, in the undergrowth. Her bright red hair would have been wet with dew, her delicate features, white and cold as marble. What had been her thoughts, as she lay down to die?

"Someone should tell her mother," she sobbed.

"I'll take care of that," said James, "I'll give her telephone number to the officer in charge, they can contact her."

"And the Lettings Agents. I have their card somewhere."

"Cassie, you're in shock. Stop it. Just let yourself process this," Jenny said. "You need to take care of yourself, now.

James, get her a brandy will you?"

Jenny passed the box of tissues to Cassie, whose face and neck were running with tears. She hugged her hard, and patted her back rhythmically, as if comforting an infant.

James came back from the kitchen carrying a tray, on which stood three, brandy balloons, each with a large measure of brandy at the bottom.

"I thought we could all do with a snifter," he smiled, handing each of the women a glass.

"I suppose we all feared it might end like this," Jenny said.

"I realise now, just what a tortured soul she was," said Cassie, bursting into fresh tears.

"You're lucky she's dead, Cassie. She would have dragged you down with her," said James, with an uncharacteristic harshness.

Cassie did not feel lucky. She felt hollowed out.

By the time she fell into bed that night, Cassie was exhausted. She fell straight asleep, having had a further two brandies, but she slept badly. She had dream after dream about Anna: Anna attacking her, and trying to kill her, finding Anna's corpse in her bed, Anna making love to her, and Cassie opening her eyes to see only a sightless skull, where Anna's face should have been.

It was a relief, in the morning, to wake from these nightmares and face a day ahead, with the joy and innocence of the Bond children. In the days and weeks that followed, Cassie tried to look for another place to live, but James and Jenny insisted she stay with them until everything was over.

Stella found another au pair, at last, so Cassie's services

were no longer required. Sophie seemed to have returned to her ebullient self. Charles and Stella hoped no lasting damage had been done.

Carla Hardwick, as next of kin, refused to come over to identify her daughter. Cassie was the obvious next choice, but James vetoed that, and volunteered himself. He also was with her for the police interview. Cassie did not know how she would have coped, without her friends. She would, forever, be grateful, for the support the Moores gave her, through this terrible time in her life.

The post-mortem confirmed that Anna had taken a massive overdose, of a concoction of drugs, together with alcohol. Once the body was released, the coroner issued an interim certificate, so that a funeral could take place. Carla Hardwick was asked if she wanted the body, or to arrange the funeral, but she again declined.

Cassie took it upon herself to arrange a quiet funeral at Mortlake Crematorium. She sent all the details to Anna's mother, including her own mobile number, and Jenny's address. Mrs Hardwick (or *Miss* Hardwick, as she really was) did not turn up to the sad little gathering, that came to say farewell to Anna Hardwick. There was only Cassie, Jenny and James, and the loyal Flick, who travelled up from Swansea, just to support Cassie.

The Bonds, understandably, stayed away. When Cassie had told her family all that had happened, everyone offered to come and support her at the funeral, even Portia, which was touching, but Cassie declined them all.

The service was short and impersonal, but as the curtains parted, to allow the coffin to slide away, Cassie, despite it all, was overcome with grief, for the Anna that she had loved.

Chapter 32

Cassie moved out at the end of August. School would be re-starting soon, and she had found another little bedsit, within walking distance of St Anne's, that was on the ground floor, and had a little outside space. Jenny insisted she take Kit with her, but Cassie felt guilty at the thought of wrenching the cat away from Jenny and James, after all this time.

"Nonsense," Jenny said, "that cat loves you, and you love him. I can bear his loss, because, guess what?"

Cassie looked at her expectantly.

"I'm twelve weeks pregnant!"

Cassie shrieked, and circled Jenny's waist to dance her around her kitchen. They were both laughing, and crying.

"Jen, I could not be more delighted for you. You and James are going to be marvellous parents, I know."

Abruptly, she released Jenny, and looked crestfallen, as she faced her friend.

"I feel awful, that with everything that's been going on, I didn't once give a thought, or ask you about how the IVF was going."

"Don't be silly, of course you didn't, with everything you've been going through. As you can see, though, it's going swimmingly!"

They laughed again. Jenny looked radiant with happiness, and they toasted the baby with their coffee cups.

Some weeks later, after term had started, the date of the

inquest came through. When Cassie told Jenny in the staff room, she insisted that she and James should come with her. Despite Cassie's protests, that Jenny needed to take care of herself in her condition, and not put any additional stress on herself, Jenny was adamant that Cassie should not do this alone. When the day dawned, Cassie felt so thankful that Jenny had prevailed. It was a horrible experience, sitting there listening to the evidence about Anna. The Coroner's conclusion was, of course, suicide.

As they came out of the Court, James turned to her and said, "That's it now, Cass. Closure, as they say. You can put this whole sorry business behind you and get on with your life."

James was wrong, however. Two weeks after the inquest Jenny came into the staffroom and handed Cassie a bulky, legal-looking envelope, addressed to Cassie, at Jenny's house.

"How on earth has this arrived for me, at yours?" Cassie exclaimed.

They sat side by side, on the battered sofa, as Cassie tore open the envelope. She read the letterhead: *Messers Lawton, Lawton &Black Solicitors 3 Water Court Grays Inn London WC1*, and scanned down the long letter, with increasing disbelief and shock.

"Jesus," she breathed. She re-read it, and passed it to Jenny. As Jenny looked through it, Cassie sat motionless, staring straight ahead. How could this be? Jenny, like Cassie, needed to start at the beginning again, to take it all in. At last she exhaled noisily, and turned to Cassie,

"This is unbelievable! She has made you her sole beneficiary of her inheritance from her grandfather, sorry, *father!* That's the chateau, when her mother dies, and four million pounds now. This is incredible. Who knew she was worth that much?"

"I don't want any of it," said Cassie, tears coursing down her cheeks.

Jenny fished out some tissues, and handed them to her.

"I know it's a shock, Cass, but you would be mad to refuse this. You'll be set up for life. You won't have to worry about anything for the rest of your natural. Are you crazy?"

"It's blood money – my blood, and hers. I can't accept it."

"Think of the good you could do, Cass, with that sort of money. You could make reparation for what Anna did to Sophie, or indeed, for what was done to her and her mother. You could give some money to charities, that help abused children, or something like that. Don't do anything hasty, until you have time to digest this, and think it through."

"This is what her mother was on about, wasn't it? She wasn't left a penny, just allowed to stay in the chateau until her death. No wonder she was bitter. After all, apart from suffering the same abuse as Anna, both from the age of three, for God's sake, she was the one who had to give birth to two products of incest. It's just too horrible."

"I know, darling, but this shows that Anna did care about you, as far as she was able. And what will happen to it, if you don't accept the legacy? The money will probably just go to the government, here or in France. I don't know how it works."

"I thought it was all over, Jen, and now this. I don't want any more, I just want to get on with my ordinary life."

"I know. Look, why don't I arrange supper with the Bonds, and James, you and I? We'll talk it through, all of us together. It might help you clarify your thinking. They're offering you an appointment, the solicitors, to go up and see them to talk it through. You know Charles' brother's a barrister. Maybe he could ask him for some advice for you?"

Cassie nodded, dumbly. She had a class to teach.

"How on earth did they track me down to yours?" she asked, as the improbability of it struck her.

Jenny frowned, and thought for a moment. "It's Carla Hardwick, isn't it? You gave her your mobile and my address when you were sorting the funeral. She must have told them of her death and given them your contact details."

"Oh, yeah." Cassie shook her head in wonder.

The Bonds, the Moores, and Cassie met at a restaurant in Barnes, the following Friday. During the course of the meal, arguments went back and forth, until finally Cassie was persuaded that she should consider accepting the legacy, and giving a proportion to charities dealing with the victims of abuse.

She had already had time to process the startling news, before their meet-up. She could not help thinking how wonderful it would be, to be able to buy her own little house, and garden. She could afford to travel a little , which she had never been able to do on her teacher's salary, with the high cost of living in London.

So it was that she caught the tube into London, in the week of half term, to meet with Mr Black at Gray's Inn. It struck her, that it was almost a year ago that she had first met Anna. What a lot can happen in such a little amount of time, she thought. She was a different person now. She felt years older, and worn down by all that had passed. It was unseasonably warm for October, so she had picked a short-sleeved black linen shift, with her black court shoes. All the stress of the last months meant any excess weight had dropped off her.

The premises of *Lawton, Lawton and Black* were in an old building, but the interior was modern and sleek. The receptionist offered her coffee, and told her to make herself comfortable, that Mr Black would not be very long. She pinned a badge on Cassie saying *visitor*. For some reason, Cassie felt nervous. She checked her phone: there was a text from Flick saying, *Go for it, heiress!* and one from Jenny, *Good luck. Thinking of you.* She smiled.

"Miss Davies?"

She looked up to see a man who did not resemble what she was expecting. For a start, he was young, maybe late thirties or early forties, and exceptionally handsome. He held out his hand.

"Hi, I'm Gideon Black. Pleased to meet you."

She shook his hand. It was a nice hand, strong but soft.

"Do come through," he said.

He showed her to a spacious office, and motioned her to the leather chair in front of his desk.

"First, I have to impart some shocking news. Did you know Anna Hardwick's mother, Carla Hardwick?"

"I only met her the once, and had a couple of phone calls with her, that's all."

"Well, I'm afraid, that like her daughter, Carla Hardwick has taken her own life. We heard a few weeks back."

He paused to allow her to take this in.

"Oh, my goodness," was all Cassie could think to say.

"Yes, a very sad business, all round. They were... let's say, an unusual family. What this does mean, of course, is that the chateau is now yours as well, with no restrictions. You can do with it what you will, live in it, sell it, whatever."

Cassie outlined to him her reluctance to accept the legacy, her wish to give a large part of the estate to charities, and why. His eyes widened.

"And I understand you and Anna Hardwick were partners?" he asked, unspoken questions clouding his face.

"Yes," said Cassie, blushing, "but, of course I didn't know anything about her... er... predilections."

"No, quite," he said, looking briefly down at his desk.

"I'd never been with a woman before," she said, quite unnecessarily, and blushed even deeper.

His lips twitched slightly.

"I see," he said solemnly. "This must have all been very difficult for you, but, I must say, you are a remarkable young woman to want to give away some of such a large fortune."

"But, don't you see, it's tainted money, and I never asked for it."

"I understand," he added more softly.

He talked then about how he might help her negotiate the transfer of funds to the charities of her choice, arrange the transfer of the remaining funds to her, and how she might safeguard, and invest her portion.

It was a long meeting, and when it concluded, they shook hands warmly, and discussed further appointments. Cassie handed her visitor's badge to the receptionist, and stepped out into the sunshine. She paused on the threshold of the offices, and took a deep breath. She looked up at the sky, and straightened her shoulders. Tomorrow was, indeed, another day.

ABOUT THE AUTHOR

Piper S. Winn is a therapist, writer and artist. She has written an autobiographical family saga which has been distributed privately. *Loving Anna* is her first published novel, and she is now working on her next. In a life dedicated to patients, children, and now, grandchildren, Piper has continued to express her creativity in myriad ways and to live her life to the full.

If you have enjoyed reading this book, please take the time to write a review of it on Amazon.